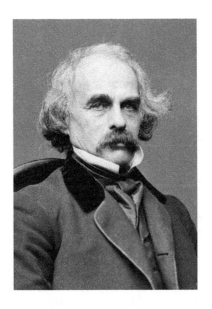

Nathaniel Hawthorne (July 4, 1804 – May 19, 1864) was an American novelist, dark romantic, and short story writer. His works often focus on history, morality, and religion. He was born in 1804 in Salem, Massachusetts, to Nathaniel Hathorne and the former Elizabeth Clarke Manning. His ancestors include John Hathorne, the only judge involved in the Salem witch trials who never repented of his actions. He entered Bowdoin College in 1821, was elected to Phi Beta Kappa in 1824, and graduated in 1825. He published his first work in 1828, the novel Fanshawe; he later tried to suppress it, feeling that it was not equal to the standard of his later work. He published several short stories in periodicals, which he collected in 1837 as Twice-Told Tales. The next year, he became engaged to Sophia Peabody. He worked at the Boston Custom House and joined Brook Farm, a transcendentalist community, before marrying Peabody in 1842. The couple moved to The Old Manse in Concord, Massachusetts, later moving to Salem, the Berkshires, then to The Wayside in Concord. (Source: Wikipedia)

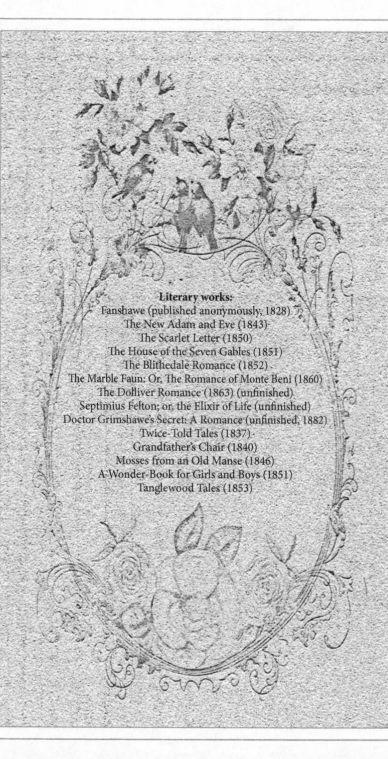

Literary works:
Fanshawe (published anonymously, 1828)
The New Adam and Eve (1843)
The Scarlet Letter (1850)
The House of the Seven Gables (1851)
The Blithedale Romance (1852)
The Marble Faun: Or, The Romance of Monte Beni (1860)
The Dolliver Romance (1863) (unfinished)
Septimius Felton; or, the Elixir of Life (unfinished)
Doctor Grimshawe's Secret: A Romance (unfinished, 1882)
Twice-Told Tales (1837)
Grandfather's Chair (1840)
Mosses from an Old Manse (1846)
A Wonder-Book for Girls and Boys (1851)
Tanglewood Tales (1853)

THE MARBLE FAUN
VOL. 2
NATHANIEL HAWTHORNE

PRINCE CLASSICS

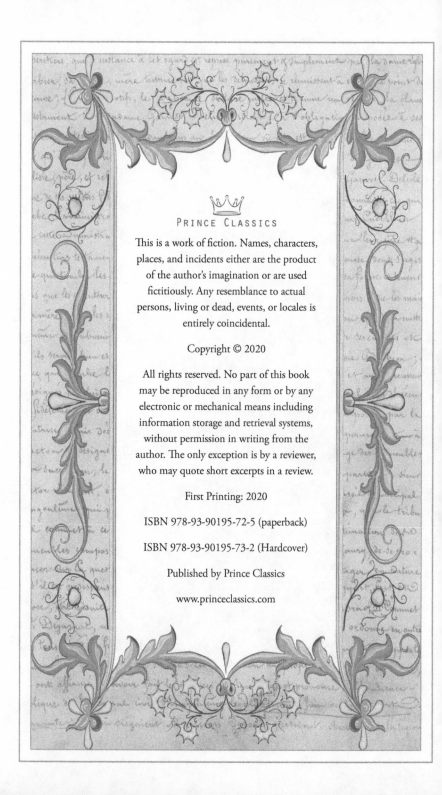

PRINCE CLASSICS

First Printing: 2020

ISBN 978-93-90195-72-5 (paperback)

ISBN 978-93-90195-73-2 (Hardcover)

Published by Prince Classics

www.princeclassics.com

Contents

THE MARBLE FAUN
VOL. 2

CHAPTER XXIV. THE TOWER AMONG THE APENNINES

It was in June that the sculptor, Kenyon, arrived on horseback at the gate of an ancient country house (which, from some of its features, might almost be called a castle) situated in a part of Tuscany somewhat remote from the ordinary track of tourists. Thither we must now accompany him, and endeavor to make our story flow onward, like a streamlet, past a gray tower that rises on the hillside, overlooking a spacious valley, which is set in the grand framework of the Apennines.

The sculptor had left Rome with the retreating tide of foreign residents. For, as summer approaches, the Niobe of Nations is made to bewail anew, and doubtless with sincerity, the loss of that large part of her population which she derives from other lands, and on whom depends much of whatever remnant of prosperity she still enjoys. Rome, at this season, is pervaded and overhung with atmospheric terrors, and insulated within a charmed and deadly circle. The crowd of wandering tourists betake themselves to Switzerland, to the Rhine, or, from this central home of the world, to their native homes in England or America, which they are apt thenceforward to look upon as provincial, after once having yielded to the spell of the Eternal City. The artist, who contemplates an indefinite succession of winters in this home of art (though his first thought was merely to improve himself by a brief visit), goes forth, in the summer time, to sketch scenery and costume among the Tuscan hills, and pour, if he can, the purple air of Italy over his canvas. He studies the old schools of art in the mountain towns where they were born, and where they are still to be seen in the faded frescos of Giotto and Cimabue, on the walls of many a church, or in the dark chapels, in which the sacristan draws aside the veil from a treasured picture of Perugino. Thence, the happy painter goes to walk the long, bright galleries of Florence, or to steal glowing colors from the miraculous works, which he finds in a score of Venetian palaces. Such summers as these, spent amid whatever is exquisite in art, or wild and picturesque in nature, may not inadequately repay him for the chill neglect and disappointment through which he has probably languished, in his Roman winter. This sunny, shadowy, breezy, wandering life, in which he seeks for beauty as his treasure, and gathers for his winter's honey what is but a passing fragrance to all other men, is worth living for, come afterwards what may. Even if he die unrecognized, the artist has had his share of enjoyment and success.

Kenyon had seen, at a distance of many miles, the old villa or castle towards which his journey lay, looking from its height over a broad expanse of valley. As he drew nearer, however, it had been hidden among the inequalities of the hillside, until the winding road brought him almost to the iron gateway. The sculptor found this substantial barrier fastened with lock and bolt. There was no bell, nor other instrument of sound; and, after summoning the invisible garrison with his voice, instead of a trumpet, he had leisure to take a glance at the exterior of the fortress.

About thirty yards within the gateway rose a square tower, lofty enough to be a very prominent object in the landscape, and more than sufficiently massive in proportion to its height. Its antiquity was evidently such that, in a climate of more abundant moisture, the ivy would have mantled it from head to foot in a garment that might, by this time, have been centuries old, though ever new. In the dry Italian air, however, Nature had only so far adopted this old pile of stonework as to cover almost every hand's-breadth of it with close-clinging lichens and yellow moss; and the immemorial growth of these kindly productions rendered the general hue of the tower soft and venerable, and took away the aspect of nakedness which would have made its age drearier than now.

Up and down the height of the tower were scattered three or four windows, the lower ones grated with iron bars, the upper ones vacant both of window frames and glass. Besides these larger openings, there were several loopholes and little square apertures, which might be supposed to light the staircase, that doubtless climbed the interior towards the battlemented and machicolated summit. With this last-mentioned warlike garniture upon its stern old head and brow, the tower seemed evidently a stronghold of times long past. Many a crossbowman had shot his shafts from those windows and loop-holes, and from the vantage height of those gray battlements; many a flight of arrows, too, had hit all round about the embrasures above, or the apertures below, where the helmet of a defender had momentarily glimmered. On festal nights, moreover, a hundred lamps had often gleamed afar over the valley, suspended from the iron hooks that were ranged for the purpose beneath the battlements and every window.

Connected with the tower, and extending behind it, there seemed to be a very spacious residence, chiefly of more modern date. It perhaps owed much of its fresher appearance, however, to a coat of stucco and yellow wash, which is a sort of renovation very much in vogue with the Italians. Kenyon noticed over a doorway, in the portion of the edifice immediately adjacent to the tower, a cross, which, with a bell suspended above the roof, indicated that this was a consecrated precinct, and the chapel of the mansion.

Meanwhile, the hot sun so incommoded the unsheltered traveller, that he shouted forth another impatient summons. Happening, at the same moment, to look upward, he saw a figure leaning from an embrasure of the battlements, and gazing down at him.

"Ho, Signore Count!" cried the sculptor, waving his straw hat, for he recognized the face, after a moment's doubt. "This is a warm reception, truly! Pray bid your porter let me in, before the sun shrivels me quite into a cinder."

"I will come myself," responded Donatello, flinging down his voice out of the clouds, as it were; "old Tomaso and old Stella are both asleep, no doubt, and the rest of the people are in the vineyard. But I have expected you, and you are welcome!"

The young Count—as perhaps we had better designate him in his ancestral tower—vanished from the battlements; and Kenyon saw his figure appear successively at each of the windows, as he descended. On every reappearance, he turned his face towards the sculptor and gave a nod and smile; for a kindly impulse prompted him thus to assure his visitor of a welcome, after keeping him so long at an inhospitable threshold.

Kenyon, however (naturally and professionally expert at reading the expression of the human countenance), had a vague sense that this was not

11

the young friend whom he had known so familiarly in Rome; not the sylvan and untutored youth, whom Miriam, Hilda, and himself had liked, laughed at, and sported with; not the Donatello whose identity they had so playfully mixed up with that of the Faun of Praxiteles.

Finally, when his host had emerged from a side portal of the mansion, and approached the gateway, the traveller still felt that there was something lost, or something gained (he hardly knew which), that set the Donatello of to-day irreconcilably at odds with him of yesterday. His very gait showed it, in a certain gravity, a weight and measure of step, that had nothing in common with the irregular buoyancy which used to distinguish him. His face was paler and thinner, and the lips less full and less apart.

"I have looked for you a long while," said Donatello; and, though his voice sounded differently, and cut out its words more sharply than had been its wont, still there was a smile shining on his face, that, for the moment, quite brought back the Faun. "I shall be more cheerful, perhaps, now that you have come. It is very solitary here."

"I have come slowly along, often lingering, often turning aside," replied Kenyon; "for I found a great deal to interest me in the mediaeval sculpture hidden away in the churches hereabouts. An artist, whether painter or sculptor, may be pardoned for loitering through such a region. But what a fine old tower! Its tall front is like a page of black letter, taken from the history of the Italian republics."

"I know little or nothing of its history," said the Count, glancing upward at the battlements, where he had just been standing. "But I thank my forefathers for building it so high. I like the windy summit better than the world below, and spend much of my time there, nowadays."

"It is a pity you are not a star-gazer," observed Kenyon, also looking up. "It is higher than Galileo's tower, which I saw, a week or two ago, outside of the walls of Florence."

"A star-gazer? I am one," replied Donatello. "I sleep in the tower, and often watch very late on the battlements. There is a dismal old staircase to climb, however, before reaching the top, and a succession of dismal chambers, from story to story. Some of them were prison chambers in times past, as old Tomaso will tell you."

The repugnance intimated in his tone at the idea of this gloomy staircase and these ghostly, dimly lighted rooms, reminded Kenyon of the original Donatello, much more than his present custom of midnight vigils on the battlements.

"I shall be glad to share your watch," said the guest; "especially by moonlight. The prospect of this broad valley must be very fine. But I was not aware, my friend, that these were your country habits. I have fancied you in a sort of Arcadian life, tasting rich figs, and squeezing the juice out of the sunniest grapes, and sleeping soundly all night, after a day of simple pleasures."

"I may have known such a life, when I was younger," answered the Count gravely. "I am not a boy now. Time flies over us, but leaves its shadow behind."

The sculptor could not but smile at the triteness of the remark, which, nevertheless, had a kind of originality as coming from Donatello. He had thought it out from his own experience, and perhaps considered himself as communicating a new truth to mankind.

They were now advancing up the courtyard; and the long extent of the villa, with its iron-barred lower windows and balconied upper ones, became visible, stretching back towards a grove of trees.

"At some period of your family history," observed Kenyon, "the Counts of Monte Beni must have led a patriarchal life in this vast house. A great-grandsire and all his descendants might find ample verge here, and with space, too, for each separate brood of little ones to play within its own precincts. Is your present household a large one?"

"Only myself," answered Donatello, "and Tomaso, who has been butler since my grandfather's time, and old Stella, who goes sweeping and dusting about the chambers, and Girolamo, the cook, who has but an idle life of it.

He shall send you up a chicken forthwith. But, first of all, I must summon one of the contadini from the farmhouse yonder, to take your horse to the stable."

Accordingly, the young Count shouted again, and with such effect that, after several repetitions of the outcry, an old gray woman protruded her head and a broom-handle from a chamber window; the venerable butler emerged from a recess in the side of the house, where was a well, or reservoir, in which he had been cleansing a small wine cask; and a sunburnt contadino, in his shirt-sleeves, showed himself on the outskirts of the vineyard, with some kind of a farming tool in his hand. Donatello found employment for all these retainers in providing accommodation for his guest and steed, and then ushered the sculptor into the vestibule of the house.

It was a square and lofty entrance-room, which, by the solidity of its construction, might have been an Etruscan tomb, being paved and walled with heavy blocks of stone, and vaulted almost as massively overhead. On two sides there were doors, opening into long suites of anterooms and saloons; on the third side, a stone staircase of spacious breadth, ascending, by dignified degrees and with wide resting-places, to another floor of similar extent. Through one of the doors, which was ajar, Kenyon beheld an almost interminable vista of apartments, opening one beyond the other, and reminding him of the hundred rooms in Blue Beard's castle, or the countless halls in some palace of the Arabian Nights.

It must have been a numerous family, indeed, that could ever have sufficed to people with human life so large an abode as this, and impart social warmth to such a wide world within doors. The sculptor confessed to himself, that Donatello could allege reason enough for growing melancholy, having only his own personality to vivify it all.

"How a woman's face would brighten it up!" he ejaculated, not intending to be overheard.

But, glancing at Donatello, he saw a stern and sorrowful look in his eyes, which altered his youthful face as if it had seen thirty years of trouble; and, at the same moment, old Stella showed herself through one of the doorways, as the only representative of her sex at Monte Beni.

14

CHAPTER XXV. SUNSHINE

"Come," said the Count, "I see you already find the old house dismal. So do I, indeed! And yet it was a cheerful place in my boyhood. But, you see, in my father's days (and the same was true of all my endless line of grandfathers, as I have heard), there used to be uncles, aunts, and all manner of kindred, dwelling together as one family. They were a merry and kindly race of people, for the most part, and kept one another's hearts warm."

"Two hearts might be enough for warmth," observed the sculptor, "even in so large a house as this. One solitary heart, it is true, may be apt to shiver a little. But, I trust, my friend, that the genial blood of your race still flows in many veins besides your own?"

"I am the last," said Donatello gloomily. "They have all vanished from me, since my childhood. Old Tomaso will tell you that the air of Monte Beni is not so favorable to length of days as it used to be. But that is not the secret of the quick extinction of my kindred."

"Then you are aware of a more satisfactory reason?" suggested Kenyon.

"I thought of one, the other night, while I was gazing at the stars," answered Donatello; "but, pardon me, I do not mean to tell it. One cause, however, of the longer and healthier life of my forefathers was, that they had many pleasant customs, and means of making themselves glad, and their guests and friends along with them. Nowadays we have but one!"

"And what is that?" asked the sculptor.

"You shall see!" said his young host.

By this time, he had ushered the sculptor into one of the numberless saloons; and, calling for refreshment, old Stella placed a cold fowl upon the table, and quickly followed it with a savory omelet, which Girolamo had lost no time in preparing. She also brought some cherries, plums, and apricots, and a plate full of particularly delicate figs, of last year's growth. The butler showing his white head at the door, his master beckoned to him. "Tomaso, bring some Sunshine!" said he. The readiest method of obeying this order, one might suppose, would have been to fling wide the green window-blinds, and let the glow of the summer noon into the carefully shaded room. But, at Monte Beni, with provident caution against the wintry days, when there is little sunshine, and the rainy ones, when there is none, it was the hereditary custom to keep their Sunshine stored away in the cellar. Old Tomaso quickly produced some of it in a small, straw-covered flask, out of which he extracted the cork, and inserted a little cotton wool, to absorb the olive oil that kept the precious liquid from the air.

"This is a wine," observed the Count, "the secret of making which has been kept in our family for centuries upon centuries; nor would it avail any man to steal the secret, unless he could also steal the vineyard, in which alone the Monte Beni grape can be produced. There is little else left me, save that patch of vines. Taste some of their juice, and tell me whether it is worthy to be called Sunshine! for that is its name." "A glorious name, too!" cried the sculptor. "Taste it," said Donatello, filling his friend's glass, and pouring likewise a little into his own. "But first smell its fragrance; for the wine is very lavish of it, and will scatter it all abroad."

"Ah, how exquisite!" said Kenyon. "No other wine has a bouquet like this. The flavor must be rare, indeed, if it fulfill the promise of this fragrance, which is like the airy sweetness of youthful hopes, that no realities will ever satisfy!"

This invaluable liquor was of a pale golden hue, like other of the rarest Italian wines, and, if carelessly and irreligiously quaffed, might have been mistaken for a very fine sort of champagne. It was not, however, an effervescing wine, although its delicate piquancy produced a somewhat similar effect upon the palate. Sipping, the guest longed to sip again; but the wine demanded so deliberate a pause, in order to detect the hidden peculiarities and subtle exquisiteness of its flavor, that to drink it was really more a moral than a physical enjoyment. There was a deliciousness in it that eluded analysis, and—like whatever else is superlatively good—was perhaps better appreciated in the memory than by present consciousness.

One of its most ethereal charms lay in the transitory life of the wine's richest qualities; for, while it required a certain leisure and delay, yet, if you lingered too long upon the draught, it became disenchanted both of its fragrance and its flavor.

The lustre should not be forgotten, among the other admirable endowments of the Monte Beni wine; for, as it stood in Kenyon's glass, a little circle of light glowed on the table round about it, as if it were really so much golden sunshine.

"I feel myself a better man for that ethereal potation," observed the sculptor. "The finest Orvieto, or that famous wine, the Est Est Est of Montefiascone, is vulgar in comparison. This is surely the wine of the Golden Age, such as Bacchus himself first taught mankind to press from the choicest of his grapes. My dear Count, why is it not illustrious? The pale, liquid gold, in every such flask as that, might be solidified into golden scudi, and would quickly make you a millionaire!"

Tomaso, the old butler, who was standing by the table, and enjoying the praises of the wine quite as much as if bestowed upon himself, made answer,—"We have a tradition, Signore," said he, "that this rare wine of our vineyard would lose all its wonderful qualities, if any of it were sent to market. The Counts of Monte Beni have never parted with a single flask of it for gold. At their banquets, in the olden time, they have entertained princes, cardinals, and once an emperor and once a pope, with this delicious wine, and always, even to this day, it has been their custom to let it flow freely, when those whom they love and honor sit at the board. But the grand duke himself could not drink that wine, except it were under this very roof!"

"What you tell me, my good friend," replied Kenyon, "makes me venerate the Sunshine of Monte Beni even more abundantly than before. As I understand you, it is a sort of consecrated juice, and symbolizes the holy virtues of hospitality and social kindness?"

"Why, partly so, Signore," said the old butler, with a shrewd twinkle in his eye; "but, to speak out all the truth, there is another excellent reason why neither a cask nor a flask of our precious vintage should ever be sent to market. The wine, Signore, is so fond of its native home, that a transportation of even a few miles turns it quite sour. And yet it is a wine that keeps well in the cellar, underneath this floor, and gathers fragrance, flavor, and brightness, in its dark dungeon. That very flask of Sunshine, now, has kept itself for you, sir guest (as a maid reserves her sweetness till her lover comes for it), ever since a merry vintage-time, when the Signore Count here was a boy!"

"You must not wait for Tomaso to end his discourse about the wine, before drinking off your glass," observed Donatello. "When once the flask is uncorked, its finest qualities lose little time in making their escape. I doubt whether your last sip will be quite so delicious as you found the first."

And, in truth, the sculptor fancied that the Sunshine became almost imperceptibly clouded, as he approached the bottom of the flask. The effect of the wine, however, was a gentle exhilaration, which did not so speedily pass away.

Being thus refreshed, Kenyon looked around him at the antique saloon in which they sat. It was constructed in a most ponderous style, with a stone floor, on which heavy pilasters were planted against the wall, supporting arches that crossed one another in the vaulted ceiling. The upright walls, as well as the compartments of the roof, were completely Covered with frescos, which doubtless had been brilliant when first executed, and perhaps for generations afterwards. The designs were of a festive and joyous character, representing Arcadian scenes, where nymphs, fauns, and satyrs disported themselves among mortal youths and maidens; and Pan, and the god of wine, and he of sunshine and music, disdained not to brighten some sylvan merry-making with the scarcely veiled glory of their presence. A wreath of dancing figures, in admirable variety of shape and motion, was festooned quite round the cornice of the room.

In its first splendor, the saloon must have presented an aspect both gorgeous and enlivening; for it invested some of the cheerfullest ideas and emotions of which the human mind is susceptible with the external reality of beautiful form, and rich, harmonious glow and variety of color. But the frescos were now very ancient. They had been rubbed and scrubbed by old Stein

18

and many a predecessor, and had been defaced in one spot, and retouched in another, and had peeled from the wall in patches, and had hidden some of their brightest portions under dreary dust, till the joyousness had quite vanished out of them all. It was often difficult to puzzle out the design; and even where it was more readily intelligible, the figures showed like the ghosts of dead and buried joys,—the closer their resemblance to the happy past, the gloomier now. For it is thus, that with only an inconsiderable change, the gladdest objects and existences become the saddest; hope fading into disappointment; joy darkening into grief, and festal splendor into funereal duskiness; and all evolving, as their moral, a grim identity between gay things and sorrowful ones. Only give them a little time, and they turn out to be just alike!

"There has been much festivity in this saloon, if I may judge by the character of its frescos," remarked Kenyon, whose spirits were still upheld by the mild potency of the Monte Beni wine. "Your forefathers, my dear Count, must have been joyous fellows, keeping up the vintage merriment throughout the year. It does me good to think of them gladdening the hearts of men and women, with their wine of Sunshine, even in the Iron Age, as Pan and Bacchus, whom we see yonder, did in the Golden one!"

"Yes; there have been merry times in the banquet hall of Monte Beni, even within my own remembrance," replied Donatello, looking gravely at the painted walls. "It was meant for mirth, as you see; and when I brought my own cheerfulness into the saloon, these frescos looked cheerful too. But, methinks, they have all faded since I saw them last."

"It would be a good idea," said the sculptor, falling into his companion's vein, and helping him out with an illustration which Donatello himself could not have put into shape, "to convert this saloon into a chapel; and when the priest tells his hearers of the instability of earthly joys, and would show how drearily they vanish, he may point to these pictures, that were so joyous and are so dismal. He could not illustrate his theme so aptly in any other way."

"True, indeed," answered the Count, his former simplicity strangely mixing itself up with ah experience that had changed him; "and yonder, where the minstrels used to stand, the altar shall be placed. A sinful man might do all the more effective penance in this old banquet hall."

"But I should regret to have suggested so ungenial a transformation in your hospitable saloon," continued Kenyon, duly noting the change in Donatello's characteristics. "You startle me, my friend, by so ascetic a design! It would hardly have entered your head, when we first met. Pray do not,—if I may take the freedom of a somewhat elder man to advise you," added he, smiling,—"pray do not, under a notion of improvement, take upon yourself to be sombre, thoughtful, and penitential, like all the rest of us."

Donatello made no answer, but sat awhile, appearing to follow with his eyes one of the figures, which was repeated many times over in the groups upon the walls and ceiling. It formed the principal link of an allegory, by which (as is often the case in such pictorial designs) the whole series of frescos were bound together, but which it would be impossible, or, at least, very wearisome, to unravel. The sculptor's eyes took a similar direction, and soon began to trace through the vicissitudes,—once gay, now sombre,—in which the old artist had involved it, the same individual figure. He fancied a resemblance in it to Donatello himself; and it put him in mind of one of the purposes with which he had come to Monte Beni.

"My dear Count," said he, "I have a proposal to make. You must let me employ a little of my leisure in modelling your bust. You remember what a striking resemblance we all of us—Hilda, Miriam, and I—found between your features and those of the Faun of Praxiteles. Then, it seemed an identity; but now that I know your face better, the likeness is far less apparent. Your head in marble would be a treasure to me. Shall I have it?"

"I have a weakness which I fear I cannot overcome," replied the Count, turning away his face. "It troubles me to be looked at steadfastly."

"I have observed it since we have been sitting here, though never before," rejoined the sculptor. "It is a kind of nervousness, I apprehend, which you caught in the Roman air, and which grows upon you, in your solitary life. It need be no hindrance to my taking your bust; for I will catch the likeness and expression by side glimpses, which (if portrait painters and bust makers did but know it) always bring home richer results than a broad stare."

"You may take me if you have the power," said Donatello; but, even as he spoke, he turned away his face; "and if you can see what makes me shrink from you, you are welcome to put it in the bust. It is not my will, but my necessity, to avoid men's eyes. Only," he added, with a smile which made Kenyon doubt whether he might not as well copy the Faun as model a new bust,—"only, you know, you must not insist on my uncovering these ears of mine!"

"Nay; I never should dream of such a thing," answered the sculptor, laughing, as the young Count shook his clustering curls. "I could not hope to persuade you, remembering how Miriam once failed!"

Nothing is more unaccountable than the spell that often lurks in a spoken word. A thought may be present to the mind, so distinctly that no utterance could make it more so; and two minds may be conscious of the same thought, in which one or both take the profoundest interest; but as long as it remains unspoken, their familiar talk flows quietly over the hidden idea, as a rivulet may sparkle and dimple over something sunken in its bed. But speak the word, and it is like bringing up a drowned body out of the deepest pool of the rivulet, which has been aware of the horrible secret all along, in spite of its smiling surface.

And even so, when Kenyon chanced to make a distinct reference to Donatello's relations with Miriam (though the subject was already in both their minds), a ghastly emotion rose up out of the depths of the young Count's heart. He trembled either with anger or terror, and glared at the sculptor with wild eyes, like a wolf that meets you in the forest, and hesitates whether to flee or turn to bay. But, as Kenyon still looked calmly at him, his aspect gradually became less disturbed, though far from resuming its former quietude.

"You have spoken her name," said he, at last, in an altered and tremulous tone; "tell me, now, all that you know of her."

"I scarcely think that I have any later intelligence than yourself," answered Kenyon; "Miriam left Rome at about the time of your own departure. Within a day or two after our last meeting at the Church of the Capuchins, I called at her studio and found it vacant. Whither she has gone, I cannot tell."

21

Donatello asked no further questions.

They rose from table, and strolled together about the premises, whiling away the afternoon with brief intervals of unsatisfactory conversation, and many shadowy silences. The sculptor had a perception of change in his companion,—possibly of growth and development, but certainly of change,—which saddened him, because it took away much of the simple grace that was the best of Donatello's peculiarities.

Kenyon betook himself to repose that night in a grim, old, vaulted apartment, which, in the lapse of five or six centuries, had probably been the birth, bridal, and death chamber of a great many generations of the Monte Beni family. He was aroused, soon after daylight, by the clamor of a tribe of beggars who had taken their stand in a little rustic lane that crept beside that portion of the villa, and were addressing their petitions to the open windows. By and by they appeared to have received alms, and took their departure.

"Some charitable Christian has sent those vagabonds away," thought the sculptor, as he resumed his interrupted nap; "who could it be? Donatello has his own rooms in the tower; Stella, Tomaso, and the cook are a world's width off; and I fancied myself the only inhabitant in this part of the house."

In the breadth and space which so delightfully characterize an Italian villa, a dozen guests might have had each his suite of apartments without infringing upon one another's ample precincts. But, so far as Kenyon knew, he was the only visitor beneath Donatello's widely extended roof.

CHAPTER XXVI. THE PEDIGREE OF MONTE BENI

From the old butler, whom he found to be a very gracious and affable personage, Kenyon soon learned many curious particulars about the family history and hereditary peculiarities of the Counts of Monte Beni. There was a pedigree, the later portion of which—that is to say, for a little more than a thousand years—a genealogist would have found delight in tracing out, link by link, and authenticating by records and documentary evidences. It would have been as difficult, however, to follow up the stream of Donatello's ancestry to its dim source, as travellers have found it to reach the mysterious fountains of the Nile. And, far beyond the region of definite and demonstrable fact, a romancer might have strayed into a region of old poetry, where the rich soil, so long uncultivated and untrodden, had lapsed into nearly its primeval state of wilderness. Among those antique paths, now overgrown with tangled and riotous vegetation, the wanderer must needs follow his own guidance, and arrive nowhither at last.

The race of Monte Beni, beyond a doubt, was one of the oldest in Italy, where families appear to survive at least, if not to flourish, on their half-decayed roots, oftener than in England or France. It came down in a broad track from the Middle Ages; but, at epochs anterior to those, it was distinctly visible in the gloom of the period before chivalry put forth its flower; and further still, we are almost afraid to say, it was seen, though with a fainter and wavering course, in the early morn of Christendom, when the Roman Empire had hardly begun to show symptoms of decline. At that venerable distance, the heralds gave up the lineage in despair.

But where written record left the genealogy of Monte Beni, tradition took it up, and carried it without dread or shame beyond the Imperial ages into the times of the Roman republic; beyond those, again, into the epoch of kingly rule. Nor even so remotely among the mossy centuries did it pause, but strayed onward into that gray antiquity of which there is no token left, save its cavernous tombs, and a few bronzes, and some quaintly wrought ornaments of gold, and gems with mystic figures and inscriptions. There, or thereabouts, the line was supposed to have had its origin in the sylvan life of Etruria, while Italy was yet guiltless of Rome.

Of course, as we regret to say, the earlier and very much the larger portion of this respectable descent—and the same is true of many briefer pedigrees—must be looked upon as altogether mythical. Still, it threw a romantic interest around the unquestionable antiquity of the Monte Beni family, and over that tract of their own vines and fig-trees beneath the shade of which they had unquestionably dwelt for immemorial ages. And there they had laid the foundations of their tower, so long ago that one half of its height was said to be sunken under the surface and to hide subterranean chambers which once were cheerful with the olden sunshine.

One story, or myth, that had mixed itself up with their mouldy genealogy, interested the sculptor by its wild, and perhaps grotesque, yet not unfascinating peculiarity. He caught at it the more eagerly, as it afforded a shadowy and whimsical semblance of explanation for the likeness which he, with Miriam and Hilda, had seen or fancied between Donatello and the Faun of Praxiteles.

The Monte Beni family, as this legend averred, drew their origin from the Pelasgic race, who peopled Italy in times that may be called prehistoric. It was the same noble breed of men, of Asiatic birth, that settled in Greece; the same happy and poetic kindred who dwelt in Arcadia, and—whether they ever lived such life or not—enriched the world with dreams, at least, and fables, lovely, if unsubstantial, of a Golden Age. In those delicious times, when deities and demigods appeared familiarly on earth, mingling with its inhabitants as friend with friend,—when nymphs, satyrs, and the whole train of classic faith or fable hardly took pains to hide themselves in the primeval woods,—at that auspicious period the lineage of Monte Beni had its rise. Its progenitor was a being not altogether human, yet partaking so largely of the gentlest human qualities, as to be neither awful nor shocking to the imagination. A sylvan creature, native among the woods, had loved a mortal maiden, and—perhaps by kindness, and the subtile courtesies which love might teach to his simplicity, or possibly by a ruder wooing—had won her to his haunts. In due time he gained her womanly affection; and, making their bridal bower, for aught we know, in the hollow of a great tree, the pair spent a happy wedded life in that ancient neighborhood where now stood Donatello's tower.

From this union sprang a vigorous progeny that took its place unquestioned among human families. In that age, however, and long afterwards, it showed the ineffaceable lineaments of its wild paternity: it was a pleasant and kindly race of men, but capable of savage fierceness, and never quite restrainable within the trammels of social law. They were strong, active, genial, cheerful as the sunshine, passionate as the tornado. Their lives were rendered blissful by art unsought harmony with nature.

But, as centuries passed away, the Faun's wild blood had necessarily been attempered with constant intermixtures from the more ordinary streams of human life. It lost many of its original qualities, and served for the most part only to bestow an unconquerable vigor, which kept the family from extinction, and enabled them to make their own part good throughout the perils and rude emergencies of their interminable descent. In the constant wars with which Italy was plagued, by the dissensions of her petty states and republics, there was a demand for native hardihood.

The successive members of the Monte Beni family showed valor and policy enough' at all events, to keep their hereditary possessions out of the clutch of grasping neighbors, and probably differed very little from the other feudal barons with whom they fought and feasted. Such a degree of conformity with the manners of the generations through which it survived, must have been essential to the prolonged continuance of the race.

It is well known, however, that any hereditary peculiarity—as a supernumerary finger, or an anomalous shape of feature, like the Austrian lip—is wont to show itself in a family after a very wayward fashion. It skips at its own pleasure along the line, and, latent for half a century or so, crops out again in a great-grandson. And thus, it was said, from a period beyond memory or record, there had ever and anon been a descendant of the Monte Benis bearing nearly all the characteristics that were attributed to the original founder of the race. Some traditions even went so far as to enumerate the ears, covered with a delicate fur, and shaped like a pointed leaf, among the proofs of authentic descent which were seen in these favored individuals. We appreciate the beauty of such tokens of a nearer kindred to the great family of nature than other mortals bear; but it would be idle to ask credit for a statement which might be deemed to partake so largely of the grotesque.

But it was indisputable that, once in a century or oftener, a son of Monte Beni gathered into himself the scattered qualities of his race, and reproduced the character that had been assigned to it from immemorial times. Beautiful, strong, brave, kindly, sincere, of honest impulses, and endowed with simple tastes and the love of homely pleasures, he was believed to possess gifts by which he could associate himself with the wild things of the forests, and with the fowls of the air, and could feel a sympathy even with the trees; among which it was his joy to dwell. On the other hand, there were deficiencies both of intellect and heart, and especially, as it seemed, in the development of the higher portion of man's nature. These defects were less perceptible in early youth, but showed themselves more strongly with advancing age, when, as the animal spirits settled down upon a lower level, the representative of the Monte Benis was apt to become sensual, addicted to gross pleasures, heavy, unsympathizing, and insulated within the narrow limits of a surly selfishness.

A similar change, indeed, is no more than what we constantly observe to take place in persons who are not careful to substitute other graces for those which they inevitably lose along with the quick sensibility and joyous vivacity of youth. At worst, the reigning Count of Monte Beni, as his hair grew white, was still a jolly old fellow over his flask of wine, the wine that Bacchus himself was fabled to have taught his sylvan ancestor how to express, and from what choicest grapes, which would ripen only in a certain divinely favored portion of the Monte Beni vineyard.

The family, be it observed, were both proud and ashamed of these legends; but whatever part of them they might consent to incorporate into their ancestral history, they steadily repudiated all that referred to their one distinctive feature, the pointed and furry ears. In a great many years past, no sober credence had been yielded to the mythical portion of the pedigree. It might, however, be considered as typifying some such assemblage of qualities—in this case, chiefly remarkable for their simplicity and naturalness—as, when they reappear in successive generations, constitute what we call family character. The sculptor found, moreover, on the evidence of some old portraits, that the physical features of the race had long been similar to what he now saw them in Donatello. With accumulating years, it is true, the Monte Beni face had a tendency to look grim and savage; and, in two or three instances, the family pictures glared at the spectator in the eyes like some surly animal, that had lost its good humor when it outlived its playfulness.

The young Count accorded his guest full liberty to investigate the personal annals of these pictured worthies, as well as all the rest of his progenitors; and ample materials were at hand in many chests of worm-eaten papers and yellow parchments, that had been gathering into larger and dustier piles ever since the dark ages. But, to confess the truth, the information afforded by these musty documents was so much more prosaic than what Kenyon acquired from Tomaso's legends, that even the superior authenticity of the former could not reconcile him to its dullness. What especially delighted the sculptor was the analogy between Donatello's character, as he himself knew it, and those peculiar traits which the old butler's narrative assumed to have been long hereditary in the race. He was amused at finding, too, that not only Tomaso but the peasantry of the estate and neighboring village recognized his friend as a genuine Monte Beni, of the original type. They seemed to cherish a great affection for the young Count, and were full of stories about his sportive childhood; how he had played among the little rustics, and been at once the wildest and the sweetest of them all; and how, in his very infancy, he had plunged into the deep pools of the streamlets and never been drowned, and had clambered to the topmost branches of tall trees without ever breaking his neck. No such mischance could happen to the sylvan child because, handling all the elements of nature so fearlessly and freely, nothing had either the power or the will to do him harm.

He grew up, said these humble friends, the playmate not only of all mortal kind, but of creatures of the woods; although, when Kenyon pressed them for some particulars of this latter mode of companionship, they could remember little more than a few anecdotes of a pet fox, which used to growl and snap at everybody save Donatello himself.

But they enlarged—and never were weary of the theme—upon the blithesome effects of Donatello's presence in his rosy childhood and budding youth. Their hovels had always glowed like sunshine when he entered them; so that, as the peasants expressed it, their young master had never darkened a doorway in his life. He was the soul of vintage festivals. While he was a mere infant, scarcely able to run alone, it had been the custom to make him tread the winepress with his tender little feet, if it were only to crush one cluster of the grapes. And the grape-juice that gushed beneath his childish tread, be it ever so small in quantity, sufficed to impart a pleasant flavor to a whole cask of wine. The race of Monte Beni—so these rustic chroniclers assured the sculptor—had possessed the gift from the oldest of old times of expressing good wine from ordinary grapes, and a ravishing liquor from the choice growth of their vineyard.

In a word, as he listened to such tales as these, Kenyon could have imagined that the valleys and hillsides about him were a veritable Arcadia; and that Donatello was not merely a sylvan faun, but the genial wine god in his very person. Making many allowances for the poetic fancies of Italian peasants, he set it down for fact that his friend, in a simple way and among rustic folks, had been an exceedingly delightful fellow in his younger days.

But the contadini sometimes added, shaking their heads and sighing, that the young Count was sadly changed since he went to Rome. The village girls now missed the merry smile with which he used to greet them.

The sculptor inquired of his good friend Tomaso, whether he, too, had noticed the shadow which was said to have recently fallen over Donatello's life.

"Ah, yes, Signore!" answered the old butler, "it is even so, since he came back from that wicked and miserable city. The world has grown either too evil, or else too wise and sad, for such men as the old Counts of Monte Beni used to be. His very first taste of it, as you see, has changed and spoilt my poor young lord. There had not been a single count in the family these hundred years or more, who was so true a Monte Beni, of the antique stamp, as this poor signorino; and now it brings the tears into my eyes to hear him sighing over a cup of Sunshine! Ah, it is a sad world now!"

"Then you think there was a merrier world once?" asked Kenyon.

"Surely, Signore," said Tomaso; "a merrier world, and merrier Counts of Monte Beni to live in it! Such tales of them as I have heard, when I was a child on my grandfather's knee! The good old man remembered a lord of Monte Beni—at least, he had heard of such a one, though I will not make oath upon the holy crucifix that my grandsire lived in his time who used to go into the woods and call pretty damsels out of the fountains, and out of the trunks of the old trees. That merry lord was known to dance with them a whole long summer afternoon! When shall we see such frolics in our days?"

"Not soon, I am afraid," acquiesced the sculptor. "You are right, excellent Tomaso; the world is sadder now!"

And, in truth, while our friend smiled at these wild fables, he sighed in the same breath to think how the once genial earth produces, in every successive generation, fewer flowers than used to gladden the preceding ones. Not that the modes and seeming possibilities of human enjoyment are rarer in our refined and softened era,—on the contrary, they never before were nearly so abundant,—but that mankind are getting so far beyond the childhood of their race that they scorn to be happy any longer. A simple and joyous character can find no place for itself among the sage and sombre figures that would put his unsophisticated cheerfulness to shame. The entire system of man's affairs, as at present established, is built up purposely to exclude the careless and happy soul. The very children would upbraid the wretched individual who should endeavor to take life and the world as w what we might naturally suppose them meant for—a place and opportunity for enjoyment.

It is the iron rule in our day to require an object and a purpose in life. It makes us all parts of a complicated scheme of progress, which can only result in our arrival at a colder and drearier region than we were born in. It insists upon everybody's adding somewhat—a mite, perhaps, but earned by incessant effort—to an accumulated pile of usefulness, of which the only use will be, to burden our posterity with even heavier thoughts and more inordinate labor than our own. No life now wanders like an unfettered stream; there is a mill-wheel for the tiniest rivulet to turn. We go all wrong, by too strenuous a resolution to go all right.

Therefore it was—so, at least, the sculptor thought, although partly suspicious of Donatello's darker misfortune—that the young Count found it impossible nowadays to be what his forefathers had been. He could not live their healthy life of animal spirits, in their sympathy with nature, and brotherhood with all that breathed around them. Nature, in beast, fowl, and tree, and earth, flood, and sky, is what it was of old; but sin, care, and self-consciousness have set the human portion of the world askew; and thus the simplest character is ever the soonest to go astray.

"At any rate, Tomaso," said Kenyon, doing his best to comfort the old man, "let us hope that your young lord will still enjoy himself at vintage time. By the aspect of the vineyard, I judge that this will be a famous year for the golden wine of Monte Beni. As long as your grapes produce that admirable liquor, sad as you think the world, neither the Count nor his guests will quite forget to smile."

"Ah, Signore," rejoined the butler with a sigh, "but he scarcely wets his lips with the sunny juice."

"There is yet another hope," observed Kenyon; "the young Count may fall in love, and bring home a fair and laughing wife to chase the gloom out of yonder old frescoed saloon. Do you think he could do a better thing, my good Tomaso?"

"Maybe not, Signore," said the sage butler, looking earnestly at him; "and, maybe, not a worse!"

The sculptor fancied that the good old man had it partly in his mind to make some remark, or communicate some fact, which, on second thoughts, he resolved to keep concealed in his own breast. He now took his departure cellarward, shaking his white head and muttering to himself, and did not reappear till dinner-time, when he favored Kenyon, whom he had taken far into his good graces, with a choicer flask of Sunshine than had yet blessed his palate.

To say the truth, this golden wine was no unnecessary ingredient towards making the life of Monte Beni palatable. It seemed a pity that Donatello did not drink a little more of it, and go jollily to bed at least, even if he should awake with an accession of darker melancholy the next morning.

Nevertheless, there was no lack of outward means for leading an agreeable life in the old villa. Wandering musicians haunted the precincts of Monte Beni, where they seemed to claim a prescriptive right; they made the lawn and shrubbery tuneful with the sound of fiddle, harp, and flute, and now and then with the tangled squeaking of a bagpipe. Improvisatori likewise came and told tales or recited verses to the contadini—among whom Kenyon was often an auditor—after their day's work in the vineyard. Jugglers, too, obtained permission to do feats of magic in the hall, where they set even the sage Tomaso, and Stella, Girolamo, and the peasant girls from the farmhouse, all of a broad grin, between merriment and wonder. These good people got food and lodging for their pleasant pains, and some of the small wine of Tuscany, and a reasonable handful of the Grand Duke's copper coin, to keep up the hospitable renown of Monte Beni. But very seldom had they the young Count as a listener or a spectator.

There were sometimes dances by moonlight on the lawn, but never since he came from Rome did Donatello's presence deepen the blushes of the pretty contadinas, or his footstep weary out the most agile partner or competitor, as once it was sure to do.

Paupers—for this kind of vermin infested the house of Monte Beni worse than any other spot in beggar-haunted Italy—stood beneath all the windows, making loud supplication, or even establishing themselves on the marble steps of the grand entrance. They ate and drank, and filled their bags, and pocketed the little money that was given them, and went forth on their devious ways, showering blessings innumerable on the mansion and its lord,

31

and on the souls of his deceased forefathers, who had always been just such simpletons as to be compassionate to beggary. But, in spite of their favorable prayers, by which Italian philanthropists set great store, a cloud seemed to hang over these once Arcadian precincts, and to be darkest around the summit of the tower where Donatello was wont to sit and brood.

CHAPTER XXVII. MYTHS

After the sculptor's arrival, however, the young Count sometimes came down from his forlorn elevation, and rambled with him among the neighboring woods and hills. He led his friend to many enchanting nooks, with which he himself had been familiar in his childhood. But of late, as he remarked to Kenyon, a sort of strangeness had overgrown them, like clusters of dark shrubbery, so that he hardly recognized the places which he had known and loved so well.

To the sculptor's eye, nevertheless, they were still rich with beauty. They were picturesque in that sweetly impressive way where wildness, in a long lapse of years, has crept over scenes that have been once adorned with the careful art and toil of man; and when man could do no more for them, time and nature came, and wrought hand in hand to bring them to a soft and venerable perfection. There grew the fig-tree that had run wild and taken to wife the vine, which likewise had gone rampant out of all human control; so that the two wild things had tangled and knotted themselves into a wild marriage bond, and hung their various progeny—the luscious figs, the grapes, oozy with the Southern juice, and both endowed with a wild flavor that added the final charm—on the same bough together.

In Kenyon's opinion, never was any other nook so lovely as a certain little dell which he and Donatello visited. It was hollowed in among the hills, and open to a glimpse of the broad, fertile valley. A fountain had its birth here, and fell into a marble basin, which was all covered with moss and shaggy with water-weeds. Over the gush of the small stream, with an urn in her arms, stood a marble nymph, whose nakedness the moss had kindly clothed as with a garment; and the long trails and tresses of the maidenhair had done what they could in the poor thing's behalf, by hanging themselves about her waist, In former days—it might be a remote antiquity—this lady of the fountain had first received the infant tide into her urn and poured it thence into the marble basin. But now the sculptured urn had a great crack from top to bottom; and the discontented nymph was compelled to see the basin fill itself through a channel which she could not control, although with water long ago consecrated to her.

For this reason, or some other, she looked terribly forlorn; and you might have fancied that the whole fountain was but the overflow of her lonely tears.

"This was a place that I used greatly to delight in," remarked Donatello, sighing. "As a child, and as a boy, I have been very happy here."

"And, as a man, I should ask no fitter place to be happy in," answered Kenyon. "But you, my friend, are of such a social nature, that I should hardly have thought these lonely haunts would take your fancy. It is a place for a poet to dream in, and people it with the beings of his imagination."

"I am no poet, that I know of," said Donatello, "but yet, as I tell you, I have been very happy here, in the company of this fountain and this nymph. It is said that a Faun, my oldest forefather, brought home hither to this very spot a human maiden, whom he loved and wedded. This spring of delicious water was their household well."

"It is a most enchanting fable!" exclaimed Kenyon; "that is, if it be not a fact."

"And why not a fact?" said the simple Donatello. "There is, likewise, another sweet old story connected with this spot. But, now that I remember it, it seems to me more sad than sweet, though formerly the sorrow, in which it closes, did not so much impress me. If I had the gift of tale-telling, this one would be sure to interest you mightily."

"Pray tell it," said Kenyon; "no matter whether well or ill. These wild legends have often the most powerful charm when least artfully told."

So the young Count narrated a myth of one of his Progenitors,—he might have lived a century ago, or a thousand years, or before the Christian epoch, for anything that Donatello knew to the contrary,—who had made acquaintance with a fair creature belonging to this fountain. Whether woman or sprite was a mystery, as was all else about her, except that her life and soul were somehow interfused throughout the gushing water. She was a fresh, cool, dewy thing, sunny and shadowy, full of pleasant little mischiefs, fitful and changeable with the whim of the moment, but yet as constant as her native stream, which kept the same gush and flow forever, while marble crumbled over and around it. The fountain woman loved the youth,—a knight, as Donatello called him,—for, according to the legend, his race was akin to hers. At least, whether kin or no, there had been friendship and sympathy of old betwixt an ancestor of his, with furry ears, and the long-lived lady of the fountain. And, after all those ages, she was still as young as a May morning, and as frolicsome as a bird upon a tree, or a breeze that makes merry with the leaves.

She taught him how to call her from her pebbly source, and they spent many a happy hour together, more especially in the fervor of the summer days. For often as he sat waiting for her by the margin of the spring, she would suddenly fall down around him in a shower of sunny raindrops, with a rainbow glancing through them, and forthwith gather herself up into the likeness of a beautiful girl, laughing—or was it the warble of the rill over the pebbles?—to see the youth's amazement.

Thus, kind maiden that she was, the hot atmosphere became deliciously cool and fragrant for this favored knight; and, furthermore, when he knelt down to drink out of the spring, nothing was more common than for a pair of rosy lips to come up out of its little depths, and touch his mouth with the thrill of a sweet, cool, dewy kiss!

"It is a delightful story for the hot noon of your Tuscan summer," observed the sculptor, at this point. "But the deportment of the watery lady must have had a most chilling influence in midwinter. Her lover would find it, very literally, a cold reception!"

"I suppose," said Donatello rather sulkily, "you are making fun of the story. But I see nothing laughable in the thing itself, nor in what you say about it."

He went on to relate, that for a long While the knight found infinite pleasure and comfort in the friendship of the fountain nymph. In his merriest hours, she gladdened him with her sportive humor. If ever he was annoyed with earthly trouble, she laid her moist hand upon his brow, and charmed the fret and fever quite away.

But one day—one fatal noontide—the young knight came rushing with hasty and irregular steps to the accustomed fountain. He called the nymph; but—no doubt because there was something unusual and frightful in his tone she did not appear, nor answer him. He flung himself down, and washed his hands and bathed his feverish brow in the cool, pure water. And then there was a sound of woe; it might have been a woman's voice; it might have been only the sighing of the brook over the pebbles. The water shrank away from the youth's hands, and left his brow as dry and feverish as before.

Donatello here came to a dead pause.

"Why did the water shrink from this unhappy knight?" inquired the sculptor.

"Because he had tried to wash off a bloodstain!" said the young Count, in a horror-stricken whisper. "The guilty man had polluted the pure water. The nymph might have comforted him in sorrow, but could not cleanse his conscience of a crime."

"And did he never behold her more?" asked Kenyon.

"Never but once," replied his friend. "He never beheld her blessed face but once again, and then there was a blood-stain on the poor nymph's brow; it was the stain his guilt had left in the fountain where he tried to wash it off. He mourned for her his whole life long, and employed the best sculptor of the time to carve this statue of the nymph from his description of her aspect. But, though my ancestor would fain have had the image wear her happiest look, the artist, unlike yourself, was so impressed with the mournfulness of the story, that, in spite of his best efforts, he made her forlorn, and forever weeping, as you see!"

Kenyon found a certain charm in this simple legend. Whether so intended or not, he understood it as an apologue, typifying the soothing and genial effects of an habitual intercourse with nature in all ordinary cares and griefs; while, on the other hand, her mild influences fall short in their effect upon the ruder passions, and are altogether powerless in the dread fever-fit or deadly chill of guilt.

"Do you say," he asked, "that the nymph's race has never since been shown to any mortal? Methinks you, by your native qualities, are as well entitled to her favor as ever your progenitor could have been. Why have you not summoned her?"

"I called her often when I was a silly child," answered Donatello; and he added, in an inward voice, "Thank Heaven, she did not come!"

"Then you never saw her?" said the sculptor.

"Never in my life!" rejoined the Count. "No, my dear friend, I have not seen the nymph; although here, by her fountain, I used to make many strange acquaintances; for, from my earliest childhood, I was familiar with whatever creatures haunt the woods. You would have laughed to see the friends I had among them; yes, among the wild, nimble things, that reckon man their deadliest enemy! How it was first taught me, I cannot tell; but there was a charm—a voice, a murmur, a kind of chant—by which I called the woodland inhabitants, the furry people, and the feathered people, in a language that they seemed to understand."

"I have heard of such a gift," responded the sculptor gravely, "but never before met with a person endowed with it. Pray try the charm; and lest I should frighten your friends away, I will withdraw into this thicket, and merely peep at them."

"I doubt," said Donatello, "whether they will remember my voice now. It changes, you know, as the boy grows towards manhood."

Nevertheless, as the young Count's good-nature and easy persuadability were among his best characteristics, he set about complying with Kenyon's request. The latter, in his concealment among the shrubberies, heard him send forth a sort of modulated breath, wild, rude, yet harmonious. It struck the auditor as at once the strangest and the most natural utterance that had ever reached his ears. Any idle boy, it should seem, singing to himself and setting his wordless song to no other or more definite tune than the play of his own pulses, might produce a sound almost identical with this; and yet, it was as individual as a murmur of the breeze. Donatello tried it, over and over again, with many breaks, at first, and pauses of uncertainty; then with more confidence, and a fuller swell, like a wayfarer groping out of obscurity into the light, and moving with freer footsteps as it brightens around him.

Anon, his voice appeared to fill the air, yet not with an obtrusive clangor. The sound was of a murmurous character, soft, attractive, persuasive, friendly. The sculptor fancied that such might have been the original voice and utterance of the natural man, before the sophistication of the human intellect formed what we now call language. In this broad dialect—broad as the sympathies of nature—the human brother might have spoken to his inarticulate brotherhood that prowl the woods, or soar upon the wing, and have been intelligible to such extent as to win their confidence.

The sound had its pathos too. At some of its simple cadences, the tears came quietly into Kenyon's eyes. They welled up slowly from his heart, which was thrilling with an emotion more delightful than he had often felt before, but which he forbore to analyze, lest, if he seized it, it should at once perish in his grasp.

Donatello paused two or three times, and seemed to listen,—then, recommencing, he poured his spirit and life more earnestly into the strain. And finally,—or else the sculptor's hope and imagination deceived him,—soft treads were audible upon the fallen leaves. There was a rustling among the shrubbery; a whir of wings, moreover, that hovered in the air. It may have been all an illusion; but Kenyon fancied that he could distinguish the stealthy, cat-like movement of some small forest citizen, and that he could even see its doubtful shadow, if not really its substance. But, all at once, whatever might be the reason, there ensued a hurried rush and scamper of little feet; and then the sculptor heard a wild, sorrowful cry, and through the crevices of the thicket beheld Donatello fling himself on the ground.

Emerging from his hiding-place, he saw no living thing, save a brown lizard (it was of the tarantula species) rustling away through the sunshine.

To all present appearance, this venomous reptile was the only creature that had responded to the young Count's efforts to renew his intercourse with the lower orders of nature.

"What has happened to you?" exclaimed Kenyon, stooping down over his friend, and wondering at the anguish which he betrayed.

"Death, death!" sobbed Donatello. "They know it!"

He grovelled beside the fountain, in a fit of such passionate sobbing and weeping, that it seemed as if his heart had broken, and spilt its wild sorrows upon the ground. His unrestrained grief and childish tears made Kenyon sensible in how small a degree the customs and restraints of society had really acted upon this young man, in spite of the quietude of his ordinary deportment. In response to his friend's efforts to console him, he murmured words hardly more articulate than the strange chant which he had so recently been breathing into the air.

"They know it!" was all that Kenyon could yet distinguish,—"they know it!"

"Who know it?" asked the sculptor. "And what is it their know?" "They know it!" repeated Donatello, trembling. "They shun me! All nature shrinks from me, and shudders at me! I live in the midst of a curse, that hems me round with a circle of fire! No innocent thing can come near me."

"Be comforted, my dear friend," said Kenyon, kneeling beside him. "You labor under some illusion, but no curse. As for this strange, natural spell, which you have been exercising, and of which I have heard before, though I never believed in, nor expected to witness it, I am satisfied that you still possess it. It was my own half-concealed presence, no doubt, and some involuntary little movement of mine, that scared away your forest friends."

"They are friends of mine no longer," answered Donatello.

"We all of us, as we grow older," rejoined Kenyon, "lose somewhat of our proximity to nature. It is the price we pay for experience."

"A heavy price, then!" said Donatello, rising from the ground. "But we will speak no more of it. Forget this scene, my dear friend. In your eyes, it must look very absurd. It is a grief, I presume, to all men, to find the pleasant privileges and properties of early life departing from them. That grief has now befallen me. Well; I shall waste no more tears for such a cause!"

Nothing else made Kenyon so sensible of a change in Donatello, as his newly acquired power of dealing with his own emotions, and, after a struggle more or less fierce, thrusting them down into the prison cells where he usually kept them confined. The restraint, which he now put upon himself, and the mask of dull composure which he succeeded in clasping over his still beautiful, and once faun-like face, affected the sensitive sculptor more sadly than even the unrestrained passion of the preceding scene. It is a very miserable epoch, when the evil necessities of life, in our tortuous world, first get the better of us so far as to compel us to attempt throwing a cloud over our transparency. Simplicity increases in value the longer we can keep it, and the further we carry it onward into life; the loss of a child's simplicity, in the inevitable lapse of years, causes but a natural sigh or two, because even his mother feared that he could not keep it always. But after a young man has brought it through his childhood, and has still worn it in his bosom, not as an early dewdrop, but as a diamond of pure white lustre,—it is a pity to lose it, then. And thus, when Kenyon saw how much his friend had now to hide, and how well he hid it, he would have wept, although his tears would have been even idler than those which Donatello had just shed.

They parted on the lawn before the house, the Count to climb his tower, and the sculptor to read an antique edition of Dante, which he had found among some old volumes of Catholic devotion, in a seldom-visited room, Tomaso met him in the entrance hall, and showed a desire to speak.

"Our poor signorino looks very sad to-day!" he said.

"Even so, good Tomaso," replied the sculptor. "Would that we could raise his spirits a little!"

"There might be means, Signore," answered the old butler, "if one might but be sure that they were the right ones. We men are but rough nurses for a sick body or a sick spirit."

"Women, you would say, my good friend, are better," said the sculptor, struck by an intelligence in the butler's face. "That is possible! But it depends."

"Ah; we will wait a little longer," said Tomaso, with the customary shake of his head.

CHAPTER XXVIII. THE OWL TOWER

"Will you not show me your tower?" said the sculptor one day to his friend.

"It is plainly enough to be seen, methinks," answered the Count, with a kind of sulkiness that often appeared in him, as one of the little symptoms of inward trouble.

"Yes; its exterior is visible far and wide," said Kenyon. "But such a gray, moss-grown tower as this, however valuable as an object of scenery, will certainly be quite as interesting inside as out. It cannot be less than six hundred years old; the foundations and lower story are much older than that, I should judge; and traditions probably cling to the walls within quite as plentifully as the gray and yellow lichens cluster on its face without."

"No doubt," replied Donatello,—"but I know little of such things, and never could comprehend the interest which some of you Forestieri take in them. A year or two ago an English signore, with a venerable white beard— they say he was a magician, too—came hither from as far off as Florence, just to see my tower."

"Ah, I have seen him at Florence," observed Kenyon. "He is a necromancer, as you say, and dwells in an old mansion of the Knights Templars, close by the Ponte Vecchio, with a great many ghostly books, pictures, and antiquities, to make the house gloomy, and one bright-eyed little girl, to keep it cheerful!"

"I know him only by his white beard," said Donatello; "but he could have told you a great deal about the tower, and the sieges which it has stood, and the prisoners who have been confined in it. And he gathered up all the traditions of the Monte Beni family, and, among the rest, the sad one which I told you at the fountain the other day. He had known mighty poets, he said, in his earlier life; and the most illustrious of them would have rejoiced to preserve such a legend in immortal rhyme,—especially if he could have had some of our wine of Sunshine to help out his inspiration!"

"Any man might be a poet, as well as Byron, with such wine and such a theme," rejoined the sculptor. "But shall we climb your tower The thunderstorm gathering yonder among the hills will be a spectacle worth witnessing."

"Come, then," said the Count, adding, with a sigh, "it has a weary staircase, and dismal chambers, and it is very lonesome at the summit!"

"Like a man's life, when he has climbed to eminence," remarked the sculptor; "or, let us rather say, with its difficult steps, and the dark prison cells you speak of, your tower resembles the spiritual experience of many a sinful soul, which, nevertheless, may struggle upward into the pure air and light of Heaven at last!"

Donatello sighed again, and led the way up into the tower.

Mounting the broad staircase that ascended from the entrance hall, they traversed the great wilderness of a house, through some obscure passages, and came to a low, ancient doorway. It admitted them to a narrow turret stair which zigzagged upward, lighted in its progress by loopholes and iron-barred windows. Reaching the top of the first flight, the Count threw open a door of worm-eaten oak, and disclosed a chamber that occupied the whole area of the tower. It was most pitiably forlorn of aspect, with a brick-paved floor, bare holes through the massive walls, grated with iron, instead of windows, and for furniture an old stool, which increased the dreariness of the place tenfold, by suggesting an idea of its having once been tenanted.

"This was a prisoner's cell in the old days," said Donatello; "the whitebearded necromancer, of whom I told you, found out that a certain famous monk was confined here, about five hundred years ago. He was a very holy man, and was afterwards burned at the stake in the Grand-ducal Square at Firenze. There have always been stories, Tomaso says, of a hooded monk creeping up and down these stairs, or standing in the doorway of this chamber. It must needs be the ghost of the ancient prisoner. Do you believe in ghosts?"

"I can hardly tell," replied Kenyon; "on the whole, I think not."

"Neither do I," responded the Count; "for, if spirits ever come back, I should surely have met one within these two months past. Ghosts never rise! So much I know, and am glad to know it!"

Following the narrow staircase still higher, they came to another room of similar size and equally forlorn, but inhabited by two personages of a race which from time immemorial have held proprietorship and occupancy in ruined towers. These were a pair of owls, who, being doubtless acquainted with Donatello, showed little sign of alarm at the entrance of visitors. They gave a dismal croak or two, and hopped aside into the darkest corner, since it was not yet their hour to flap duskily abroad.

"They do not desert me, like my other feathered acquaintances," observed the young Count, with a sad smile, alluding to the scene which Kenyon had witnessed at the fountain-side. "When I was a wild, playful boy, the owls did not love me half so well."

He made no further pause here, but led his friend up another flight of steps—while, at every stage, the windows and narrow loopholes afforded Kenyon more extensive eye-shots over hill and valley, and allowed him to taste the cool purity of mid-atmosphere. At length they reached the topmost chamber, directly beneath the roof of the tower.

"This is my own abode," said Donatello; "my own owl's nest."

In fact, the room was fitted up as a bedchamber, though in a style of the utmost simplicity. It likewise served as an oratory; there being a crucifix in one corner, and a multitude of holy emblems, such as Catholics judge it necessary to help their devotion withal. Several ugly little prints, representing the sufferings of the Saviour, and the martyrdoms of saints, hung on the wall; and behind the crucifix there was a good copy of Titian's Magdalen of the Pitti Palace, clad only in the flow of her golden ringlets. She had a confident look (but it was Titian's fault, not the penitent woman's), as if expecting to win heaven by the free display of her earthly charms. Inside of a glass case appeared an image of the sacred Bambino, in the guise of a little waxen boy, very prettily made, reclining among flowers, like a Cupid, and holding up a heart that resembled a bit of red sealing-wax. A small vase of precious marble was full of holy water.

Beneath the crucifix, on a table, lay a human skull, which looked as if it might have been dug up out of some old grave. But, examining it more closely, Kenyon saw that it was carved in gray alabaster; most skillfully done to the death, with accurate imitation of the teeth, the sutures, the empty eye-caverns, and the fragile little bones of the nose. This hideous emblem rested on a cushion of white marble, so nicely wrought that you seemed to see the impression of the heavy skull in a silken and downy substance.

Donatello dipped his fingers into the holy-water vase, and crossed himself. After doing so he trembled.

"I have no right to make the sacred symbol on a sinful breast!" he said.

"On what mortal breast can it be made, then?" asked the sculptor. "Is there one that hides no sin?"

"But these blessed emblems make you smile, I fear," resumed the Count, looking askance at his friend. "You heretics, I know, attempt to pray without even a crucifix to kneel at."

"I, at least, whom you call a heretic, reverence that holy symbol," answered Kenyon. "What I am most inclined to murmur at is this death's head. I could laugh, moreover, in its ugly face! It is absurdly monstrous, my dear friend, thus to fling the dead weight of our mortality upon our immortal hopes. While we live on earth, 't is true, we must needs carry our skeletons about with us; but, for Heaven's sake, do not let us burden our spirits with them, in our feeble efforts to soar upward! Believe me, it will change the whole aspect of death, if you can once disconnect it, in your idea, with that corruption from which it disengages our higher part."

"I do not well understand you," said Donatello; and he took up the alabaster skull, shuddering, and evidently feeling it a kind of penance to touch it. "I only know that this skull has been in my family for centuries. Old Tomaso has a story that it was copied by a famous sculptor from the skull of that same unhappy knight who loved the fountain lady, and lost her by a blood-stain. He lived and died with a deep sense of sin upon him, and on his death-bed he ordained that this token of him should go down to his posterity. And my forefathers, being a cheerful race of men in their natural disposition, found it needful to have the skull often before their eyes, because they dearly loved life and its enjoyments, and hated the very thought of death."

"I am afraid," said Kenyon, "they liked it none the better, for seeing its face under this abominable mask."

Without further discussion, the Count led the way up one more flight of stairs, at the end of which they emerged upon the summit of the tower. The sculptor felt as if his being were suddenly magnified a hundredfold; so wide was the Umbrian valley that suddenly opened before him, set in its grand framework of nearer and more distant hills. It seemed as if all Italy lay under his eyes in that one picture. For there was the broad, sunny smile of God, which we fancy to be spread over that favored land more abundantly than on other regions, and beneath it glowed a most rich and varied fertility. The trim vineyards were there, and the fig-trees, and the mulberries, and the smoky-hued tracts of the olive orchards; there, too, were fields of every kind of grain, among which, waved the Indian corn, putting Kenyon in mind of the fondly remembered acres of his father's homestead. White villas, gray convents, church spires, villages, towns, each with its battlemented walls and towered gateway, were scattered upon this spacious map; a river gleamed across it; and lakes opened their blue eyes in its face, reflecting heaven, lest mortals should forget that better land when they beheld the earth so beautiful.

What made the valley look still wider was the two or three varieties of weather that were visible on its surface, all at the same instant of time. Here lay the quiet sunshine; there fell the great black patches of ominous shadow from the clouds; and behind them, like a giant of league-long strides, came hurrying the thunderstorm, which had already swept midway across the plain. In the rear of the approaching tempest, brightened forth again the sunny splendor, which its progress had darkened with so terrible a frown.

All round this majestic landscape, the bald-peaked or forest-crowned mountains descended boldly upon the plain. On many of their spurs and midway declivities, and even on their summits, stood cities, some of them famous of old; for these had been the seats and nurseries of early art, where the flower of beauty sprang out of a rocky soil, and in a high, keen atmosphere, when the richest and most sheltered gardens failed to nourish it.

"Thank God for letting me again behold this scene!" Said the sculptor, a devout man in his way, reverently taking off his hat. "I have viewed it from many points, and never without as full a sensation of gratitude as my heart seems capable of feeling. How it strengthens the poor human spirit in its reliance on His providence, to ascend but this little way above the common level, and so attain a somewhat wider glimpse of His dealings with mankind! He doeth all things right! His will be done!"

"You discern something that is hidden from me," observed Donatello gloomily, yet striving with unwonted grasp to catch the analogies which so cheered his friend. "I see sunshine on one spot, and cloud in another, and no reason for it in either ease. The sun on you; the cloud on me! What comfort can I draw from this?"

"Nay; I cannot preach," said Kenyon, "with a page of heaven and a page of earth spread wide open before us! Only begin to read it, and you will find it interpreting itself without the aid of words. It is a great mistake to try to put our best thoughts into human language. When we ascend into the higher regions of emotion and spiritual enjoyment, they are only expressible by such grand hieroglyphics as these around us."

They stood awhile, contemplating the scene; but, as inevitably happens after a spiritual flight, it was not long before the sculptor felt his wings flagging in the rarity of the upper atmosphere. He was glad to let himself quietly downward out of the mid-sky, as it were, and alight on the solid platform of the battlemented tower. He looked about him, and beheld growing out of the stone pavement, which formed the roof, a little shrub, with green and glossy leaves. It was the only green thing there; and Heaven knows how its seeds had ever been planted, at that airy height, or how it had found nourishment for its small life in the chinks of the stones; for it had no earth, and nothing more like soil than the crumbling mortar, which had been crammed into the crevices in a long-past age.

Yet the plant seemed fond of its native site; and Donatello said it had always grown there from his earliest remembrance, and never, he believed, any smaller or any larger than they saw it now.

"I wonder if the shrub teaches you any good lesson," said he, observing the interest with which Kenyon examined it. "If the wide valley has a great meaning, the plant ought to have at least a little one; and it has been growing on our tower long enough to have learned how to speak it."

"O, certainly!" answered the sculptor; "the shrub has its moral, or it would have perished long ago. And, no doubt, it is for your use and edification, since you have had it before your eyes all your lifetime, and now are moved to ask what may be its lesson."

"It teaches me nothing," said the simple Donatello, stooping over the plant, and perplexing himself with a minute scrutiny. "But here was a worm that would have killed it; an ugly creature, which I will fling over the battlements."

CHAPTER XXIX. ON THE BATTLEMENTS

The sculptor now looked through art embrasure, and threw down a bit of lime, watching its fall, till it struck upon a stone bench at the rocky foundation of the tower, and flew into many fragments.

"Pray pardon me for helping Time to crumble away your ancestral walls," said he. "But I am one of those persons who have a natural tendency to climb heights, and to stand on the verge of them, measuring the depth below. If I were to do just as I like, at this moment, I should fling myself down after that bit of lime. It is a very singular temptation, and all but irresistible; partly, I believe, because it might be so easily done, and partly because such momentous consequences would ensue, without my being compelled to wait a moment for them. Have you never felt this strange impulse of an evil spirit at your back, shoving you towards a precipice?"

"Ah, no!" cried. Donatello, shrinking from the battlemented wall with a face of horror. "I cling to life in a way which you cannot conceive; it has been so rich, so warm, so sunny!—and beyond its verge, nothing but the chilly dark! And then a fall from a precipice is such an awful death!"

"Nay; if it be a great height," said Kenyon, "a man would leave his life in the air, and never feel the hard shock at the bottom."

"That is not the way with this kind of death!" exclaimed Donatello, in a low, horror-stricken voice, which grew higher and more full of emotion as he proceeded. "Imagine a fellow creature,—breathing now, and looking you in the face,—and now tumbling down, down, down, with a long shriek wavering after him, all the way! He does not leave his life in the air! No; but it keeps in him till he thumps against the stones, a horribly long while; then he lies there frightfully quiet, a dead heap of bruised flesh and broken bones! A quiver runs through the crushed mass; and no more movement after that! No; not if you would give your soul to make him stir a finger! Ah, terrible! Yes, yes; I would fain fling myself down for the very dread of it, that I might endure it once for all, and dream of it no more!"

"How forcibly, how frightfully you conceive this!" said the sculptor, aghast at the passionate horror which was betrayed in the Count's words, and still more in his wild gestures and ghastly look. "Nay, if the height of your tower affects your imagination thus, you do wrong to trust yourself here in solitude, and in the night-time, and at all unguarded hours. You are not safe in your chamber. It is but a step or two; and what if a vivid dream should lead you up hither at midnight, and act itself out as a reality!"

Donatello had hidden his face in his hands, and was leaning against the parapet.

"No fear of that!" said he. "Whatever the dream may be, I am too genuine a coward to act out my own death in it."

The paroxysm passed away, and the two friends continued their desultory talk, very much as if no such interruption had occurred. Nevertheless, it affected the sculptor with infinite pity to see this young man, who had been born to gladness as an assured heritage, now involved in a misty bewilderment of grievous thoughts, amid which he seemed to go staggering blindfold. Kenyon, not without an unshaped suspicion of the definite fact, knew that his condition must have resulted from the weight and gloom of life, now first, through the agency of a secret trouble, making themselves felt on a character that had heretofore breathed only an atmosphere of joy. The effect of this hard lesson, upon Donatello's intellect and disposition, was very striking. It was perceptible that he had already had glimpses of strange and subtle matters in those dark caverns, into which all men must descend, if they would know anything beneath the surface and illusive pleasures of existence. And when they emerge, though dazzled and blinded by the first glare of daylight, they take truer and sadder views of life forever afterwards.

From some mysterious source, as the sculptor felt assured, a soul had been inspired into the young Count's simplicity, since their intercourse in Rome. He now showed a far deeper sense, and an intelligence that began to deal with high subjects, though in a feeble and childish way. He evinced, too, a more definite and nobler individuality, but developed out of grief and pain, and fearfully conscious of the pangs that had given it birth. Every human life, if it ascends to truth or delves down to reality, must undergo a similar change; but sometimes, perhaps, the instruction comes without the sorrow; and oftener the sorrow teaches no lesson that abides with us. In Donatello's case, it was pitiful, and almost ludicrous, to observe the confused struggle that he made; how completely he was taken by surprise; how ill-prepared he stood, on this old battlefield of the world, to fight with such an inevitable foe as mortal calamity, and sin for its stronger ally.

"And yet," thought Kenyon, "the poor fellow bears himself like a hero, too! If he would only tell me his trouble, or give me an opening to speak frankly about it, I might help him; but he finds it too horrible to be uttered, and fancies himself the only mortal that ever felt the anguish of remorse. Yes; he believes that nobody ever endured his agony before; so that—sharp enough in itself—it has all the additional zest of a torture just invented to plague him individually."

The sculptor endeavored to dismiss the painful subject from his mind; and, leaning against the battlements, he turned his face southward and westward, and gazed across the breadth of the valley. His thoughts flew far beyond even those wide boundaries, taking an air-line from Donatello's tower to another turret that ascended into the sky of the summer afternoon, invisibly to him, above the roofs of distant Rome. Then rose tumultuously into his consciousness that strong love for Hilda, which it was his habit to confine in one of the heart's inner chambers, because he had found no encouragement to bring it forward. But now he felt a strange pull at his heart-strings. It could not have been more perceptible, if all the way between these battlements and Hilda's dove-cote had stretched an exquisitely sensitive cord, which, at the hither end, was knotted with his aforesaid heart-strings, and, at the remoter one, was grasped by a gentle hand. His breath grew tremulous. He put his hand to his breast; so distinctly did he seem to feel that cord drawn once, and again, and again, as if—though still it was bashfully intimated there were an importunate demand for his presence. O for the white wings of Hilda's doves, that he might, have flown thither, and alighted at the Virgin's shrine!

But lovers, and Kenyon knew it well, project so lifelike a copy of their mistresses out of their own imaginations, that it can pull at the heartstrings almost as perceptibly as the genuine original. No airy intimations are to be trusted; no evidences of responsive affection less positive than whispered and broken words, or tender pressures of the hand, allowed and half returned; or glances, that distil many passionate avowals into one gleam of richly colored light. Even these should be weighed rigorously, at the instant; for, in another instant, the imagination seizes on them as its property, and stamps them with its own arbitrary value. But Hilda's maidenly reserve had given her lover no such tokens, to be interpreted either by his hopes or fears.

"Yonder, over mountain and valley, lies Rome," said the sculptor; "shall you return thither in the autumn?"

"Never! I hate Rome," answered Donatello; "and have good cause."

"And yet it was a pleasant winter that we spent there," observed Kenyon, "and with pleasant friends about us. You would meet them again there—all of them."

"All?" asked Donatello.

"All, to the best of my belief," said the sculptor: "but you need not go to Rome to seek them. If there were one of those friends whose lifetime was twisted with your own, I am enough of a fatalist to feel assured that you will meet that one again, wander whither you may. Neither can we escape the companions whom Providence assigns for us, by climbing an old tower like this."

"Yet the stairs are steep and dark," rejoined the Count; "none but yourself would seek me here, or find me, if they sought."

As Donatello did not take advantage of this opening which his friend had kindly afforded him to pour out his hidden troubles, the latter again threw aside the subject, and returned to the enjoyment of the scene before him. The thunder-storm, which he had beheld striding across the valley, had passed to the left of Monte Beni, and was continuing its march towards the hills that formed the boundary on the eastward. Above the whole valley, indeed, the sky was heavy with tumbling vapors, interspersed with which were tracts of blue, vividly brightened by the sun; but, in the east, where the tempest was yet trailing its ragged skirts, lay a dusky region of cloud and sullen mist, in which some of the hills appeared of a dark purple hue. Others became so indistinct, that the spectator could not tell rocky height from impalpable cloud. Far into this misty cloud region, however,—within the domain of chaos, as it were,—hilltops were seen brightening in the sunshine; they looked like fragments of the world, broken adrift and based on nothingness, or like portions of a sphere destined to exist, but not yet finally compacted.

The sculptor, habitually drawing many of the images and illustrations of his thoughts from the plastic art, fancied that the scene represented the process of the Creator, when he held the new, imperfect earth in his hand, and modelled it.

"What a magic is in mist and vapor among the mountains!" he exclaimed. "With their help, one single scene becomes a thousand. The cloud scenery gives such variety to a hilly landscape that it would be worth while to journalize its aspect from hour to hour. A cloud, however,—as I have myself experienced,—is apt to grow solid and as heavy as a stone the instant that you take in hand to describe it, But, in my own heart, I have found great use in clouds. Such silvery ones as those to the northward, for example, have often suggested sculpturesque groups, figures, and attitudes; they are especially rich in attitudes of living repose, which a sculptor only hits upon by the rarest good fortune. When I go back to my dear native land, the clouds along the horizon will be my only gallery of art!"

"I can see cloud shapes, too," said Donatello; "yonder is one that shifts strangely; it has been like people whom I knew. And now, if I watch it a little longer, it will take the figure of a monk reclining, with his cowl about his head and drawn partly over his face, and—well! did I not tell you so?"

"I think," remarked Kenyon, "we can hardly be gazing at the same cloud. What I behold is a reclining figure, to be sure, but feminine, and with a despondent air, wonderfully well expressed in the wavering outline from head to foot. It moves my very heart by something indefinable that it suggests."

"I see the figure, and almost the face," said the Count; adding, in a lower voice, "It is Miriam's!"

"No, not Miriam's," answered the sculptor. While the two gazers thus found their own reminiscences and presentiments floating among the clouds, the day drew to its close, and now showed them the fair spectacle of an Italian sunset. The sky was soft and bright, but not so gorgeous as Kenyon had seen it, a thousand times, in America; for there the western sky is wont to be set aflame with breadths and depths of color with which poets seek in vain to dye their verses, and which painters never dare to copy. As beheld from the tower of Monte Beni, the scene was tenderly magnificent, with mild gradations of hue and a lavish outpouring of gold, but rather such gold as we see on the leaf of a bright flower than the burnished glow of metal from the mine. Or, if metallic, it looked airy and unsubstantial, like the glorified dreams of an alchemist. And speedily—more speedily than in our own clime—came the twilight, and, brightening through its gray transparency, the stars.

A swarm of minute insects that had been hovering all day round the battlements were now swept away by the freshness of a rising breeze. The two owls in the chamber beneath Donatello's uttered their soft melancholy cry,—which, with national avoidance of harsh sounds, Italian owls substitute for the hoot of their kindred in other countries,—and flew darkling forth among the shrubbery. A convent bell rang out near at hand, and was not only echoed among the hills, but answered by another bell, and still another, which doubtless had farther and farther responses, at various distances along the valley; for, like the English drumbeat around the globe, there is a chain of convent bells from end to end, and crosswise, and in all possible directions over priest-ridden Italy.

"Come," said the sculptor, "the evening air grows cool. It is time to descend."

"Time for you, my friend," replied the Count; and he hesitated a little before adding, "I must keep a vigil here for some hours longer. It is my frequent custom to keep vigils,—and sometimes the thought occurs to me whether it were not better to keep them in yonder convent, the bell of which just now seemed to summon me. Should I do wisely, do you think, to exchange this old tower for a cell?"

"What! Turn monk?" exclaimed his friend. "A horrible idea!"

"True," said Donatello, sighing. "Therefore, if at all, I purpose doing it."

"Then think of it no more, for Heaven's sake!" cried the sculptor. "There are a thousand better and more poignant methods of being miserable than that, if to be miserable is what you wish. Nay; I question whether a monk keeps himself up to the intellectual and spiritual height which misery implies. A monk I judge from their sensual physiognomies, which meet me at every turn—is inevitably a beast! Their souls, if they have any to begin with, perish out of them, before their sluggish, swinish existence is half done. Better, a million times, to stand star-gazing on these airy battlements, than to smother your new germ of a higher life in a monkish cell!"

"You make me tremble," said Donatello, "by your bold aspersion of men who have devoted themselves to God's service!"

"They serve neither God nor man, and themselves least of all, though their motives be utterly selfish," replied Kenyon. "Avoid the convent, my dear friend, as you would shun the death of the soul! But, for my own part, if I had an insupportable burden,—if, for any cause, I were bent upon sacrificing every earthly hope as a peace-offering towards Heaven,—I would make the wide world my cell, and good deeds to mankind my prayer. Many penitent men have done this, and found peace in it."

"Ah, but you are a heretic!" said the Count.

Yet his face brightened beneath the stars; and, looking at it through the twilight, the sculptor's remembrance went back to that scene in the Capitol, where, both in features and expression, Donatello had seemed identical with the Faun. And still there was a resemblance; for now, when first the idea was suggested of living for the welfare of his fellow-creatures, the original beauty, which sorrow had partly effaced, came back elevated and spiritualized. In the black depths the Faun had found a soul, and was struggling with it towards the light of heaven.

The illumination, it is true, soon faded out of Donatello's face. The idea of lifelong and unselfish effort was too high to be received by him with more than a momentary comprehension. An Italian, indeed, seldom dreams of being philanthropic, except in bestowing alms among the paupers, who appeal to his beneficence at every step; nor does it occur to him that there are fitter modes of propitiating Heaven than by penances, pilgrimages, and offerings at shrines. Perhaps, too, their system has its share of moral advantages; they, at all events, cannot well pride themselves, as our own more energetic benevolence is apt to do, upon sharing in the counsels of Providence and kindly helping out its otherwise impracticable designs.

And now the broad valley twinkled with lights, that glimmered through its duskiness like the fireflies in the garden of a Florentine palace. A gleam of lightning from the rear of the tempest showed the circumference of hills and the great space between, as the last cannon-flash of a retreating army reddens across the field where it has fought. The sculptor was on the point of descending the turret stair, when, somewhere in the darkness that lay beneath them, a woman's voice was heard, singing a low, sad strain.

"Hark!" said he, laying his hand on Donatello's arm.

And Donatello had said "Hark!" at the same instant.

The song, if song it could be called, that had only a wild rhythm, and flowed forth in the fitful measure of a wind-harp, did not clothe itself in the sharp brilliancy of the Italian tongue. The words, so far as they could be distinguished, were German, and therefore unintelligible to the Count, and hardly less so to the sculptor; being softened and molten, as it were, into the melancholy richness of the voice that sung them. It was as the murmur of a soul bewildered amid the sinful gloom of earth, and retaining only enough memory of a better state to make sad music of the wail, which would else have been a despairing shriek. Never was there profounder pathos than breathed through that mysterious voice; it brought the tears into the sculptor's eyes, with remembrances and forebodings of whatever sorrow he had felt or apprehended; it made Donatello sob, as chiming in with the anguish that he found unutterable, and giving it the expression which he vaguely sought.

But, when the emotion was at its profoundest depth, the voice rose out of it, yet so gradually that a gloom seemed to pervade it, far upward from the abyss, and not entirely to fall away as it ascended into a higher and purer region. At last, the auditors would have fancied that the melody, with its rich sweetness all there, and much of its sorrow gone, was floating around the very summit of the tower.

"Donatello," said the sculptor, when there was silence again, "had that voice no message for your ear?"

"I dare not receive it," said Donatello; "the anguish of which it spoke abides with me: the hope dies away with the breath that brought it hither. It is not good for me to hear that voice."

The sculptor sighed, and left the poor penitent keeping his vigil on the tower.

CHAPTER XXX. DONATELLO'S BUST

Kenyon, it will be remembered, had asked Donatello's permission to model his bust. The work had now made considerable progress, and necessarily kept the sculptor's thoughts brooding much and often upon his host's personal characteristics. These it was his difficult office to bring out from their depths, and interpret them to all men, showing them what they could not discern for themselves, yet must be compelled to recognize at a glance, on the surface of a block of marble.

He had never undertaken a portrait-bust which gave him so much trouble as Donatello's; not that there was any special difficulty in hitting the likeness, though even in this respect the grace and harmony of the features seemed inconsistent with a prominent expression of individuality; but he was chiefly perplexed how to make this genial and kind type of countenance the index of the mind within. His acuteness and his sympathies, indeed, were both somewhat at fault in their efforts to enlighten him as to the moral phase through which the Count was now passing. If at one sitting he caught a glimpse of what appeared to be a genuine and permanent trait, it would probably be less perceptible on a second occasion, and perhaps have vanished entirely at a third. So evanescent a show of character threw the sculptor into despair; not marble or clay, but cloud and vapor, was the material in which it ought to be represented. Even the ponderous depression which constantly weighed upon Donatello's heart could not compel him into the kind of repose which the plastic art requires.

Hopeless of a good result, Kenyon gave up all preconceptions about the character of his subject, and let his hands work uncontrolled with the clay, somewhat as a spiritual medium, while holding a pen, yields it to an unseen guidance other than that of her own will. Now and then he fancied that this plan was destined to be the successful one. A skill and insight beyond his consciousness seemed occasionally to take up the task. The mystery, the miracle, of imbuing an inanimate substance with thought, feeling, and all the intangible attributes of the soul, appeared on the verge of being wrought. And now, as he flattered himself, the true image of his friend was about to emerge from the facile material, bringing with it more of Donatello's character than the keenest observer could detect at any one moment in the face of the original Vain expectation!—some touch, whereby the artist thought to improve or hasten the result, interfered with the design of his unseen spiritual assistant, and spoilt the whole. There was still the moist, brown clay, indeed, and the features of Donatello, but without any semblance of intelligent and sympathetic life.

"The difficulty will drive me mad, I verily believe!" cried the sculptor nervously. "Look at the wretched piece of work yourself, my dear friend, and tell me whether you recognize any manner of likeness to your inner man?"

"None," replied Donatello, speaking the simple truth. "It is like looking a stranger in the face."

This frankly unfavorable testimony so wrought with the sensitive artist, that he fell into a passion with the stubborn image, and cared not what might happen to it thenceforward. Wielding that wonderful power which sculptors possess over moist clay, however refractory it may show itself in certain respects, he compressed, elongated, widened, and otherwise altered the features of the bust in mere recklessness, and at every change inquired of the Count whether the expression became anywise more satisfactory.

"Stop!" cried Donatello at last, catching the sculptor's hand. "Let it remain so!" By some accidental handling of the clay, entirely independent of his own will, Kenyon had given the countenance a distorted and violent look, combining animal fierceness with intelligent hatred. Had Hilda, or had Miriam, seen the bust, with the expression which it had now assumed, they might have recognized Donatello's face as they beheld it at that terrible moment when he held his victim over the edge of the precipice.

"What have I done?" said the sculptor, shocked at his own casual production. "It were a sin to let the clay which bears your features harden into a look like that. Cain never wore an uglier one."

59

"For that very reason, let it remain!" answered the Count, who had grown pale as ashes at the aspect of his crime, thus strangely presented to him in another of the many guises under which guilt stares the criminal in the face. "Do not alter it! Chisel it, rather, in eternal marble! I will set it up in my oratory and keep it continually before my eyes. Sadder and more horrible is a face like this, alive with my own crime, than the dead skull which my forefathers handed down to me!"

But, without in the least heeding Donatello's remonstrances, the sculptor again applied his artful fingers to the clay, and compelled the bust to dismiss the expression that had so startled them both.

"Believe me," said he, turning his eyes upon his friend, full of grave and tender sympathy, "you know not what is requisite for your spiritual growth, seeking, as you do, to keep your soul perpetually in the unwholesome region of remorse. It was needful for you to pass through that dark valley, but it is infinitely dangerous to linger there too long; there is poison in the atmosphere, when we sit down and brood in it, instead of girding up our loins to press onward. Not despondency, not slothful anguish, is what you now require,—but effort! Has there been an unalterable evil in your young life? Then crowd it out with good, or it will lie corrupting there forever, and cause your capacity for better things to partake its noisome corruption!"

"You stir up many thoughts," said Donatello, pressing his hand upon his brow, "but the multitude and the whirl of them make me dizzy."

They now left the sculptor's temporary studio, without observing that his last accidental touches, with which he hurriedly effaced the look of deadly rage, had given the bust a higher and sweeter expression than it had hitherto worn. It is to be regretted that Kenyon had not seen it; for only an artist, perhaps, can conceive the irksomeness, the irritation of brain, the depression of spirits, that resulted from his failure to satisfy himself, after so much toil and thought as he had bestowed on Donatello's bust. In case of success, indeed, all this thoughtful toil would have been reckoned, not only as well bestowed, but as among the happiest hours of his life; whereas, deeming himself to have failed, it was just so much of life that had better never have been lived; for thus does the good or ill result of his labor throw back sunshine or gloom upon the artist's mind. The sculptor, therefore, would have done well to glance again at his work; for here were still the features of the antique Faun, but now illuminated with a higher meaning, such as the old marble never bore.

Donatello having quitted him, Kenyon spent the rest of the day strolling about the pleasant precincts of Monte Beni, where the summer was now so far advanced that it began, indeed, to partake of the ripe wealth of autumn. Apricots had long been abundant, and had passed away, and plums and cherries along with them. But now came great, juicy pears, melting and delicious, and peaches of goodly size and tempting aspect, though cold and watery to the palate, compared with the sculptor's rich reminiscences of that fruit in America. The purple figs had already enjoyed their day, and the white ones were luscious now. The contadini (who, by this time, knew Kenyon well) found many clusters of ripe grapes for him, in every little globe of which was included a fragrant draught of the sunny Monte Beni wine.

Unexpectedly, in a nook close by the farmhouse, he happened upon a spot where the vintage had actually commenced. A great heap of early ripened grapes had been gathered, and thrown into a mighty tub. In the middle of it stood a lusty and jolly contadino, nor stood, merely, but stamped with all his might, and danced amain; while the red juice bathed his feet, and threw its foam midway up his brown and shaggy legs. Here, then, was the very process that shows so picturesquely in Scripture and in poetry, of treading out the wine-press and dyeing the feet and garments with the crimson effusion as with the blood of a battlefield. The memory of the process does not make the Tuscan wine taste more deliciously. The contadini hospitably offered Kenyon a sample of the new liquor, that had already stood fermenting for a day or two. He had tried a similar draught, however, in years past, and was little inclined to make proof of it again; for he knew that it would be a sour and bitter juice, a wine of woe and tribulation, and that the more a man drinks of such liquor, the sorrier he is likely to be.

The scene reminded the sculptor of our New England vintages, where the big piles of golden and rosy apples lie under the orchard trees, in the mild, autumnal sunshine; and the creaking cider-mill, set in motion by a circumgyratory horse, is all a-gush with the luscious juice. To speak frankly, the cider-making is the more picturesque sight of the two, and the new, sweet cider an infinitely better drink than the ordinary, unripe Tuscan wine. Such as it is, however, the latter fills thousands upon thousands of small, flat barrels, and, still growing thinner and sharper, loses the little life it had, as wine, and becomes apotheosized as a more praiseworthy vinegar.

Yet all these vineyard scenes, and the processes connected with the culture of the grape, had a flavor of poetry about them. The toil that produces those kindly gifts of nature which are not the substance of life, but its luxury, is unlike other toil. We are inclined to fancy that it does not bend the sturdy frame and stiffen the overwrought muscles, like the labor that is devoted in sad, hard earnest to raise grain for sour bread. Certainly, the sunburnt young men and dark-cheeked, laughing girls, who weeded the rich acres of Monte Beni, might well enough have passed for inhabitants of an unsophisticated Arcadia. Later in the season, when the true vintage time should come, and the wine of Sunshine gush into the vats, it was hardly too wild a dream that Bacchus himself might revisit the haunts which he loved of old. But, alas! where now would he find the Faun with whom we see him consorting in so many an antique group?

Donatello's remorseful anguish saddened this primitive and delightful life. Kenyon had a pain of his own, moreover, although not all a pain, in the never quiet, never satisfied yearning of his heart towards Hilda. He was authorized to use little freedom towards that shy maiden, even in his visions; so that he almost reproached himself when sometimes his imagination pictured in detail the sweet years that they might spend together, in a retreat like this. It had just that rarest quality of remoteness from the actual and ordinary world B a remoteness through which all delights might visit them freely, sifted from all troubles—which lovers so reasonably insist upon, in their ideal arrangements for a happy union. It is possible, indeed, that even Donatello's grief and Kenyon's pale, sunless affection lent a charm to Monte Beni, which it would not have retained amid a more abundant joyousness. The sculptor strayed amid its vineyards and orchards, its dells and tangled shrubberies, with somewhat the sensations of an adventurer who should find his way to the site of ancient Eden, and behold its loveliness through the transparency of that gloom which has been brooding over those haunts of innocence ever since the fall. Adam saw it in a brighter sunshine, but never knew the shade of Pensive beauty which Eden won from his expulsion.

It was in the decline of the afternoon that Kenyon returned from his long, musing ramble, Old Tomaso—between whom and himself for some time past there had been a mysterious understanding,—met him in the entrance hall, and drew him a little aside.

"The signorina would speak with you," he whispered.

"In the chapel?" asked the sculptor.

"No; in the saloon beyond it," answered the butler: "the entrance you once saw the signorina appear through it is near the altar, hidden behind the tapestry."

Kenyon lost no time in obeying the summons.

CHAPTER XXXI. THE MARBLE SALOON

In an old Tuscan villa, a chapel ordinarily makes one among the numerous apartments; though it often happens that the door is permanently closed, the key lost, and the place left to itself, in dusty sanctity, like that chamber in man's heart where he hides his religious awe. This was very much the case with the chapel of Monte Beni. One rainy day, however, in his wanderings through the great, intricate house, Kenyon had unexpectedly found his way into it, and been impressed by its solemn aspect. The arched windows, high upward in the wall, and darkened with dust and cobweb, threw down a dim light that showed the altar, with a picture of a martyrdom above, and some tall tapers ranged before it. They had apparently been lighted, and burned an hour or two, and been extinguished perhaps half a century before. The marble vase at the entrance held some hardened mud at the bottom, accruing from the dust that had settled in it during the gradual evaporation of the holy water; and a spider (being an insect that delights in pointing the moral of desolation and neglect) had taken pains to weave a prodigiously thick tissue across the circular brim. An old family banner, tattered by the moths, drooped from the vaulted roof. In niches there were some mediaeval busts of Donatello's forgotten ancestry; and among them, it might be, the forlorn visage of that hapless knight between whom and the fountain-nymph had occurred such tender love passages.

Throughout all the jovial prosperity of Monte Beni, this one spot within the domestic walls had kept itself silent, stern, and sad. When the individual or the family retired from song and mirth, they here sought those realities which men do not invite their festive associates to share. And here, on the occasion above referred to, the sculptor had discovered—accidentally, so far as he was concerned, though with a purpose on her part—that there was a guest under Donatello's roof, whose presence the Count did not suspect. An interview had since taken place, and he was now summoned to another.

He crossed the chapel, in compliance with Tomaso's instructions, and, passing through the side entrance, found himself in a saloon, of no great size, but more magnificent than he had supposed the villa to contain. As it was vacant, Kenyon had leisure to pace it once or twice, and examine it with a careless sort of scrutiny, before any person appeared.

This beautiful hall was floored with rich marbles, in artistically arranged figures and compartments. The walls, likewise, were almost entirely cased in marble of various kinds, the prevalent, variety being giallo antico, intermixed with verd-antique, and others equally precious. The splendor of the giallo antico, however, was what gave character to the saloon; and the large and deep niches, apparently intended for full length statues, along the walls, were lined with the same costly material. Without visiting Italy, one can have no idea of the beauty and magnificence that are produced by these fittings-up of polished marble. Without such experience, indeed, we do not even know what marble means, in any sense, save as the white limestone of which we carve our mantelpieces. This rich hall of Monte Beni, moreover, was adorned, at its upper end, with two pillars that seemed to consist of Oriental alabaster; and wherever there was a space vacant of precious and variegated marble, it was frescoed with ornaments in arabesque. Above, there was a coved and vaulted ceiling, glowing with pictured scenes, which affected Kenyon with a vague sense of splendor, without his twisting his neck to gaze at them.

It is one of the special excellences of such a saloon of polished and richly colored marble, that decay can never tarnish it. Until the house crumbles down upon it, it shines indestructibly, and, with a little dusting, looks just as brilliant in its three hundredth year as the day after the final slab of giallo antico was fitted into the wall. To the sculptor, at this first View of it, it seemed a hall where the sun was magically imprisoned, and must always shine. He anticipated Miriam's entrance, arrayed in queenly robes, and beaming with even more than the singular beauty that had heretofore distinguished her.

While this thought was passing through his mind, the pillared door, at the upper end of the saloon, was partly opened, and Miriam appeared. She was very pale, and dressed in deep mourning. As she advanced towards the sculptor, the feebleness of her step was so apparent that he made haste to meet her, apprehending that she might sink down on the marble floor, without the instant support of his arm.

But, with a gleam of her natural self-reliance, she declined his aid, and, after touching her cold hand to his, went and sat down on one of the cushioned divans that were ranged against the wall.

"You are very ill, Miriam!" said Kenyon, much shocked at her appearance. "I had not thought of this."

"No; not so ill as I seem to you," she answered; adding despondently, "yet I am ill enough, I believe, to die, unless some change speedily occurs."

"What, then, is your disorder?" asked the sculptor; "and what the remedy?"

"The disorder!" repeated Miriam. "There is none that I know of save too much life and strength, without a purpose for one or the other. It is my too redundant energy that is slowly—or perhaps rapidly—wearing me away, because I can apply it to no use. The object, which I am bound to consider my only one on earth, fails me utterly. The sacrifice which I yearn to make of myself, my hopes, my everything, is coldly put aside. Nothing is left for me but to brood, brood, brood, all day, all night, in unprofitable longings and repinings."

"This is very sad, Miriam," said Kenyon.

"Ay, indeed; I fancy so," she replied, with a short, unnatural laugh.

"With all your activity of mind," resumed he, "so fertile in plans as I have known you, can you imagine no method of bringing your resources into play?"

"My mind is not active any longer," answered Miriam, in a cold, indifferent tone. "It deals with one thought and no more. One recollection paralyzes it. It is not remorse; do not think it! I put myself out of the question, and feel neither regret nor penitence on my own behalf. But what benumbs me, what robs me of all power,-it is no secret for a woman to tell a man, yet I care not though you know it, —is the certainty that I am, and must ever be, an object of horror in Donatello's sight."

The sculptor—a young man, and cherishing a love which insulated him from the wild experiences which some men gather—was startled to perceive how Miriam's rich, ill-regulated nature impelled her to fling herself, conscience and all, on one passion, the object of which intellectually seemed far beneath her.

"How have you obtained the certainty of which you speak?" asked he, after a pause.

"O, by a sure token," said Miriam; "a gesture, merely; a shudder, a cold shiver, that ran through him one sunny morning when his hand happened to touch mine! But it was enough."

"I firmly believe, Miriam," said the sculptor, "that he loves you still."

She started, and a flush of color came tremulously over the paleness of her cheek.

"Yes," repeated Kenyon, "if my interest in Donatello—and in yourself, Miriam—endows me with any true insight, he not only loves you still, but with a force and depth proportioned to the stronger grasp of his faculties, in their new development."

"Do not deceive me," said Miriam, growing pale again.

"Not for the world!" replied Kenyon. "Here is what I take to be the truth. There was an interval, no doubt, when the horror of some calamity, which I need not shape out in my conjectures, threw Donatello into a stupor of misery. Connected with the first shock there was an intolerable pain and shuddering repugnance attaching themselves to all the circumstances and surroundings of the event that so terribly affected him. Was his dearest friend involved within the horror of that moment? He would shrink from her as he shrank most of all from himself. But as his mind roused itself,—as it rose to a higher life than he had hitherto experienced,—whatever had been true and permanent within him revived by the selfsame impulse. So has it been with his love."

"But, surely," said Miriam, "he knows that I am here! Why, then, except that I am odious to him, does he not bid me welcome?"

"He is, I believe, aware of your presence here," answered the sculptor. "Your song, a night or two ago, must have revealed it to him, and, in truth, I had fancied that there was already a consciousness of it in his mind. But, the more passionately he longs for your society, the more religiously he deems himself bound to avoid it. The idea of a lifelong penance has taken strong possession of Donatello. He gropes blindly about him for some method of sharp self-torture, and finds, of course, no other so efficacious as this."

"But he loves me," repeated Miriam, in a low voice, to herself. "Yes; he loves me!"

It was strange to observe the womanly softness that came over her, as she admitted that comfort into her bosom. The cold, unnatural indifference of her manner, a kind of frozen passionateness which had shocked and chilled the sculptor, disappeared. She blushed, and turned away her eyes, knowing that there was more surprise and joy in their dewy glances than any man save one ought to detect there.

"In other respects," she inquired at length, "is he much changed?"

"A wonderful process is going forward in Donatello's mind," answered the sculptor. "The germs of faculties that have heretofore slept are fast springing into activity. The world of thought is disclosing itself to his inward sight. He startles me, at times, with his perception of deep truths; and, quite as often, it must be owned, he compels me to smile by the intermixture of his former simplicity with a new intelligence. But he is bewildered with the revelations that each day brings. Out of his bitter agony, a soul and intellect, I could almost say, have been inspired into him."

"Ah, I could help him here!" cried Miriam, clasping her hands. "And how sweet a toil to bend and adapt my whole nature to do him good! To instruct, to elevate, to enrich his mind with the wealth that would flow in upon me, had I such a motive for acquiring it! Who else can perform the task? Who else has the tender sympathy which he requires? Who else, save only me,—a woman, a sharer in the same dread secret, a partaker in one identical guilt,—

could meet him on such terms of intimate equality as the case demands? With this object before me, I might feel a right to live! Without it, it is a shame for me to have lived so long."

"I fully agree with you," said Kenyon, "that your true place is by his side."

"Surely it is," replied Miriam. "If Donatello is entitled to aught on earth, it is to my complete self-sacrifice for his sake. It does not weaken his claim, methinks, that my only prospect of happiness a fearful word, however lies in the good that may accrue to him from our intercourse. But he rejects me! He will not listen to the whisper of his heart, telling him that she, most wretched, who beguiled him into evil, might guide him to a higher innocence than that from which he fell. How is this first great difficulty to be obviated?"

"It lies at your own option, Miriam, to do away the obstacle, at any moment," remarked the sculptor. "It is but to ascend Donatello's tower, and you will meet him there, under the eye of God."

"I dare not," answered Miriam. "No; I dare not!"

"Do you fear," asked the sculptor, "the dread eye-witness whom I have named?"

"No; for, as far as I can see into that cloudy and inscrutable thing, my heart, it has none but pure motives," replied Miriam. "But, my friend, you little know what a weak or what a strong creature a woman is! I fear not Heaven, in this case, at least, but—shall I confess it? I am greatly in dread of Donatello. Once he shuddered at my touch. If he shudder once again, or frown, I die!"

Kenyon could not but marvel at the subjection into which this proud and self-dependent woman had willfully flung herself, hanging her life upon the chance of an angry or favorable regard from a person who, a little while before, had seemed the plaything of a moment. But, in Miriam's eyes, Donatello was always, thenceforth, invested with the tragic dignity of their hour of crime; and, furthermore, the keen and deep insight, with which her love endowed her, enabled her to know him far better than he could be known by ordinary observation. Beyond all question, since she loved him so, there was a force in Donatello worthy of her respect and love.

"You see my weakness," said Miriam, flinging out her hands, as a person does when a defect is acknowledged, and beyond remedy. "What I need, now, is an opportunity to show my strength."

"It has occurred to me," Kenyon remarked, "that the time is come when it may be desirable to remove Donatello from the complete seclusion in which he buries himself. He has struggled long enough with one idea. He now needs a variety of thought, which cannot be otherwise so readily supplied to him, as through the medium of a variety of scenes. His mind is awakened, now; his heart, though full of pain, is no longer benumbed. They should have food and solace. If he linger here much longer, I fear that he may sink back into a lethargy. The extreme excitability, which circumstances have imparted to his moral system, has its dangers and its advantages; it being one of the dangers, that an obdurate scar may supervene upon its very tenderness. Solitude has done what it could for him; now, for a while, let him be enticed into the outer world."

"What is your plan, then?" asked Miriam.

"Simply," replied Kenyon, "to persuade Donatello to be my companion in a ramble among these hills and valleys. The little adventures and vicissitudes of travel will do him infinite good. After his recent profound experience, he will re-create the world by the new eyes with which he will regard it. He will escape, I hope, out of a morbid life, and find his way into a healthy one."

"And what is to be my part in this process?" inquired Miriam sadly, and not without jealousy. "You are taking him from me, and putting yourself, and all manner of living interests, into the place which I ought to fill!"

"It would rejoice me, Miriam, to yield the entire responsibility of this office to yourself," answered the sculptor. "I do not pretend to be the guide and counsellor whom Donatello needs; for, to mention no other obstacle, I am a man, and between man and man there is always an insuperable gulf.

They can never quite grasp each other's hands; and therefore man never derives any intimate help, any heart sustenance, from his brother man, but from woman—his mother, his sister, or his wife. Be Donatello's friend at need, therefore, and most gladly will I resign him!"

"It is not kind to taunt me thus," said Miriam. "I have told you that I cannot do what you suggest, because I dare not."

"Well, then," rejoined the sculptor, "see if there is any possibility of adapting yourself to my scheme. The incidents of a journey often fling people together in the oddest and therefore the most natural way. Supposing you were to find yourself on the same route, a reunion with Donatello might ensue, and Providence have a larger hand in it than either of us."

"It is not a hopeful plan," said Miriam, shaking her head, after a moment's thought; "yet I will not reject it without a trial. Only in case it fail, here is a resolution to which I bind myself, come what come may! You know the bronze statue of Pope Julius in the great square of Perugia? I remember standing in the shadow of that statue one sunny noontime, and being impressed by its paternal aspect, and fancying that a blessing fell upon me from its outstretched hand. Ever since, I have had a superstition, you will call it foolish, but sad and ill-fated persons always dream such things,—that, if I waited long enough in that same spot, some good event would come to pass. Well, my friend, precisely a fortnight after you begin your tour,—unless we sooner meet,—bring Donatello, at noon, to the base of the statue. You will find me there!"

Kenyon assented to the proposed arrangement, and, after some conversation respecting his contemplated line of travel, prepared to take his leave. As he met Miriam's eyes, in bidding farewell, he was surprised at the new, tender gladness that beamed out of them, and at the appearance of health and bloom, which, in this little while, had overspread her face.'

"May I tell you, Miriam," said he, smiling, "that you are still as beautiful as ever?"

"You have a right to notice it," she replied, "for, if it be so, my faded bloom has been revived by the hopes you give me. Do you, then, think me beautiful? I rejoice, most truly. Beauty—if I possess it—shall be one of the instruments by which I will try to educate and elevate him, to whose good I solely dedicate myself."

The sculptor had nearly reached the door, when, hearing her call him, he turned back, and beheld Miriam still standing where he had left her, in the magnificent hall which seemed only a fit setting for her beauty. She beckoned him to return.

"You are a man of refined taste," said she; "more than that,—a man of delicate sensibility. Now tell me frankly, and on your honor! Have I not shocked you many times during this interview by my betrayal of woman's cause, my lack of feminine modesty, my reckless, passionate, most indecorous avowal, that I live only in the life of one who, perhaps, scorns and shudders at me?"

Thus adjured, however difficult the point to which she brought him, the sculptor was not a man to swerve aside from the simple truth.

"Miriam," replied he, "you exaggerate the impression made upon my mind; but it has been painful, and somewhat of the character which you suppose."

"I knew it," said Miriam, mournfully, and with no resentment. "What remains of my finer nature would have told me so, even if it had not been perceptible in all your manner. Well, my dear friend, when you go back to Rome, tell Hilda what her severity has done! She was all womanhood to me; and when she cast me off, I had no longer any terms to keep with the reserves and decorums of my sex. Hilda has set me free! Pray tell her so, from Miriam, and thank her!"

"I shall tell Hilda nothing that will give her pain," answered Kenyon. "But, Miriam, though I know not what passed between her and yourself, I feel,—and let the noble frankness of your disposition forgive me if I say so,—I feel that she was right. You have a thousand admirable qualities. Whatever mass of evil may have fallen into your life, —pardon me, but your own words suggest it,—you are still as capable as ever of many high and heroic virtues. But the white shining purity of Hilda's nature is a thing apart; and she is bound, by the undefiled material of which God moulded her, to keep that severity which I, as well as you, have recognized."

"O, you are right!" said Miriam; "I never questioned it; though, as I told you, when she cast me off, it severed some few remaining bonds between me and decorous womanhood. But were there anything to forgive, I do forgive her. May you win her virgin heart; for methinks there can be few men in this evil world who are not more unworthy of her than yourself."

CHAPTER XXXII. SCENES BY THE WAY

When it came to the point of quitting the reposeful life of Monte Beni, the sculptor was not without regrets, and would willingly have dreamed a little longer of the sweet paradise on earth that Hilda's presence there might make. Nevertheless, amid all its repose, he had begun to be sensible of a restless melancholy, to which the cultivators of the ideal arts are more liable than sturdier men. On his own part, therefore, and leaving Donatello out of the case, he would have judged it well to go. He made parting visits to the legendary dell, and to other delightful spots with which he had grown familiar; he climbed the tower again, and saw a sunset and a moonrise over the great valley; he drank, on the eve of his departure, one flask, and then another, of the Monte Beni Sunshine, and stored up its flavor in his memory as the standard of what is exquisite in wine. These things accomplished, Kenyon was ready for the journey.

Donatello had not very easily been stirred out of the peculiar sluggishness, which enthralls and bewitches melancholy people. He had offered merely a passive resistance, however, not an active one, to his friend's schemes; and when the appointed hour came, he yielded to the impulse which Kenyon failed not to apply; and was started upon the journey before he had made up his mind to undertake it. They wandered forth at large, like two knights-errant, among the valleys, and the mountains, and the old mountain towns of that picturesque and lovely region. Save to keep the appointment with Miriam, a fortnight thereafter, in the great square of Perugia, there was nothing more definite in the sculptor's plan than that they should let themselves be blown hither and thither like Winged seeds, that mount upon each wandering breeze. Yet there was an idea of fatality implied in the simile of the winged seeds which did not altogether suit Kenyon's fancy; for, if you look closely into the matter, it will be seen that whatever appears most vagrant, and utterly purposeless, turns out, in the end, to have been impelled the most surely on a preordained and unswerving track. Chance and change love to deal with men's settled plans, not with their idle vagaries. If we desire unexpected and unimaginable events, we should contrive an iron framework, such as we fancy may compel the future to take one inevitable shape; then comes in the unexpected, and shatters our design in fragments.

The travellers set forth on horseback, and purposed to perform much of their aimless journeyings under the moon, and in the cool of the morning or evening twilight; the midday sun, while summer had hardly begun to trail its departing skirts over Tuscany, being still too fervid to allow of noontide exposure.

For a while, they wandered in that same broad valley which Kenyon had viewed with such delight from the Monte Beni tower. The sculptor soon began to enjoy the idle activity of their new life, which the lapse of a day or two sufficed to establish as a kind of system; it is so natural for mankind to be nomadic, that a very little taste of that primitive mode of existence subverts the settled habits of many preceding years. Kenyon's cares, and whatever gloomy ideas before possessed him, seemed to be left at Monte Beni, and were scarcely remembered by the time that its gray tower grew undistinguishable on the brown hillside. His perceptive faculties, which had found little exercise of late, amid so thoughtful a way of life, became keen, and kept his eyes busy with a hundred agreeable scenes.

He delighted in the picturesque bits of rustic character and manners, so little of which ever comes upon the surface of our life at home. There, for example, were the old women, tending pigs or sheep by the wayside. As they followed the vagrant steps of their charge, these venerable ladies kept spinning yarn with that elsewhere forgotten contrivance, the distaff; and so wrinkled and stern looking were they, that you might have taken them for the Parcae, spinning the threads of human destiny. In contrast with their great-grandmothers were the children, leading goats of shaggy beard, tied by the horns, and letting them browse on branch and shrub. It is the fashion of Italy to add the petty industry of age and childhood to the hum of human toil. To the eyes of an observer from the Western world, it was a strange spectacle to see sturdy, sunburnt creatures, in petticoats, but otherwise manlike, toiling side by side with male laborers, in the rudest work of the fields. These sturdy women (if as such we must recognize them) wore the high-crowned, broad brimmed hat of Tuscan straw, the customary female head-apparel; and, as every breeze blew back its breadth of brim, the sunshine constantly added depth to the brown glow of their cheeks. The elder sisterhood, however, set off their witch-like ugliness to the worst advantage with black felt hats, bequeathed them, one would fancy, by their long-buried husbands.

Another ordinary sight, as sylvan as the above and more agreeable, was a girl, bearing on her back a huge bundle of green twigs and shrubs, or grass, intermixed with scarlet poppies and blue flowers; the verdant burden being sometimes of such size as to hide the bearer's figure, and seem a self-moving mass of fragrant bloom and verdure. Oftener, however, the bundle reached only halfway down the back of the rustic nymph, leaving in sight her well-developed lower limbs, and the crooked knife, hanging behind her, with which she had been reaping this strange harvest sheaf. A pre-Raphaelite artist (he, for instance, who painted so marvellously a wind-swept heap of autumnal leaves) might find an admirable subject in one of these Tuscan girls, stepping with a free, erect, and graceful carriage. The miscellaneous herbage and tangled twigs and blossoms of her bundle, crowning her head (while her ruddy, comely face looks out between the hanging side festoons like a larger flower), would give the painter boundless scope for the minute delineation which he loves.

Though mixed up with what was rude and earthlike, there was still a remote, dreamlike, Arcadian charm, which is scarcely to be found in the daily toil of other lands. Among the pleasant features of the wayside were always the vines, clambering on fig-trees, or other sturdy trunks; they wreathed themselves in huge and rich festoons from one tree to another, suspending clusters of ripening grapes in the interval between. Under such careless mode of culture, the luxuriant vine is a lovelier spectacle than where it produces a more precious liquor, and is therefore more artificially restrained and trimmed. Nothing can be more picturesque than an old grapevine, with almost a trunk of its own, clinging fast around its supporting tree. Nor does the picture lack its moral. You might twist it to more than one grave purpose, as you saw how the knotted, serpentine growth imprisoned within its strong embrace the friend that had supported its tender infancy; and how (as seemingly flexible natures are prone to do) it converted the sturdier tree entirely to its own selfish ends, extending its innumerable arms on every bough, and permitting hardly a leaf to sprout except its own. It occurred to Kenyon, that the enemies of the vine, in his native land, might here have seen an emblem of the remorseless gripe, which the habit of vinous enjoyment lays upon its victim, possessing him wholly, and letting him live no life but such as it bestows.

The scene was not less characteristic when their path led the two wanderers through some small, ancient town. There, besides the peculiarities of present life, they saw tokens of the life that had long ago been lived and flung aside. The little town, such as we see in our mind's eye, would have its gate and its surrounding walls, so ancient and massive that ages had not sufficed to crumble them away; but in the lofty upper portion of the gateway, still standing over the empty arch, where there was no longer a gate to shut, there would be a dove-cote, and peaceful doves for the only warders. Pumpkins lay ripening in the open chambers of the structure. Then, as for the town wall, on the outside an orchard extends peacefully along its base, full, not of apple-trees, but of those old humorists with gnarled trunks and twisted boughs, the olives. Houses have been built upon the ramparts, or burrowed out of their ponderous foundation. Even the gray, martial towers, crowned with ruined turrets, have been converted into rustic habitations, from the windows of which hang ears of Indian corn. At a door, that has been broken through the massive stonework where it was meant to be strongest, some contadini are winnowing grain. Small windows, too, are pierced through the whole line of ancient wall, so that it seems a row of dwellings with one continuous front, built in a strange style of needless strength; but remnants of the old battlements and machicolations are interspersed with the homely chambers and earthen-tiled housetops; and all along its extent both grapevines and running flower-shrubs are encouraged to clamber and sport over the roughness of its decay.

Finally the long grass, intermixed with weeds and wild flowers, waves on the uppermost height of the shattered rampart; and it is exceedingly pleasant in the golden sunshine of the afternoon to behold the warlike precinct so friendly in its old days, and so overgrown with rural peace. In its guard rooms, its prison chambers, and scooped out of its ponderous breadth, there are dwellings nowadays where happy human lives are spent. Human parents and broods of children nestle in them, even as the swallows nestle in the little crevices along the broken summit of the wall.

Passing through the gateway of this same little town, challenged only by those watchful sentinels, the pigeons, we find ourselves in a long, narrow street, paved from side to side with flagstones, in the old Roman fashion. Nothing can exceed the grim ugliness of the houses, most of which are three or four stories high, stone built, gray, dilapidated, or half-covered with plaster in patches, and contiguous all along from end to end of the town. Nature, in the shape of tree, shrub, or grassy sidewalk, is as much shut out from the one street of the rustic village as from the heart of any swarming city. The dark and half ruinous habitations, with their small windows, many of which are drearily closed with wooden shutters, are but magnified hovels, piled story upon story, and squalid with the grime that successive ages have left behind them. It would be a hideous scene to contemplate in a rainy day, or when no human life pervaded it. In the summer noon, however, it possesses vivacity enough to keep itself cheerful; for all the within-doors of the village then bubbles over upon the flagstones, or looks out from the small windows, and from here and there a balcony. Some of the populace are at the butcher's shop; others are at the fountain, which gushes into a marble basin that resembles an antique sarcophagus. A tailor is sewing before his door with a young priest seated sociably beside him; a burly friar goes by with an empty wine-barrel on his head; children are at play; women, at their own doorsteps, mend clothes, embroider, weave hats of Tuscan straw, or twirl the distaff. Many idlers, meanwhile, strolling from one group to another, let the warm day slide by in the sweet, interminable task of doing nothing.

From all these people there comes a babblement that seems quite disproportioned to the number of tongues that make it. So many words are not uttered in a New England village throughout the year—except it be at a political canvass or town-meeting—as are spoken here, with no especial purpose, in a single day. Neither so many words, nor so much laughter; for people talk about nothing as if they were terribly in earnest, and make merry at nothing as if it were the best of all possible jokes. In so long a time as they have existed, and within such narrow precincts, these little walled towns are brought into a closeness of society that makes them but a larger household. All the inhabitants are akin to each, and each to all; they assemble in the street as their common saloon, and thus live and die in a familiarity of intercourse, such as never can be known where a village is open at either end, and all roundabout, and has ample room within itself.

Stuck up beside the door of one house, in this village street, is a withered bough; and on a stone seat, just under the shadow of the bough, sits a party of jolly drinkers, making proof of the new wine, or quaffing the old, as their often-tried and comfortable friend. Kenyon draws bridle here (for the bough, or bush, is a symbol of the wine-shop at this day in Italy, as it was three hundred years ago in England), and calls for a goblet of the deep, mild, purple juice, well diluted with water from the fountain. The Sunshine of Monte Beni would be welcome now. Meanwhile, Donatello has ridden onward, but alights where a shrine, with a burning lamp before it, is built into the wall of an inn stable. He kneels and crosses himself, and mutters a brief prayer, without attracting notice from the passers-by, many of whom are parenthetically devout in a similar fashion. By this time the sculptor has drunk off his wine-and-water, and our two travellers resume their way, emerging from the opposite gate of the village.

Before them, again, lies the broad valley, with a mist so thinly scattered over it as to be perceptible only in the distance, and most so in the nooks of the hills. Now that we have called it mist, it seems a mistake not rather to have called it sunshine; the glory of so much light being mingled with so little gloom, in the airy material of that vapor. Be it mist or sunshine, it adds a touch of ideal beauty to the scene, almost persuading the spectator that this valley and those hills are visionary, because their visible atmosphere is so like the substance of a dream.

Immediately about them, however, there were abundant tokens that the country was not really the paradise it looked to be, at a casual glance. Neither the wretched cottages nor the dreary farmhouses seemed to partake of the prosperity, with which so kindly a climate, and so fertile a portion of Mother

Earth's bosom, should have filled them, one and all. But possibly the peasant inhabitants do not exist in so grimy a poverty, and in homes so comfortless, as a stranger, with his native ideas of those matters, would be likely to imagine. The Italians appear to possess none of that emulative pride which we see in our New England villages, where every householder, according to his taste and means, endeavors to make his homestead an ornament to the grassy and elm-shadowed wayside. In Italy there are no neat doorsteps and thresholds; no pleasant, vine-sheltered porches; none of those grass-plots or smoothly shorn lawns, which hospitably invite the imagination into the sweet domestic interiors of English life. Everything, however sunny and luxuriant may be the scene around, is especially disheartening in the immediate neighborhood of an Italian home.

An artist, it is true, might often thank his stars for those old houses, so picturesquely time-stained, and with the plaster falling in blotches from the ancient brick-work. The prison-like, iron-barred windows, and the wide arched, dismal entrance, admitting on one hand to the stable, on the other to the kitchen, might impress him as far better worth his pencil than the newly painted pine boxes, in which—if he be an American—his countrymen live and thrive. But there is reason to suspect that a people are waning to decay and ruin the moment that their life becomes fascinating either in the poet's imagination or the painter's eye.

As usual on Italian waysides, the wanderers passed great, black crosses, hung with all the instruments of the sacred agony and passion: there were the crown of thorns, the hammer and nails, the pincers, the spear, the sponge; and perched over the whole, the cock that crowed to St. Peter's remorseful conscience. Thus, while the fertile scene showed the never-failing beneficence of the Creator towards man in his transitory state, these symbols reminded each wayfarer of the Saviour's infinitely greater love for him as an immortal spirit. Beholding these consecrated stations, the idea seemed to strike Donatello of converting the otherwise aimless journey into a penitential pilgrimage. At each of them he alighted to kneel and kiss the cross, and humbly press his forehead against its foot; and this so invariably, that the sculptor soon learned to draw bridle of his own accord. It may be, too, heretic as he was, that Kenyon likewise put up a prayer, rendered more fervent by the symbols before his eyes, for the peace of his friend's conscience and the pardon of the sin that so oppressed him.

Not only at the crosses did Donatello kneel, but at each of the many shrines, where the Blessed Virgin in fresco—faded with sunshine and half washed out with showers—looked benignly at her worshipper; or where she was represented in a wooden image, or a bas-relief of plaster or marble, as accorded with the means of the devout person who built, or restored from a mediaeval antiquity, these places of wayside worship. They were everywhere: under arched niches, or in little penthouses with a brick tiled roof just large enough to shelter them; or perhaps in some bit of old Roman masonry, the founders of which had died before the Advent; or in the wall of a country inn or farmhouse; or at the midway point of a bridge; or in the shallow cavity of a natural rock; or high upward in the deep cuts of the road. It appeared to the sculptor that Donatello prayed the more earnestly and the more hopefully at these shrines, because the mild face of the Madonna promised him to intercede as a tender mother betwixt the poor culprit and the awfulness of judgment.

It was beautiful to observe, indeed, how tender was the soul of man and woman towards the Virgin mother, in recognition of the tenderness which, as their faith taught them, she immortally cherishes towards all human souls. In the wire-work screen 'before each shrine hung offerings of roses, or whatever flower was sweetest and most seasonable; some already wilted and withered, some fresh with that very morning's dewdrops. Flowers there were, too, that, being artificial, never bloomed on earth, nor would ever fade. The thought occurred to Kenyon, that flower-pots with living plants might be set within the niches, or even that rose-trees, and all kinds of flowering shrubs, might be reared under the shrines, and taught to twine and wreathe themselves around; so that the Virgin should dwell within a bower of verdure, bloom, and fragrant freshness, symbolizing a homage perpetually new. There are many things in the religious customs of these people that seem good; many things, at least, that might be both good and beautiful, if the soul of goodness and the sense of beauty were as much alive in the Italians now as they must have been when those customs were first imagined and adopted. But, instead of blossoms on the shrub, or freshly gathered, with the dewdrops on their leaves, their worship, nowadays, is best symbolized by the artificial flower.

The sculptor fancied, moreover (but perhaps it was his heresy that suggested the idea), that it would be of happy influence to place a comfortable and shady seat beneath every wayside shrine. Then the weary and sun-scorched traveller, while resting himself under her protecting shadow, might thank the Virgin for her hospitality. Nor, perchance, were he to regale himself, even in such a consecrated spot, with the fragrance of a pipe, would it rise to heaven more offensively than the smoke of priestly incense. We do ourselves wrong, and too meanly estimate the Holiness above us, when we deem that any act or enjoyment, good in itself, is not good to do religiously.

Whatever may be the iniquities of the papal system, it was a wise and lovely sentiment that set up the frequent shrine and cross along the roadside. No wayfarer, bent on whatever worldly errand, can fail to be reminded, at every mile or two, that this is not the business which most concerns him. The pleasure-seeker is silently admonished to look heavenward for a joy infinitely greater than he now possesses. The wretch in temptation beholds the cross, and is warned that, if he yield, the Saviour's agony for his sake will have been endured in vain. The stubborn criminal, whose heart has long been like a stone, feels it throb anew with dread and hope; and our poor Donatello, as he went kneeling from shrine to cross, and from cross to shrine, doubtless found an efficacy in these symbols that helped him towards a higher penitence.

Whether the young Count of Monte Beni noticed the fact, or no, there was more than one incident of their journey that led Kenyon to believe that they were attended, or closely followed, or preceded, near at hand, by some one who took an interest in their motions. As it were, the step, the sweeping garment, the faintly heard breath, of an invisible companion, was beside them, as they went on their way. It was like a dream that had strayed out of their slumber, and was haunting them in the daytime, when its shadowy substance could have neither density nor outline, in the too obtrusive light. After sunset, it grew a little more distinct.

"On the left of that last shrine," asked the sculptor, as they rode, under the moon, "did you observe the figure of a woman kneeling, with her, face hidden in her hands?"

"I never looked that way," replied Donatello. "I was saying my own prayer. It was some penitent, perchance. May the Blessed Virgin be the more gracious to the poor soul, because she is a woman."

CHAPTER XXXIII. PICTURED WINDOWS

After wide wanderings through the valley, the two travellers directed their course towards its boundary of hills. Here, the natural scenery and men's modifications of it immediately took a different aspect from that of the fertile and smiling plain. Not unfrequently there was a convent on the hillside; or, on some insulated promontory, a mined castle, once the den of a robber chieftain, who was accustomed to dash down from his commanding height upon the road that wound below. For ages back, the old fortress had been flinging down its crumbling ramparts, stone by stone, towards the grimy village at its foot.

Their road wound onward among the hills, which rose steep and lofty from the scanty level space that lay between them. They continually thrust their great bulks before the wayfarers, as if grimly resolute to forbid their passage, or closed abruptly behind them, when they still dared to proceed. A gigantic hill would set its foot right down before them, and only at the last moment would grudgingly withdraw it, just far enough to let them creep towards another obstacle. Adown these rough heights were visible the dry tracks of many a mountain torrent that had lived a life too fierce and passionate to be a long one. Or, perhaps, a stream was yet hurrying shyly along the edge of a far wider bed of pebbles and shelving rock than it seemed to need, though not too wide for the swollen rage of which this shy rivulet was capable. A stone bridge bestrode it, the ponderous arches of which were upheld and rendered indestructible by the weight of the very stones that threatened to crush them down. Old Roman toil was perceptible in the foundations of that massive bridge; the first weight that it ever bore was that of an army of the Republic.

Threading these defiles, they would arrive at some immemorial city, crowning the high summit of a hill with its cathedral, its many churches, and public edifices, all of Gothic architecture. With no more level ground than a single piazza in the midst, the ancient town tumbled its crooked and narrow streets down the mountainside, through arched passages and by steps of stone. The aspect of everything was awfully old; older, indeed, in its effect on the imagination than Rome itself, because history does not lay its finger on these forgotten edifices and tell us all about their origin. Etruscan princes may have dwelt in them. A thousand years, at all events, would seem but a middle age for these structures. They are built of such huge, square stones, that their appearance of ponderous durability distresses the beholder with the idea that they can never fall,—never crumble away,—never be less fit than now for human habitation. Many of them may once have been palaces, and still retain a squalid grandeur. But, gazing at them, we recognize how undesirable it is to build the tabernacle of our brief lifetime out of permanent materials, and with a view to their being occupied by future 'generations.

All towns should be made capable of purification by fire, or of decay, within each half-century. Otherwise, they become the hereditary haunts of vermin and noisomeness, besides standing apart from the possibility of such improvements as are constantly introduced into the rest of man's contrivances and accommodations. It is beautiful, no doubt, and exceedingly satisfactory to some of our natural instincts, to imagine our far posterity dwelling under the same roof-tree as ourselves. Still, when people insist on building indestructible houses, they incur, or their children do, a misfortune analogous to that of the Sibyl, when she obtained the grievous boon of immortality. So we may build almost immortal habitations, it is true; but we cannot keep them from growing old, musty, unwholesome, dreary,—full of death scents, ghosts, and murder stains; in short, such habitations as one sees everywhere in Italy, be they hovels or palaces.

"You should go with me to my native country," observed the sculptor to Donatello. "In that fortunate land, each generation has only its own sins and sorrows to bear. Here, it seems as if all the weary and dreary Past were piled upon the back of the Present. If I were to lose my spirits in this country,—if I were to suffer any heavy misfortune here,—methinks it would be impossible to stand up against it, under such adverse influences."

"The sky itself is an old roof, now," answered the Count; "and, no doubt, the sins of mankind have made it gloomier than it used to be." "O, my poor Faun," thought Kenyon to himself, "how art thou changed!"

A city, like this of which we speak, seems a sort of stony growth out of the hillside, or a fossilized town; so ancient and strange it looks, without enough of life and juiciness in it to be any longer susceptible of decay. An earthquake would afford it the only chance of being ruined, beyond its present ruin.

Yet, though dead to all the purposes for which we live to-day, the place has its glorious recollections, and not merely rude and warlike ones, but those of brighter and milder triumphs, the fruits of which we still enjoy. Italy can count several of these lifeless towns which, four or five hundred years ago, were each the birthplace of its own school of art; nor have they yet forgotten to be proud of the dark old pictures, and the faded frescos, the pristine beauty of which was a light and gladness to the world. But now, unless one happens to be a painter, these famous works make us miserably desperate. They are poor, dim ghosts of what, when Giotto or Cimabue first created them, threw a splendor along the stately aisles; so far gone towards nothingness, in our day, that scarcely a hint of design or expression can glimmer through the dusk. Those early artists did well to paint their frescos. Glowing on the church-walls, they might be looked upon as symbols of the living spirit that made Catholicism a true religion, and that glorified it as long as it retained a genuine life; they filled the transepts with a radiant throng of saints and angels, and threw around the high altar a faint reflection—as much as mortals could see, or bear—of a Diviner Presence. But now that the colors are so wretchedly bedimmed,—now that blotches of plastered wall dot the frescos all over, like a mean reality thrusting itself through life's brightest illusions,— the next best artist to Cimabue or Giotto or Ghirlandaio or Pinturicchio will be he that shall reverently cover their ruined masterpieces with whitewash!

Kenyon, however, being an earnest student and critic of Art, lingered long before these pathetic relics; and Donatello, in his present phase of penitence, thought no time spent amiss while he could be kneeling before an altar. Whenever they found a cathedral, therefore, or a Gothic church, the two travellers were of one mind to enter it. In some of these holy edifices they saw pictures that time had not dimmed nor injured in the least, though they perhaps belonged to as old a school of Art as any that were perishing around them. These were the painted windows; and as often as he gazed at them the sculptor blessed the medieval time, and its gorgeous contrivances of splendor; for surely the skill of man has never accomplished, nor his mind imagined, any other beauty or glory worthy to be compared with these.

It is the special excellence of pictured glass, that the light, which falls merely on the outside of other pictures, is here interfused throughout the work; it illuminates the design, and invests it with a living radiance; and in requital the unfading colors transmute the common daylight into a miracle of richness and glory in its passage through the heavenly substance of the blessed and angelic shapes which throng the high-arched window.

"It is a woeful thing," cried Kenyon, while one of these frail yet enduring and fadeless pictures threw its hues on his face, and on the pavement of the church around him,—"a sad necessity that any Christian soul should pass from earth without once seeing an antique painted window, with the bright Italian sunshine glowing through it! There is no other such true symbol of the glories of the better world, where a celestial radiance will be inherent in all things and persons, and render each continually transparent to the sight of all."

"But what a horror it would be," said Donatello sadly, "if there were a soul among them through which the light could not be transfused!"

"Yes; and perhaps this is to be the punishment of sin," replied the sculptor; "not that it shall be made evident to the universe, which can profit nothing by such knowledge, but that it shall insulate the sinner from all sweet society by rendering him impermeable to light, and, therefore, unrecognizable in the abode of heavenly simplicity and truth. Then, what remains for him, but the dreariness of infinite and eternal solitude?"

"That would be a horrible destiny, indeed!" said Donatello.

His voice as he spoke the words had a hollow and dreary cadence, as if he anticipated some such frozen solitude for himself. A figure in a dark robe was lurking in the obscurity of a side chapel close by, and made an impulsive movement forward, but hesitated as Donatello spoke again.

"But there might be a more miserable torture than to be solitary forever," said he. "Think of having a single companion in eternity, and instead of finding any consolation, or at all events variety of torture, to see your own weary, weary sin repeated in that inseparable soul."

"I think, my dear Count, you have never read Dante," observed Kenyon. "That idea is somewhat in his style, but I cannot help regretting that it came into your mind just then."

The dark-robed figure had shrunk back, and was quite lost to sight among the shadows of the chapel.

"There was an English poet," resumed Kenyon, turning again towards the window, "who speaks of the 'dim, religious light,' transmitted through painted glass. I always admired this richly descriptive phrase; but, though he was once in Italy, I question whether Milton ever saw any but the dingy pictures in the dusty windows of English cathedrals, imperfectly shown by the gray English daylight. He would else have illuminated that word 'dim' with some epithet that should not chase away the dimness, yet should make it glow like a million of rubies, sapphires, emeralds, and topazes. Is it not so with yonder window? The pictures are most brilliant in themselves, yet dim with tenderness and reverence, because God himself is shining through them."

"The pictures fill me with emotion, but not such as you seem to experience," said Donatello. "I tremble at those awful saints; and, most of all, at the figure above them. He glows with Divine wrath!"

"My dear friend," said Kenyon, "how strangely your eyes have transmuted the expression of the figure! It is divine love, not wrath!"

"To my eyes," said Donatello stubbornly, "it is wrath, not love! Each must interpret for himself."

The friends left the church, and looking up, from the exterior, at the window which they had just been contemplating within, nothing; was visible but the merest outline of dusky shapes, Neither the individual likeness of saint, angel, nor Saviour, and far less the combined scheme and purport of the picture, could anywise be made out. That miracle of radiant art, thus viewed, was nothing better than an incomprehensible obscurity, without a gleam of beauty to induce the beholder to attempt unravelling it.

"All this," thought the sculptor, "is a most forcible emblem of the different aspect of religious truth and sacred story, as viewed from the warm interior of belief, or from its cold and dreary outside. Christian faith is a grand cathedral, with divinely pictured windows. Standing without, you see no glory, nor can possibly imagine any; standing within, every ray of light reveals a harmony of unspeakable splendors."

After Kenyon and Donatello emerged from the church, however, they had better opportunity for acts of charity and mercy than for religious contemplation; being immediately surrounded by a swarm of beggars, who are the present possessors of Italy, and share the spoil of the stranger with the fleas and mosquitoes, their formidable allies. These pests—the human ones—had hunted the two travellers at every stage of their journey. From village to village, ragged boys and girls kept almost under the horses' feet; hoary grandsires and grandames caught glimpses of their approach, and hobbled to intercept them at some point of vantage; blind men stared them out of countenance with their sightless orbs; women held up their unwashed babies; cripples displayed their wooden legs, their grievous scars, their dangling, boneless arms, their broken backs, their burden of a hump, or whatever infirmity or deformity Providence had assigned them for an inheritance. On the highest mountain summit—in the most shadowy ravine—there was a beggar waiting for them. In one small village, Kenyon had the curiosity to count merely how many children were crying, whining, and bellowing all at once for alms. They proved to be more than forty of as ragged and dirty little imps as any in the world; besides whom, all the wrinkled matrons, and most of the village maids, and not a few stalwart men, held out their hands grimly, piteously, or smilingly in the forlorn hope of whatever trifle of coin might remain in pockets already so fearfully taxed. Had they been permitted, they would gladly have knelt down and worshipped the travellers, and have cursed them, without rising from their knees, if the expected boon failed to be awarded.

Yet they were not so miserably poor but that the grown people kept houses over their heads.

In the way of food, they had, at least, vegetables in their little gardens, pigs and chickens to kill, eggs to fry into omelets with oil, wine to drink, and many other things to make life comfortable. As for the children, when no more small coin appeared to be forthcoming, they began to laugh and play, and turn heels over head, showing themselves jolly and vivacious brats, and evidently as well fed as needs be. The truth is, the Italian peasantry look upon strangers as the almoners of Providence, and therefore feel no more shame in asking and receiving alms, than in availing themselves of providential bounties in whatever other form.

In accordance with his nature, Donatello was always exceedingly charitable to these ragged battalions, and appeared to derive a certain consolation from the prayers which many of them put up in his behalf. In Italy a copper coin of minute value will often make all the difference between a vindictive curse—death by apoplexy being the favorite one-mumbled in an old witch's toothless jaws, and a prayer from the same lips, so earnest that it would seem to reward the charitable soul with at least a puff of grateful breath to help him heavenward. Good wishes being so cheap, though possibly not very efficacious, and anathemas so exceedingly bitter,—even if the greater portion of their poison remain in the mouth that utters them,—it may be wise to expend some reasonable amount in the purchase of the former. Donatello invariably did so; and as he distributed his alms under the pictured window, of which we have been speaking, no less than seven ancient women lifted their hands and besought blessings on his head.

"Come," said the sculptor, rejoicing at the happier expression which he saw in his friend's face. "I think your steed will not stumble with you to-day. Each of these old dames looks as much like Horace's Atra Cura as can well be conceived; but, though there are seven of them, they will make your burden on horseback lighter instead of heavier."

"Are we to ride far?" asked the Count.

"A tolerable journey betwixt now and to-morrow noon," Kenyon replied; "for, at that hour, I purpose to be standing by the Pope's statue in the great square of Perugia."

CHAPTER XXXIV. MARKET DAY IN PERUGIA

Perugia, on its lofty hilltop, was reached by the two travellers before the sun had quite kissed away the early freshness of the morning. Since midnight, there had been a heavy, rain, bringing infinite refreshment to the scene of verdure and fertility amid which this ancient civilization stands; insomuch that Kenyon loitered, when they came to the gray city wall, and was loath to give up the prospect of the sunny wilderness that lay below. It was as green as England, and bright as Italy alone. There was all the wide valley, sweeping down and spreading away on all sides from the weed grown ramparts, and bounded afar by mountains, which lay asleep in the sun, with thin mists and silvery clouds floating about their heads by way of morning dreams.

"It lacks still two hours of noon," said the sculptor to his friend, as they stood under the arch of the gateway, waiting for their passports to be examined; "will you come with me to see some admirable frescos by Perugino? There is a hall in the Exchange, of no great magnitude, but covered with what must have been—at the time it was painted—such magnificence and beauty as the world had not elsewhere to show."

"It depresses me to look at old frescos," responded the Count; "it is a pain, yet not enough of a pain to answer as a penance."

"Will you look at some pictures by Fra Angelico in the Church of San Domenico?" asked Kenyon; "they are full of religious sincerity, When one studies them faithfully, it is like holding a conversation about heavenly things with a tender and devout-minded man."

"You have shown me some of Fra Angelico's pictures, I remember," answered Donatello; "his angels look as if they had never taken a flight out of heaven; and his saints seem to have been born saints, and always to have lived so. Young maidens, and all innocent persons, I doubt not, may find great delight and profit in looking at such holy pictures. But they are not for me."

"Your criticism, I fancy, has great moral depth," replied Kenyon; "and I see in it the reason why Hilda so highly appreciates Fra Angelico's pictures.

Well; we will let all such matters pass for to-day, and stroll about this fine old city till noon."

They wandered to and fro, accordingly, and lost themselves among the strange, precipitate passages, which, in Perugia, are called streets, Some of them are like caverns, being arched all over, and plunging down abruptly towards an unknown darkness; which, when you have fathomed its depths, admits you to a daylight that you scarcely hoped to behold again. Here they met shabby men, and the careworn wives and mothers of the people, some of whom guided children in leading strings through those dim and antique thoroughfares, where a hundred generations had passed before the little feet of to-day began to tread them. Thence they climbed upward again, and came to the level plateau, on the summit of the hill, where are situated the grand piazza and the principal public edifices.

It happened to be market day in Perugia. The great square, therefore, presented a far more vivacious spectacle than would have been witnessed in it at any other time of the week, though not so lively as to overcome the gray solemnity of the architectural portion of the scene. In the shadow of the cathedral and other old Gothic structures—seeking shelter from the sunshine that fell across the rest of the piazza—was a crowd of people, engaged as buyers or sellers in the petty traffic of a country fair. Dealers had erected booths and stalls on the pavement, and overspread them with scanty awnings, beneath which they stood, vociferously crying their merchandise; such as shoes, hats and caps, yarn stockings, cheap jewelry and cutlery, books, chiefly little volumes of a religious Character, and a few French novels; toys, tinware, old iron, cloth, rosaries of beads, crucifixes, cakes, biscuits, sugar-plums, and innumerable little odds and ends, which we see no object in advertising. Baskets of grapes, figs, and pears stood on the ground. Donkeys, bearing panniers stuffed out with kitchen vegetables, and requiring an ample roadway, roughly shouldered aside the throng.

Crowded as the square was, a juggler found room to spread out a white cloth upon the pavement, and cover it with cups, plates, balls, cards, w the whole material of his magic, in short,—wherewith he proceeded to work miracles under the noonday sun. An organ grinder at one point, and a clarion and a flute at another, accomplished what their could towards filling the wide space with tuneful noise, Their small uproar, however, was nearly drowned by the multitudinous voices of the people, bargaining, quarrelling, laughing, and babbling copiously at random; for the briskness of the mountain atmosphere, or some other cause, made everybody so loquacious, that more words were wasted in Perugia on this one market day, than the noisiest piazza of Rome would utter in a month.

Through all this petty tumult, which kept beguiling one's eyes and upper strata of thought, it was delightful to catch glimpses of the grand old architecture that stood around the square. The life of the flitting moment, existing in the antique shell of an age gone by, has a fascination which we do not find in either the past or present, taken by themselves. It might seem irreverent to make the gray cathedral and the tall, time-worn palaces echo back the exuberant vociferation of the market; but they did so, and caused the sound to assume a kind of poetic rhythm, and themselves looked only the more majestic for their condescension.

On one side, there was an immense edifice devoted to public purposes, with an antique gallery, and a range of arched and stone-mullioned windows, running along its front; and by way of entrance it had a central Gothic arch, elaborately wreathed around with sculptured semicircles, within which the spectator was aware of a stately and impressive gloom. Though merely the municipal council-house and exchange of a decayed country town, this structure was worthy to have held in one portion of it the parliament hall of a nation, and in the other, the state apartments of its ruler. On another side of the square rose the mediaeval front of the cathedral, where the imagination of a Gothic architect had long ago flowered out indestructibly, in the first place, a grand design, and then covering it with such abundant detail of ornament, that the magnitude of the work seemed less a miracle than its minuteness. You would suppose that he must have softened the stone into wax, until his most delicate fancies were modelled in the pliant material, and then had hardened it into stone again. The whole was a vast, black-letter page of the richest and quaintest poetry. In fit keeping with all this old magnificence was a great marble fountain, where again the Gothic imagination showed its overflow and gratuity of device in the manifold sculptures which it lavished as freely as the water did its shifting shapes.

Besides the two venerable structures which we have described, there were lofty palaces, perhaps of as old a date, rising story above Story, and adorned with balconies, whence, hundreds of years ago, the princely occupants had been accustomed to gaze down at the sports, business, and popular assemblages of the piazza. And, beyond all question, they thus witnessed the erection of a bronze statue, which, three centuries since, was placed on the pedestal that it still occupies.

"I never come to Perugia," said Kenyon, "without spending as much time as I can spare in studying yonder statue of Pope Julius the Third. Those sculptors of the Middle Age have fitter lessons for the professors of my art than we can find in the Grecian masterpieces. They belong to our Christian civilization; and, being earnest works, they always express something which we do not get from the antique. Will you look at it?"

"Willingly," replied the Count, "for I see, even so far off, that the statue is bestowing a benediction, and there is a feeling in my heart that I may be permitted to share it."

Remembering the similar idea which Miriam a short time before had expressed, the sculptor smiled hopefully at the coincidence. They made their way through the throng of the market place, and approached close to the iron railing that protected the pedestal of the statue.

It was the figure of a pope, arrayed in his pontifical robes, and crowned with the tiara. He sat in a bronze chair, elevated high above the pavement, and seemed to take kindly yet authoritative cognizance of the busy scene which was at that moment passing before his eye. His right hand was raised and spread abroad, as if in the act of shedding forth a benediction, which every man—so broad, so wise, and so serenely affectionate was the bronze pope's regard—might hope to feel quietly descending upon the need, or the distress, that he had closest at his heart. The statue had life and observation in it, as well as patriarchal majesty. An imaginative spectator could not but be impressed with the idea that this benignly awful representative of divine and human authority might rise from his brazen chair, should any great public exigency demand his interposition, and encourage or restrain the people by his gesture, or even by prophetic utterances worthy of so grand a presence.

And in the long, calm intervals, amid the quiet lapse of ages, the pontiff watched the daily turmoil around his seat, listening with majestic patience to the market cries, and all the petty uproar that awoke the echoes of the stately old piazza. He was the enduring friend of these men, and of their forefathers and children, the familiar face of generations.

"The pope's blessing, methinks, has fallen upon you," observed the sculptor, looking at his friend.

In truth, Donatello's countenance indicated a healthier spirit than while he was brooding in his melancholy tower. The change of scene, the breaking up of custom, the fresh flow of incidents, the sense of being homeless, and therefore free, had done something for our poor Faun; these circumstances had at least promoted a reaction, which might else have been slower in its progress. Then, no doubt, the bright day, the gay spectacle of the market place, and the sympathetic exhilaration of so many people's cheerfulness, had each their suitable effect on a temper naturally prone to be glad. Perhaps, too, he was magnetically conscious of a presence that formerly sufficed to make him happy. Be the cause what it might, Donatello's eyes shone with a serene and hopeful expression while looking upward at the bronze pope, to whose widely diffused blessing, it may be, he attributed all this good influence.

"Yes, my dear friend," said he, in reply to the sculptor's remark, "I feel the blessing upon my spirit."

"It is wonderful," said Kenyon, with a smile, "wonderful and delightful to think how long a good man's beneficence may be potent, even after his death. How great, then, must have been the efficacy of this excellent pontiff's blessing while he was alive!"

"I have heard," remarked the Count, "that there was a brazen image set up in the wilderness, the sight of which healed the Israelites of their poisonous and rankling wounds. If it be the Blessed Virgin's pleasure, why should not this holy image before us do me equal good? A wound has long been rankling in my soul, and filling it with poison."

"I did wrong to smile," answered Kenyon. "It is not for me to limit Providence in its operations on man's spirit."

While they stood talking, the clock in the neighboring cathedral told the hour, with twelve reverberating strokes, which it flung down upon the crowded market place, as if warning one and all to take advantage of the bronze pontiff's benediction, or of Heaven's blessing, however proffered, before the opportunity were lost.

"High noon," said the sculptor. "It is Miriam's hour!"

CHAPTER XXXV. THE BRONZE PONTIFF'S BENEDICTION

When the last of the twelve strokes had fallen from the cathedral clock, Kenyon threw his eyes over the busy scene of the market place, expecting to discern Miriam somewhere in the 'crowd. He looked next towards the cathedral itself, where it was reasonable to imagine that she might have taken shelter, while awaiting her appointed time. Seeing no trace of her in either direction, his eyes came back from their quest somewhat disappointed, and rested on a figure which was leaning, like Donatello and himself, on the iron balustrade that surrounded the statue. Only a moment before, they two had been alone.

It was the figure of a woman, with her head bowed on her hands, as if she deeply felt—what we have been endeavoring to convey into our feeble description—the benign and awe-inspiring influence which the pontiff's statue exercises upon a sensitive spectator. No matter though it were modelled for a Catholic chief priest, the desolate heart, whatever be its religion, recognizes in that image the likeness of a father.

"Miriam," said the sculptor, with a tremor in his voice, "is it yourself?"

"It is I," she replied; "I am faithful to my engagement, though with many fears." She lifted her head, and revealed to Kenyon—revealed to Donatello likewise—the well-remembered features of Miriam. They were pale and worn, but distinguished even now, though less gorgeously, by a beauty that might be imagined bright enough to glimmer with its own light in a dim cathedral aisle, and had no need to shrink from the severer test of the mid-day sun. But she seemed tremulous, and hardly able to go through with a scene which at a distance she had found courage to undertake.

"You are most welcome, Miriam!" said the sculptor, seeking to afford her the encouragement which he saw she so greatly required. "I have a hopeful trust that the result of this interview will be propitious. Come; let me lead you to Donatello."

"No, Kenyon, no!" whispered Miriam, shrinking back; "unless of his own accord he speaks my name,—unless he bids me stay,—no word shall ever pass between him and me. It is not that I take upon me to be proud at this late hour. Among other feminine qualities, I threw away my pride when Hilda cast me off."

"If not pride, what else restrains you?" Kenyon asked, a little angry at her unseasonable scruples, and also at this half-complaining reference to Hilda's just severity. "After daring so much, it is no time for fear! If we let him part from you without a word, your opportunity of doing him inestimable good is lost forever."

"True; it will be lost forever!" repeated Miriam sadly. "But, dear friend, will it be my fault? I willingly fling my woman's pride at his feet. But—do you not see?—his heart must be left freely to its own decision whether to recognize me, because on his voluntary choice depends the whole question whether my devotion will do him good or harm. Except he feel an infinite need of me, I am a burden and fatal obstruction to him!"

"Take your own course, then, Miriam," said Kenyon; "and, doubtless, the crisis being what it is, your spirit is better instructed for its emergencies than mine."

While the foregoing words passed between them they had withdrawn a little from the immediate vicinity of the statue, so as to be out of Donatello's hearing. Still, however, they were beneath the pontiff's outstretched hand; and Miriam, with her beauty and her sorrow, looked up into his benignant face, as if she had come thither for his pardon and paternal affection, and despaired of so vast a boon.

Meanwhile, she had not stood thus long in the public square of Perugia, without attracting the observation of many eyes. With their quick sense of beauty, these Italians had recognized her loveliness, and spared not to take their fill of gazing at it; though their native gentleness and courtesy made their homage far less obtrusive than that of Germans, French, or Anglo-Saxons might have been. It is not improbable that Miriam had planned this momentous interview, on so public a spot and at high noon, with an eye to the sort of protection that would be thrown over it by a multitude of eye-witnesses. In circumstances of profound feeling and passion, there is often a sense that too great a seclusion cannot be endured; there is an indefinite dread of being quite alone with the object of our deepest interest. The species of solitude that a crowd harbors within itself is felt to be preferable, in certain conditions of the heart, to the remoteness of a desert or the depths of an untrodden wood. Hatred, love, or whatever kind of too intense emotion, or even indifference, where emotion has once been, instinctively seeks to interpose some barrier between itself and the corresponding passion in another breast. This, we suspect, was what Miriam had thought of, in coming to the thronged piazza; partly this, and partly, as she said, her superstition that the benign statue held good influences in store.

But Donatello remained leaning against the balustrade. She dared not glance towards him, to see whether he were pale and agitated, or calm as ice. Only, she knew that the moments were fleetly lapsing away, and that his heart must call her soon, or the voice would never reach her. She turned quite away from him and spoke again to the sculptor.

"I have wished to meet you," said she, "for more than one reason. News has come to me respecting a dear friend of ours. Nay, not of mine! I dare not call her a friend of mine, though once the dearest."

"Do you speak of Hilda?" exclaimed Kenyon, with quick alarm. "Has anything befallen her? When I last heard of her, she was still in Rome, and well."

"Hilda remains in Rome," replied Miriam, "nor is she ill as regards physical health, though much depressed in spirits. She lives quite alone in her dove-cote; not a friend near her, not one in Rome, which, you know, is deserted by all but its native inhabitants. I fear for her health, if she continue long in such solitude, with despondency preying on her mind. I tell you this, knowing the interest which the rare beauty of her character has awakened in you."

"I will go to Rome!" said the sculptor, in great emotion. "Hilda has never allowed me to manifest more than a friendly regard; but, at least, she cannot prevent my watching over her at a humble distance. I will set out this very hour."

"Do not leave us now!" whispered Miriam imploringly, and laying her hand on his arm. "One moment more! Ah; he has no word for me!"

"Miriam!" said Donatello.

Though but a single word, and the first that he had spoken, its tone was a warrant of the sad and tender depth from which it came. It told Miriam things of infinite importance, and, first of all, that he still loved her. The sense of their mutual crime had stunned, but not destroyed, the vitality of his affection; it was therefore indestructible. That tone, too, bespoke an altered and deepened character; it told of a vivified intellect, and of spiritual instruction that had come through sorrow and remorse; so that instead of the wild boy, the thing of sportive, animal nature, the sylvan Faun, here was now the man of feeling and intelligence.

She turned towards him, while his voice still reverberated in the depths of her soul.

"You have called me!" said she.

"Because my deepest heart has need of you!" he replied. "Forgive, Miriam, the coldness, the hardness with which I parted from you! I was bewildered with strange horror and gloom."

"Alas! and it was I that brought it on you," said she. "What repentance, what self-sacrifice, can atone for that infinite wrong? There was something so sacred in the innocent and joyous life which you were leading! A happy person is such an unaccustomed and holy creature in this sad world! And, encountering so rare a being, and gifted with the power of sympathy with his sunny life, it was my doom, mine, to bring him within the limits of sinful, sorrowful mortality! Bid me depart, Donatello! Fling me off! No good, through my agency, can follow upon such a mighty evil!"

"Miriam," said he, "our lot lies together. Is it not so? Tell me, in Heaven's name, if it be otherwise."

Donatello's conscience was evidently perplexed with doubt, whether the communion of a crime, such as they two were jointly stained with, ought not to stifle all the instinctive motions of their hearts, impelling them one towards the other. Miriam, on the other hand, remorsefully questioned with herself whether the misery, already accruing from her influence, should not warn her to withdraw from his path. In this momentous interview, therefore, two souls were groping for each other in the darkness of guilt and sorrow, and hardly were bold enough to grasp the cold hands that they found.

The sculptor stood watching the scene with earnest sympathy.

"It seems irreverent," said he, at length; "intrusive, if not irreverent, for a third person to thrust himself between the two solely concerned in a crisis like the present. Yet, possibly as a bystander, though a deeply interested one, I may discern somewhat of truth that is hidden from you both; nay, at least interpret or suggest some ideas which you might not so readily convey to each other."

"Speak!" said Miriam. "We confide in you." "Speak!" said Donatello. "You are true and upright."

"I well know," rejoined Kenyon, "that I shall not succeed in uttering the few, deep words which, in this matter, as in all others, include the absolute truth. But here, Miriam, is one whom a terrible misfortune has begun to educate; it has taken him, and through your agency, out of a wild and happy state, which, within circumscribed limits, gave him joys that he cannot elsewhere find on earth. On his behalf, you have incurred a responsibility which you cannot fling aside. And here, Donatello, is one whom Providence marks out as intimately connected with your destiny. The mysterious process, by which our earthly life instructs us for another state of being, was begun for you by her. She has rich gifts of heart and mind, a suggestive power, a magnetic influence, a sympathetic knowledge, which, wisely and religiously exercised, are what your condition needs. She possesses what you require, and, with utter self devotion, will use it for your good. The bond betwixt you, therefore, is a true one, and never—except by Heaven's own act—should be rent asunder."

"Ah; he has spoken the truth!" cried Donatello, grasping Miriam's hand.

"The very truth, dear friend," cried Miriam.

"But take heed," resumed the sculptor, anxious not to violate the integrity of his own conscience, "take heed; for you love one another, and yet your bond is twined with such black threads that you must never look upon it as identical with the ties that unite other loving souls. It is for mutual support; it is for one another's final good; it is for effort, for sacrifice, but not for earthly happiness. If such be your motive, believe me, friends, it were better to relinquish each other's hands at this sad moment. There would be no holy sanction on your wedded life."

"None," said Donatello, shuddering. "We know it well."

"None," repeated Miriam, also shuddering. "United—miserably entangled with me, rather—by a bond of guilt, our union might be for eternity, indeed, and most intimate;—but, through all that endless duration, I should be conscious of his horror."

"Not for earthly bliss, therefore," said Kenyon, "but for mutual elevation, and encouragement towards a severe and painful life, you take each other's hands. And if, out of toil, sacrifice, prayer, penitence, and earnest effort towards right things, there comes at length a sombre and thoughtful, happiness, taste it, and thank Heaven! So that you live not for it,—so that it be a wayside flower, springing along a path that leads to higher ends,—it will be Heaven's gracious gift, and a token that it recognizes your union here below."

"Have you no more to say?" asked Miriam earnestly. "There is matter of sorrow and lofty consolation strangely mingled in your words."

"Only this, dear Miriam," said the sculptor; "if ever in your lives the highest duty should require from either of you the sacrifice of the other, meet the occasion without shrinking. This is all."

While Kenyon spoke, Donatello had evidently taken in the ideas which he propounded, and had ennobled them by the sincerity of his reception. His aspect unconsciously assumed a dignity, which, elevating his former beauty, accorded with the change that had long been taking place in his interior self. He was a man, revolving grave and deep thoughts in his breast. He still held

Miriam's hand; and there they stood, the beautiful man, the beautiful woman, united forever, as they felt, in the presence of these thousand eye-witnesses, who gazed so curiously at the unintelligible scene. Doubtless the crowd recognized them as lovers, and fancied this a betrothal that was destined to result in lifelong happiness. And possibly it might be so. Who can tell where happiness may come; or where, though an expected guest, it may never show its face? Perhaps—shy, subtle thing—it had crept into this sad marriage bond, when the partners would have trembled at its presence as a crime.

"Farewell!" said Kenyon; "I go to Rome."

"Farewell, true friend!" said Miriam.

"Farewell!" said Donatello too. "May you be happy. You have no guilt to make you shrink from happiness."

At this moment it so chanced that all the three friends by one impulse glanced upward at the statue of Pope Julius; and there was the majestic figure stretching out the hand of benediction over them, and bending down upon this guilty and repentant pair its visage of grand benignity. There is a singular effect oftentimes when, out of the midst of engrossing thought and deep absorption, we suddenly look up, and catch a glimpse of external objects. We seem at such moments to look farther and deeper into them, than by any premeditated observation; it is as if they met our eyes alive, and with all their hidden meaning on the surface, but grew again inanimate and inscrutable the instant that they became aware of our glances. So now, at that unexpected glimpse, Miriam, Donatello, and the sculptor, all three imagined that they beheld the bronze pontiff endowed with spiritual life. A blessing was felt descending upon them from his outstretched hand; he approved by look and gesture the pledge of a deep union that had passed under his auspices.

CHAPTER XXXVI. HILDA'S TOWER

When we have once known Rome, and left her where she lies, like a long-decaying corpse, retaining a trace of the noble shape it was, but with accumulated dust and a fungous growth overspreading all its more admirable features, left her in utter weariness, no doubt, of her narrow, crooked, intricate streets, so uncomfortably paved with little squares of lava that to tread over them is a penitential pilgrimage, so indescribably ugly, moreover, so cold, so alley-like, into which the sun never falls, and where a chill wind forces its deadly breath into our lungs,—left her, tired of the sight of those immense seven-storied, yellow-washed hovels, or call them palaces, where all that is dreary in domestic life seems magnified and multiplied, and weary of climbing those staircases, which ascend from a ground-floor of cook shops, cobblers' stalls, stables, and regiments of cavalry, to a middle region of princes, cardinals, and ambassadors, and an upper tier of artists, just beneath the unattainable sky,—left her, worn out with shivering at the cheerless and smoky fireside by day, and feasting with our own substance the ravenous little populace of a Roman bed at night,—left her, sick at heart of Italian trickery, which has uprooted whatever faith in man's integrity had endured till now, and sick at stomach of sour bread, sour wine, rancid butter, and bad cookery, needlessly bestowed on evil meats,—left her, disgusted with the pretence of holiness and the reality of nastiness, each equally omnipresent,—left her, half lifeless from the languid atmosphere, the vital principle of which has been used up long ago, or corrupted by myriads of slaughters,—left her, crushed down in spirit with the desolation of her ruin, and the hopelessness of her future,—left her, in short, hating her with all our might, and adding our individual curse to the infinite anathema which her old crimes have unmistakably brought down,—when we have left Rome in such mood as this, we are astonished by the discovery, by and by, that our heart-strings have mysteriously attached themselves to the Eternal City, and are drawing us thitherward again, as if it were more familiar, more intimately our home, than even the spot where we were born.

It is with a kindred sentiment, that we now follow the course of our story back through the Flaminian Gate, and, treading our way to the Via Portoghese, climb the staircase to the upper chamber of the tower where we last saw Hilda.

Hilda all along intended to pass the summer in Rome; for she had laid out many high and delightful tasks, which she could the better complete while her favorite haunts were deserted by the multitude that thronged them throughout the winter and early spring. Nor did she dread the summer atmosphere, although generally held to be so pestilential. She had already made trial of it, two years before, and found no worse effect than a kind of dreamy languor, which was dissipated by the first cool breezes that came with autumn. The thickly populated centre of the city, indeed, is never affected by the feverish influence that lies in wait in the Campagna, like a besieging foe, and nightly haunts those beautiful lawns and woodlands, around the suburban villas, just at the season when they most resemble Paradise. What the flaming sword was to the first Eden, such is the malaria to these sweet gardens and grove. We may wander through them, of an afternoon, it is true, but they cannot be made a home and a reality, and to sleep among them is death. They are but illusions, therefore, like the show of gleaming waters and shadowy foliage in a desert.

But Rome, within the walls, at this dreaded season, enjoys its festal days, and makes itself merry with characteristic and hereditary pas-times, for which its broad piazzas afford abundant room. It leads its own life with a freer spirit, now that the artists and foreign visitors are scattered abroad. No bloom, perhaps, would be visible in a cheek that should be unvisited, throughout the summer, by more invigorating winds than any within fifty miles of the city; no bloom, but yet, if the mind kept its healthy energy, a subdued and colorless well-being. There was consequently little risk in Hilda's purpose to pass the summer days in the galleries of Roman palaces, and her nights in that aerial chamber, whither the heavy breath of the city and its suburbs could not aspire. It would probably harm her no more than it did the white doves, who sought the same high atmosphere at sunset, and, when morning came, flew down into the narrow streets, about their daily business, as Hilda likewise did.

With the Virgin's aid and blessing, which might be hoped for even by a heretic, who so religiously lit the lamp before her shrine, the New England girl would sleep securely in her old Roman tower, and go forth on her pictorial pilgrimages without dread or peril. In view of such a summer, Hilda had anticipated many months of lonely, but unalloyed enjoyment. Not that she had a churlish disinclination to society, or needed to be told that we taste one intellectual pleasure twice, and with double the result, when we taste it with a friend. But, keeping a maiden heart within her bosom, she rejoiced in the freedom that enabled her still to choose her own sphere, and dwell in it, if she pleased, without another inmate.

Her expectation, however, of a delightful summer was woefully disappointed. Even had she formed no previous plan of remaining there, it is improbable that Hilda would have gathered energy to stir from Rome. A torpor, heretofore unknown to her vivacious though quiet temperament, had possessed itself of the poor girl, like a half-dead serpent knotting its cold, inextricable wreaths about her limbs. It was that peculiar despair, that chill and heavy misery, which only the innocent can experience, although it possesses many of the gloomy characteristics that mark a sense of guilt. It was that heartsickness, which, it is to be hoped, we may all of us have been pure enough to feel, once in our lives, but the capacity for which is usually exhausted early, and perhaps with a single agony. It was that dismal certainty of the existence of evil in the world, which, though we may fancy ourselves fully assured of the sad mystery long before, never becomes a portion of our practical belief until it takes substance and reality from the sin of some guide, whom we have deeply trusted and revered, or some friend whom we have dearly loved.

When that knowledge comes, it is as if a cloud had suddenly gathered over the morning light; so dark a cloud, that there seems to be no longer any sunshine behind it or above it. The character of our individual beloved one having invested itself with all the attributes of right,—that one friend being to us the symbol and representative of whatever is good and true,—when he falls, the effect is almost as if the sky fell with him, bringing down in chaotic ruin the columns that upheld our faith. We struggle forth again, no doubt, bruised and bewildered. We stare wildly about us, and discover—or, it may be, we never make the discovery—that it was not actually the sky that has tumbled down, but merely a frail structure of our own rearing, which never rose higher than the housetops, and has fallen because we founded it on nothing. But the crash, and the affright and trouble, are as overwhelming, for the time, as if the catastrophe involved the whole moral world. Remembering these things, let them suggest one generous motive for walking heedfully amid the defilement of earthly ways! Let us reflect, that the highest path is pointed out by the pure Ideal of those who look up to us, and who, if we tread less loftily, may never look so high again.

Hilda's situation was made infinitely more wretched by the necessity of Confining all her trouble within her own consciousness. To this innocent girl, holding the knowledge of Miriam's crime within her tender and delicate soul, the effect was almost the same as if she herself had participated in the guilt. Indeed, partaking the human nature of those who could perpetrate such deeds, she felt her own spotlessness impugnent.

Had there been but a single friend,—or not a friend, since friends were no longer to be confided in, after Miriam had betrayed her trust,—but, had there been any calm, wise mind, any sympathizing intelligence; or, if not these, any dull, half-listening ear into which she might have flung the dreadful secret, as into an echoless cavern, what a relief would have ensued! But this awful loneliness! It enveloped her whithersoever she went. It was a shadow in the sunshine of festal days; a mist between her eyes and the pictures at which she strove to look; a chill dungeon, which kept her in its gray twilight and fed her with its unwholesome air, fit only for a criminal to breathe and pine in! She could not escape from it. In the effort to do so, straying farther into the intricate passages of our nature, she stumbled, ever and again, over this deadly idea of mortal guilt.

Poor sufferer for another's sin! Poor wellspring of a virgin's heart, into which a murdered corpse had casually fallen, and whence it could not be drawn forth again, but lay there, day after day, night after night, tainting its sweet atmosphere with the scent of crime and ugly death!

The strange sorrow that had befallen Hilda did not fail to impress its mysterious seal upon her face, and to make itself perceptible to sensitive observers in her manner and carriage. A young Italian artist, who frequented the same galleries which Hilda haunted, grew deeply interested in her expression. One day, while she stood before Leonardo da Vinci's picture of Joanna of Aragon, but evidently without seeing it,—for, though it had attracted her eyes, a fancied resemblance to Miriam had immediately drawn away her thoughts,—this artist drew a hasty sketch which he afterwards elaborated into a finished portrait. It represented Hilda as gazing with sad and earnest horror at a bloodspot which she seemed just then to have discovered on her white robe. The picture attracted considerable notice. Copies of an engraving from it may still be found in the print shops along the Corso. By many connoisseurs, the idea of the face was supposed to have been suggested by the portrait of Beatrice Cenci; and, in fact, there was a look somewhat similar to poor Beatrice's forlorn gaze out of the dreary isolation and remoteness, in which a terrible doom had involved a tender soul. But the modern artist strenuously upheld the originality of his own picture, as well as the stainless purity its subject, and chose to call it—and was laughed at for his pains—"Innocence, dying of a Blood-stain!"

"Your picture, Signore Panini, does you credit," remarked the picture dealer, who had bought it of the young man for fifteen scudi, and afterwards sold it for ten times the sum; "but it would be worth a better price if you had given it a more intelligible title. Looking at the face and expression of this fair signorina, we seem to comprehend readily enough, that she is undergoing one or another of those troubles of the heart to which young ladies are but too liable. But what is this blood-stain? And what has innocence to do with it? Has she stabbed her perfidious lover with a bodkin?"

"She! she commit a crime!" cried the young artist. "Can you look at the innocent anguish in her face, and ask that question? No; but, as I read the mystery, a man has been slain in her presence, and the blood, spurting accidentally on her white robe, has made a stain which eats into her life."

"Then, in the name of her patron saint," exclaimed the picture dealer, "why don't she get the robe made white again at the expense of a few baiocchi to her washerwoman? No, no, my dear Panini. The picture being now my property, I shall call it 'The Signorina's Vengeance.' She has stabbed her lover overnight, and is repenting it betimes the next morning. So interpreted, the picture becomes an intelligible and very natural representation of a not uncommon fact."

Thus coarsely does the world translate all finer griefs that meet its eye. It is more a coarse world than an unkind one.

But Hilda sought nothing either from the world's delicacy or its pity, and never dreamed of its misinterpretations. Her doves often flew in through the windows of the tower, winged messengers, bringing her what sympathy they could, and uttering soft, tender, and complaining sounds, deep in their bosoms, which soothed the girl more than a distincter utterance might. And sometimes Hilda moaned quietly among the doves, teaching her voice to accord with theirs, and thus finding a temporary relief from the burden of her incommunicable sorrow, as if a little portion of it, at least, had been told to these innocent friends, and been understood and pitied.

When she trimmed the lamp before the Virgin's shrine, Hilda gazed at the sacred image, and, rude as was the workmanship, beheld, or fancied, expressed with the quaint, powerful simplicity which sculptors sometimes had five hundred years ago, a woman's tenderness responding to her gaze. If she knelt, if she prayed, if her oppressed heart besought the sympathy of divine womanhood afar in bliss, but not remote, because forever humanized by the memory of mortal griefs, was Hilda to be blamed? It was not a Catholic kneeling at an idolatrous shrine, but a child lifting its tear-stained face to seek comfort from a mother.

CHAPTER XXXVII. THE EMPTINESS OF PICTURE GALLERIES

Hilda descended, day by day, from her dove-cote, and went to one or another of the great old palaces,—the Pamfili Doria, the Corsini, the Sciarra, the Borghese, the Colonna,—where the doorkeepers knew her well, and offered her a kindly greeting. But they shook their heads and sighed, on observing the languid step with which the poor girl toiled up the grand marble staircases. There was no more of that cheery alacrity with which she used to flit upward, as if her doves had lent her their wings, nor of that glow of happy spirits which had been wont to set the tarnished gilding of the picture frames and the shabby splendor of the furniture all a-glimmer, as she hastened to her congenial and delightful toil.

An old German artist, whom she often met in the galleries, once laid a paternal hand on Hilda's head, and bade her go back to her own country.

"Go back soon," he said, with kindly freedom and directness, "or you will go never more. And, if you go not, why, at least, do you spend the whole summer-time in Rome? The air has been breathed too often, in so many thousand years, and is not wholesome for a little foreign flower like you, my child, a delicate wood-anemone from the western forest-land."

"I have no task nor duty anywhere but here," replied Hilda. "The old masters will not set me free!"

"Ah, those old masters!" cried the veteran artist, shaking his head. "They are a tyrannous race! You will find them of too mighty a spirit to be dealt with, for long together, by the slender hand, the fragile mind, and the delicate heart, of a young girl. Remember that Raphael's genius wore out that divinest painter before half his life was lived. Since you feel his influence powerfully enough to reproduce his miracles so well, it will assuredly consume you like a flame."

"That might have been my peril once," answered Hilda. "It is not so now."

"Yes, fair maiden, you stand in that peril now!" insisted the kind old man; and he added, smiling, yet in a melancholy vein, and with a German grotesqueness of idea, "Some fine morning, I shall come to the Pinacotheca of the Vatican, with my palette and my brushes, and shall look for my little American artist that sees into the very heart of the grand pictures! And what shall I behold? A heap of white ashes on the marble floor, just in front of the divine Raphael's picture of the Madonna da Foligno! Nothing more, upon my word! The fire, which the poor child feels so fervently, will have gone into her innermost, and burnt her quite up!"

"It would be a happy martyrdom!" said Hilda, faintly smiling. "But I am far from being worthy of it. What troubles me much, among other troubles, is quite the reverse of what you think. The old masters hold me here, it is true, but they no longer warm me with their influence. It is not flame consuming, but torpor chilling me, that helps to make me wretched."

"Perchance, then," said the German, looking keenly at her, "Raphael has a rival in your heart? He was your first love; but young maidens are not always constant, and one flame is sometimes extinguished by another!" Hilda shook her head, and turned away. She had spoken the truth, however, in alleging that torpor, rather than fire, was what she had to dread. In those gloomy days that had befallen her, it was a great additional calamity that she felt conscious of the present dimness of an insight which she once possessed in more than ordinary measure. She had lost—and she trembled lest it should have departed forever—the faculty of appreciating those great works of art, which heretofore had made so large a portion of her happiness. It was no wonder.

A picture, however admirable the painter's art, and wonderful his power, requires of the spectator a surrender of himself, in due proportion with the miracle which has been wrought. Let the canvas glow as it may, you must look with the eye of faith, or its highest excellence escapes you. There is always the necessity of helping out the painter's art with your own resources of sensibility and imagination. Not that these qualities shall really add anything to what the master has effected; but they must be put so entirely under his control, and work along with him to such an extent, that, in a different mood, when you are cold and critical, instead of sympathetic, you will be apt to fancy that the loftier merits of the picture were of your own dreaming, not of his creating.

Like all revelations of the better life, the adequate perception of a great work of art demands a gifted simplicity of vision. In this, and in her self-surrender, and the depth and tenderness of her sympathy, had lain Hilda's remarkable power as a copyist of the old masters. And now that her capacity of emotion was choked up with a horrible experience, it inevitably followed that she should seek in vain, among those friends so venerated and beloved, for the marvels which they had heretofore shown her. In spite of a reverence that lingered longer than her recognition, their poor worshipper became almost an infidel, and sometimes doubted whether the pictorial art be not altogether a delusion.

For the first time in her life, Hilda now grew acquainted with that icy demon of weariness, who haunts great picture galleries. He is a plausible Mephistopheles, and possesses the magic that is the destruction of all other magic. He annihilates color, warmth, and, more especially, sentiment and passion, at a touch. If he spare anything, it will be some such matter as an earthen pipkin, or a bunch of herrings by Teniers; a brass kettle, in which you can see your rice, by Gerard Douw; a furred robe, or the silken texture of a mantle, or a straw hat, by Van Mieris; or a long-stalked wineglass, transparent and full of shifting reflection, or a bit of bread and cheese, or an over-ripe peach with a fly upon it, truer than reality itself, by the school of Dutch conjurers. These men, and a few Flemings, whispers the wicked demon, were the only painters. The mighty Italian masters, as you deem them, were not human, nor addressed their work to human sympathies, but to a false intellectual taste, which they themselves were the first to create. Well might they call their doings "art," for they substituted art instead of nature. Their fashion is past, and ought, indeed, to have died and been buried along with them.

Then there is such a terrible lack of variety in their subjects. The churchmen, their great patrons, suggested most of their themes, and a dead mythology the rest. A quarter part, probably, of any large collection of pictures consists of Virgins and infant Christs, repeated over and over again

112

in pretty much an identical spirit, and generally with no more mixture of the Divine than just enough to spoil them as representations of maternity and childhood, with which everybody's heart might have something to do. Half of the other pictures are Magdalens, Flights into Egypt, Crucifixions, Depositions from the Cross, Pietas, Noli-me-tangeres, or the Sacrifice of Abraham, or martyrdoms of saints, originally painted as altar-pieces, or for the shrines of chapels, and woefully lacking the accompaniments which the artist haft in view.

The remainder of the gallery comprises mythological subjects, such as nude Venuses, Ledas, Graces, and, in short, a general apotheosis of nudity, once fresh and rosy perhaps, but yellow and dingy in our day, and retaining only a traditionary charm. These impure pictures are from the same illustrious and impious hands that adventured to call before us the august forms of Apostles and Saints, the Blessed Mother of the Redeemer, and her Son, at his death, and in his glory, and even the awfulness of Him, to whom the martyrs, dead a thousand years ago, have not yet dared to raise their eyes. They seem to take up one task or the other w the disrobed woman whom they call Venus, or the type of highest and tenderest womanhood in the mother of their Saviour with equal readiness, but to achieve the former with far more satisfactory success. If an artist sometimes produced a picture of the Virgin, possessing warmth enough to excite devotional feelings, it was probably the object of his earthly love to whom he thus paid the stupendous and fearful homage of setting up her portrait to be worshipped, not figuratively as a mortal, but by religious souls in their earnest aspirations towards Divinity. And who can trust the religious sentiment of Raphael, or receive any of his Virgins as heaven-descended likenesses, after seeing, for example, the Fornarina of the Barberini Palace, and feeling how sensual the artist must have been to paint such a brazen trollop of his own accord, and lovingly? Would the Blessed Mary reveal herself to his spiritual vision, and favor him with sittings alternately with that type of glowing earthliness, the Fornarina?

But no sooner have we given expression to this irreverent criticism, than a throng of spiritual faces look reproachfully upon us. We see cherubs by Raphael, whose baby innocence could only have been nursed in paradise;

angels by Raphael as innocent as they, but whose serene intelligence embraces both earthly and celestial things; madonnas by Raphael, on whose lips he has impressed a holy and delicate reserve, implying sanctity on earth, and into whose soft eyes he has thrown a light which he never could have imagined except by raising his own eyes with a pure aspiration heavenward. We remember, too, that divinest countenance in the Transfiguration, and withdraw all that we have said.

Poor Hilda, however, in her gloomiest moments, was never guilty of the high treason suggested in the above remarks against her beloved and honored Raphael. She had a faculty (which, fortunately for themselves, pure women often have) of ignoring all moral blotches in a character that won her admiration. She purified the objects; of her regard by the mere act of turning such spotless eyes upon them.

Hilda's despondency, nevertheless, while it dulled her perceptions in one respect, had deepened them in another; she saw beauty less vividly, but felt truth, or the lack of it, more profoundly. She began to suspect that some, at least, of her venerated painters, had left an inevitable hollowness in their works, because, in the most renowned of them, they essayed to express to the world what they had not in their own souls. They deified their light and Wandering affections, and were continually playing off the tremendous jest, alluded to above, of offering the features of some venal beauty to be enshrined in the holiest places. A deficiency of earnestness and absolute truth is generally discoverable in Italian pictures, after the art had become consummate. When you demand what is deepest, these painters have not wherewithal to respond. They substituted a keen intellectual perception, and a marvellous knack of external arrangement, instead of the live sympathy and sentiment which should have been their inspiration. And hence it happens, that shallow and worldly men are among the best critics of their works; a taste for pictorial art is often no more than a polish upon the hard enamel of an artificial character. Hilda had lavished her whole heart upon it, and found (just as if she had lavished it upon a human idol) that the greater part was thrown away.

For some of the earlier painters, however, she still retained much of her former reverence. Fra Angelico, she felt, must have breathed a humble aspiration between every two touches of his brush, in order to have made the finished picture such a visible prayer as we behold it, in the guise of a prim angel, or a saint without the human nature. Through all these dusky centuries, his works may still help a struggling heart to pray. Perugino was evidently a devout man; and the Virgin, therefore, revealed herself to him in loftier and sweeter faces of celestial womanhood, and yet with a kind of homeliness in their human mould, than even the genius of Raphael could imagine. Sodoma, beyond a question, both prayed and wept, while painting his fresco, at Siena, of Christ bound to a pillar.

In her present need and hunger for a spiritual revelation, Hilda felt a vast and weary longing to see this last-mentioned picture once again. It is inexpressibly touching. So weary is the Saviour and utterly worn out with agony, that his lips have fallen apart from mere exhaustion; his eyes seem to be set; he tries to lean his head against the pillar, but is kept from sinking down upon the ground only by the cords that bind him. One of the most striking effects produced is the sense of loneliness. You behold Christ deserted both in heaven and earth; that despair is in him which wrung forth the saddest utterance man ever made, "Why hast Thou forsaken me?" Even in this extremity, however, he is still divine. The great and reverent painter has not suffered the Son of God to be merely an object of pity, though depicting him in a state so profoundly pitiful. He is rescued from it, we know not how,—by nothing less than miracle,—by a celestial majesty and beauty, and some quality of which these are the outward garniture. He is as much, and as visibly, our Redeemer, there bound, there fainting, and bleeding from the scourge, with the cross in view, as if he sat on his throne of glory in the heavens! Sodoma, in this matchless picture, has done more towards reconciling the incongruity of Divine Omnipotence and outraged, suffering Humanity, combined in one person, than the theologians ever did.

This hallowed work of genius shows what pictorial art, devoutly exercised, might effect in behalf of religious truth; involving, as it does, deeper mysteries of revelation, and bringing them closer to man's heart, and making him tenderer to be impressed by them, than the most eloquent words of preacher or prophet.

It is not of pictures like the above that galleries, in Rome or elsewhere, are made up, but of productions immeasurably below them, and requiring to be appreciated by a very different frame of mind. Few amateurs are endowed with a tender susceptibility to the sentiment of a picture; they are not won from an evil life, nor anywise morally improved by it. The love of art, therefore, differs widely in its influence from the love of nature; whereas, if art had not strayed away from its legitimate paths and aims, it ought to soften and sweeten the lives of its worshippers, in even a more exquisite degree than the contemplation of natural objects. But, of its own potency, it has no such effect; and it fails, likewise, in that other test of its moral value which poor Hilda was now involuntarily trying upon it. It cannot comfort the heart in affliction; it grows dim when the shadow is upon us.

So the melancholy girl wandered through those long galleries, and over the mosaic pavements of vast, solitary saloons, wondering what had become of the splendor that used to beam upon her from the walls. She grew sadly critical, and condemned almost everything that she was wont to admire. Heretofore, her sympathy went deeply into a picture, yet seemed to leave a depth which it was inadequate to sound; now, on the contrary, her perceptive faculty penetrated the canvas like a steel probe, and found but a crust of paint over an emptiness. Not that she gave up all art as worthless; only it had lost its consecration. One picture in ten thousand, perhaps, ought to live in the applause of mankind, from generation to generation, until the colors fade and blacken out of sight, or the canvas rot entirely away. For the rest, let them be piled in garrets, just as the tolerable poets are shelved, when their little day is over. Is a painter more sacred than a poet?

And as for these galleries of Roman palaces, they were to Hilda, —though she still trod them with the forlorn hope of getting back her sympathies,— they were drearier than the whitewashed walls of a prison corridor. If a magnificent palace were founded, as was generally the case, on hardened guilt and a stony conscience,—if the prince or cardinal who stole the marble of his vast mansion from the Coliseum, or some Roman temple, had perpetrated still deadlier crimes, as probably he did,—there could be no fitter punishment for his ghost than to wander, perpetually through these long suites of rooms, over the cold marble or mosaic of the floors, growing chiller at every eternal footstep. Fancy the progenitor of the Dorias thus haunting those heavy halls where his posterity reside! Nor would it assuage his monotonous misery, but increase it manifold, to be compelled to scrutinize those masterpieces of art, which he collected with so much cost and care, and gazing at them unintelligently, still leave a further portion of his vital warmth at every one.

Such, or of a similar kind, is the torment of those who seek to enjoy pictures in an uncongenial mood. Every haunter of picture galleries, we should imagine, must have experienced it, in greater or less degree; Hilda never till now, but now most bitterly.

And now, for the first time in her lengthened absence, comprising so many years of her young life, she began to be acquainted with the exile's pain. Her pictorial imagination brought up vivid scenes of her native village, with its great old elm-trees; and the neat, comfortable houses, scattered along the wide, grassy margin of its street, and the white meeting-house, and her mother's very door, and the stream of gold brown water, which her taste for color had kept flowing, all this while, through her remembrance. O dreary streets, palaces, churches, and imperial sepulchres of hot and dusty Rome, with the muddy Tiber eddying through the midst, instead of the gold-brown rivulet! How she pined under this crumbly magnificence, as if it were piled all upon her human heart! How she yearned for that native homeliness, those familiar sights, those faces which she had known always, those days that never brought any strange event; that life of sober week-days, and a solemn sabbath at the close! The peculiar fragrance of a flower-bed, which Hilda used to cultivate, came freshly to her memory, across the windy sea, and through the long years since the flowers had withered. Her heart grew faint at the hundred reminiscences that were awakened by that remembered smell of dead blossoms; it was like opening a drawer, where many things were laid away, and every one of them scented with lavender and dried rose-leaves.

We ought not to betray Hilda's secret; but it is the truth, that being so sad, and so utterly alone, and in such great need of sympathy, her thoughts sometimes recurred to the sculptor. Had she met him now, her heart, indeed, might not have been won, but her confidence would have flown to him like

117

a bird to its nest. One summer afternoon, especially, Hilda leaned upon the battlements of her tower, and looked over Rome towards the distant mountains, whither Kenyon had told her that he was going.

"O that he were here!" she sighed; "I perish under this terrible secret; and he might help me to endure it. O that he were here!"

That very afternoon, as the reader may remember, Kenyon felt Hilda's hand pulling at the silken cord that was connected with his heart-strings, as he stood looking towards Rome from the battlements of Monte Beni.

CHAPTER XXXVIII. ALTARS AND INCENSE

Rome has a certain species of consolation readier at hand, for all the necessitous, than any other spot under the sun; and Hilda's despondent state made her peculiarly liable to the peril, if peril it can justly be termed, of seeking, or consenting, to be thus consoled.

Had the Jesuits known the situation of this troubled heart, her inheritance of New England Puritanism would hardly have protected the poor girl from the pious strategy of those good fathers. Knowing, as they do, how to work each proper engine, it would have been ultimately impossible for Hilda to resist the attractions of a faith, which so marvellously adapts itself to every human need. Not, indeed, that it can satisfy the soul's cravings, but, at least, it can sometimes help the soul towards a higher satisfaction than the faith contains within itself. It supplies a multitude of external forms, in which the spiritual may be clothed and manifested; it has many painted windows, as it were, through which the celestial sunshine, else disregarded, may make itself gloriously perceptible in visions of beauty and splendor. There is no one want or weakness of human nature for which Catholicism will own itself without a remedy; cordials, certainly, it possesses in abundance, and sedatives in inexhaustible variety, and what may once have been genuine medicaments, though a little the worse for long keeping.

To do it justice, Catholicism is such a miracle of fitness for its own ends, many of which might seem to be admirable ones, that it is difficult to imagine it a contrivance of mere man. Its mighty machinery was forged and put together, not on middle earth, but either above or below. If there were but angels to work it, instead of the very different class of engineers who now manage its cranks and safety valves, the system would soon vindicate the dignity and holiness of its origin.

Hilda had heretofore made many pilgrimages among the churches of Rome, for the sake of wondering at their gorgeousness. Without a glimpse at these palaces of worship, it is impossible to imagine the magnificence of the religion that reared them. Many of them shine with burnished gold. They glow with pictures. Their walls, columns, and arches seem a quarry of precious stones, so beautiful and costly are the marbles with which they are inlaid. Their pavements are often a mosaic, of rare workmanship. Around their lofty cornices hover flights of sculptured angels; and within the vault of the ceiling and the swelling interior of the dome, there are frescos of such brilliancy, and wrought with so artful a perspective, that the sky, peopled with sainted forms, appears to be opened only a little way above the spectator. Then there are chapels, opening from the side aisles and transepts, decorated by princes for their own burial places, and as shrines for their especial saints. In these, the splendor of the entire edifice is intensified and gathered to a focus. Unless words were gems, that would flame with many-colored light upon the page, and throw thence a tremulous glimmer into the reader's eyes, it were wain to attempt a description of a princely chapel.

Restless with her trouble, Hilda now entered upon another pilgrimage among these altars and shrines. She climbed the hundred steps of the Ara Coeli; she trod the broad, silent nave of St. John Lateran; she stood in the Pantheon, under the round opening in the dome, through which the blue sunny sky still gazes down, as it used to gaze when there were Roman deities in the antique niches. She went into every church that rose before her, but not now to wonder at its magnificence, when she hardly noticed more than if it had been the pine-built interior of a New England meeting-house.

She went—and it was a dangerous errand—to observe how closely and comfortingly the popish faith applied itself to all human occasions. It was impossible to doubt that multitudes of people found their spiritual advantage in it, who would find none at all in our own formless mode of worship; which, besides, so far as the sympathy of prayerful souls is concerned, can be enjoyed only at stated and too unfrequent periods. But here, whenever the hunger for divine nutriment came upon the soul, it could on the instant be appeased. At one or another altar, the incense was forever ascending; the mass always being performed, and carrying upward with it the devotion of such as had not words for their own prayer. And yet, if the worshipper had his individual petition to offer, his own heart-secret to whisper below his breath, there were divine auditors ever ready to receive it from his lips; and what encouraged him still more, these auditors had not always been divine, but kept, within their heavenly memories, the tender humility of a human experience. Now a saint in heaven, but once a man on earth.

Hilda saw peasants, citizens, soldiers, nobles, women with bare heads, ladies in their silks, entering the churches individually, kneeling for moments or for hours, and directing their inaudible devotions to the shrine of some saint of their own choice. In his hallowed person, they felt themselves possessed of an own friend in heaven. They were too humble to approach the Deity directly. Conscious of their unworthiness, they asked the mediation of their sympathizing patron, who, on the score of his ancient martyrdom, and after many ages of celestial life, might venture to talk with the Divine Presence, almost as friend with friend. Though dumb before its Judge, even despair could speak, and pour out the misery of its soul like water, to an advocate so wise to comprehend the case, and eloquent to plead it, and powerful to win pardon whatever were the guilt. Hilda witnessed what she deemed to be an example of this species of confidence between a young man and his saint. He stood before a shrine, writhing, wringing his hands, contorting his whole frame in an agony of remorseful recollection, but finally knelt down to weep and pray. If this youth had been a Protestant, he would have kept all that torture pent up in his heart, and let it burn there till it seared him into indifference.

Often and long, Hilda lingered before the shrines and chapels of the Virgin, and departed from them with reluctant steps. Here, perhaps, strange as it may seem, her delicate appreciation of art stood her in good stead, and lost Catholicism a convert. If the painter had represented Mary with a heavenly face, poor Hilda was now in the very mood to worship her, and adopt the faith in which she held so elevated a position. But she saw that it was merely the flattered portrait of an earthly beauty; the wife, at best, of the artist; or, it might be, a peasant girl of the Campagna, or some Roman princess, to whom he desired to pay his court. For love, or some even less justifiable motive, the old painter had apotheosized these women; he thus gained for them, as far as his skill would go, not only the meed of immortality, but the privilege of presiding over Christian altars, and of being worshipped with far holier fervors than while they dwelt on earth. Hilda's fine sense of the fit and decorous could not be betrayed into kneeling at such a shrine.

She never found just the virgin mother whom she needed. Here it was an earthly mother, worshipping the earthly baby in her lap, as any and every mother does, from Eve's time downward. In another picture, there was a dim sense, shown in the mother's face, of some divine quality in the child. In a third, the artist seemed to have had a higher perception, and had striven hard to shadow out the Virgin's joy at bringing the Saviour into the world, and her awe and love, inextricably mingled, of the little form which she pressed against her bosom. So far was good. But still, Hilda looked for something more; a face of celestial beauty, but human as well as heavenly, and with the shadow of past grief upon it; bright with immortal youth, yet matronly and motherly; and endowed with a queenly dignity, but infinitely tender, as the highest and deepest attribute of her divinity.

"Ah," thought Hilda to herself, "why should not there be a woman to listen to the prayers of women? A mother in heaven for all motherless girls like me? In all God's thought and care for us, can he have withheld this boon, which our weakness so much needs?"

Oftener than to the other churches, she wandered into St. Peter's. Within its vast limits, she thought, and beneath the sweep of its great dome, there should be space for all forms of Christian truth; room both for the faithful and the heretic to kneel; due help for every creature's spiritual want.

Hilda had not always been adequately impressed by the grandeur of this mighty cathedral. When she first lifted the heavy leathern curtain, at one of the doors, a shadowy edifice in her imagination had been dazzled out of sight by the reality. Her preconception of St. Peter's was a structure of no definite outline, misty in its architecture, dim and gray and huge, stretching into an interminable perspective, and overarched by a dome like the cloudy firmament. Beneath that vast breadth and height, as she had fancied them, the personal man might feel his littleness, and the soul triumph in its immensity. So, in her earlier visits, when the compassed splendor Of the actual interior glowed before her eyes, she had profanely called it a great prettiness; a gay piece of cabinet work, on a Titanic scale; a jewel casket, marvellously magnified.

This latter image best pleased her fancy; a casket, all inlaid in the inside with precious stones of various hue, so that there Should not be a hair's-breadth of the small interior unadorned with its resplendent gem. Then, conceive this minute wonder of a mosaic box, increased to the magnitude of a cathedral, without losing the intense lustre of its littleness, but all its petty glory striving to be sublime. The magic transformation from the minute to the vast has not been so cunningly effected but that the rich adornment still counteracts the impression of space and loftiness. The spectator is more sensible of its limits than of its extent.

Until after many visits, Hilda continued to mourn for that dim, illimitable interior, which with her eyes shut she had seen from childhood, but which vanished at her first glimpse through the actual door. Her childish vision seemed preferable to the cathedral which Michael Angelo, and all the great architects, had built; because, of the dream edifice, she had said, "How vast it is!" while of the real St. Peter's she could only say, "After all, it is not so immense!" Besides, such as the church is, it can nowhere be made visible at one glance. It stands in its own way. You see an aisle, or a transept; you see the nave, or the tribune; but, on account of its ponderous piers and other obstructions, it is only by this fragmentary process that you get an idea of the cathedral.

There is no answering such objections. The great church smiles calmly upon its critics, and, for all response, says, "Look at me!" and if you still murmur for the loss of your shadowy perspective, there comes no reply, save, "Look at me!" in endless repetition, as the one thing to be said. And, after looking many times, with long intervals between, you discover that the cathedral has gradually extended itself over the whole compass of your idea; it covers all the site of your visionary temple, and has room for its cloudy pinnacles beneath the dome.

One afternoon, as Hilda entered St. Peter's in sombre mood, its interior beamed upon her with all the effect of a new creation. It seemed an embodiment of whatever the imagination could conceive, or the heart desire, as a magnificent, comprehensive, majestic symbol of religious faith. All splendor was included within its verge, and there was space for all. She gazed with delight even at the multiplicity of ornament. She was glad at the cherubim that fluttered upon the pilasters, and of the marble doves, hovering unexpectedly, with green olive-branches of precious stones. She could spare nothing, now, of the manifold magnificence that had been lavished, in a hundred places, richly enough to have made world-famous shrines in any other church, but which here melted away into the vast sunny breadth, and were of no separate account. Yet each contributed its little all towards the grandeur of the whole.

She would not have banished one of those grim popes, who sit each over his own tomb, scattering cold benedictions out of their marble hands; nor a single frozen sister of the Allegoric family, to whom—as, like hired mourners at an English funeral, it costs them no wear and tear of heart—is assigned the office of weeping for the dead. If you choose to see these things, they present themselves; if you deem them unsuitable and out of place, they vanish, individually, but leave their life upon the walls.

The pavement! it stretched out illimitably, a plain of many-colored marble, where thousands of worshippers might kneel together, and shadowless angels tread among them without brushing their heavenly garments against those earthly ones. The roof! the dome! Rich, gorgeous, filled with sunshine, cheerfully sublime, and fadeless after centuries, those lofty depths seemed to translate the heavens to mortal comprehension, and help the spirit upward to a yet higher and wider sphere. Must not the faith, that built this matchless edifice, and warmed, illuminated, and overflowed from it, include whatever can satisfy human aspirations at the loftiest, or minister to human necessity at the sorest? If Religion had a material home, was it not here?

As the scene which we but faintly suggest shone calmly before the New England maiden at her entrance, she moved, as if by very instinct, to one of the vases of holy water, upborne against a column by two mighty cherubs. Hilda dipped her fingers, and had almost signed the cross upon her breast, but forbore, and trembled, while shaking the water from her finger-tips. She felt as if her mother's spirit, somewhere within the dome, were looking down upon her child, the daughter of Puritan forefathers, and weeping to behold her ensnared by these gaudy superstitions. So she strayed sadly onward, up the nave, and towards the hundred golden lights that swarm before the high altar. Seeing a woman; a priest, and a soldier kneel to kiss the toe of the brazen St. Peter, who protrudes it beyond his pedestal for the purpose, polished bright with former salutations, while a child stood on tiptoe to do the same, the glory of the church was darkened before Hilda's eyes. But again she went onward into remoter regions. She turned into the right transept, and thence found her way to a shrine, in the extreme corner of the edifice, which is adorned with a mosaic copy of Guido's beautiful Archangel, treading on the prostrate fiend.

This was one of the few pictures, which, in these dreary days, had not faded nor deteriorated in Hilda's estimation; not that it was better than many in which she no longer took an interest; but the subtile delicacy of the painter's genius was peculiarly adapted to her character. She felt, while gazing at it, that the artist had done a great thing, not merely for the Church of Rome, but for the cause of Good. The moral of the picture, the immortal youth and loveliness of virtue, and its irresistibles might against ugly Evil, appealed as much to Puritans as Catholics.

Suddenly, and as if it were done in a dream, Hilda found herself kneeling before the shrine, under the ever-burning lamp that throws its rays upon the Archangel's face. She laid her forehead on the marble steps before the altar, and sobbed out a prayer; she hardly knew to whom, whether Michael, the Virgin, or the Father; she hardly knew for what, save only a vague longing, that thus the burden of her spirit might be lightened a little.

In an instant she snatched herself up, as it were, from her knees, all a-throb with the emotions which were struggling to force their way out of her heart by the avenue that had so nearly been opened for them. Yet there was a strange sense of relief won by that momentary, passionate prayer; a strange joy, moreover, whether from what she had done, or for what she had escaped doing, Hilda could not tell. But she felt as one half stifled, who has stolen a breath of air.

Next to the shrine where she had knelt there is another, adorned with a picture by Guercino, representing a maiden's body in the jaws of the sepulchre, and her lover weeping over it; while her beatified spirit looks down upon the scene, in the society of the Saviour and a throng of saints. Hilda wondered if it were not possible, by some miracle of faith, so to rise above her present despondency that she might look down upon what she was, just as Petronilla in the picture looked at her own corpse. A hope, born of hysteric trouble, fluttered in her heart. A presentiment, or what she fancied such, whispered her, that, before she had finished the circuit of the cathedral, relief would come.

The unhappy are continually tantalized by similar delusions of succor near at hand; at least, the despair is very dark that has no such will-o'-the-wisp to glimmer in it.

CHAPTER XXXIX. THE WORLD'S CATHEDRAL

Still gliding onward, Hilda now looked up into the dome, where the sunshine came through the western windows, and threw across long shafts of light. They rested upon the mosaic figures of two evangelists above the cornice. These great beams of radiance, traversing what seemed the empty space, were made visible in misty glory, by the holy cloud of incense, else unseen, which had risen into the middle dome. It was to Hilda as if she beheld the worship of the priest and people ascending heavenward, purified from its alloy of earth, and acquiring celestial substance in the golden atmosphere to which it aspired, She wondered if angels did not sometimes hover within the dome, and show themselves, in brief glimpses, floating amid the sunshine and the glorified vapor, to those who devoutly worshipped on the pavement.

She had now come into the southern transept. Around this portion of the church are ranged a number of confessionals. They are small tabernacles of carved wood, with a closet for the priest in the centre; and, on either side, a space for a penitent to kneel, and breathe his confession through a perforated auricle into the good father's ear. Observing this arrangement, though already familiar to her, our poor Hilda was anew impressed with the infinite convenience—if we may use so poor a phrase—of the Catholic religion to its devout believers.

Who, in truth, that considers the matter, can resist a similar impression! In the hottest fever-fit of life, they can always find, ready for their need, a cool, quiet, beautiful place of worship. They may enter its sacred precincts at any hour, leaving the fret and trouble of the world behind them, and purifying themselves with a touch of holy water at the threshold. In the calm interior, fragrant of rich and soothing incense, they may hold converse with some saint, their awful, kindly friend. And, most precious privilege of all, whatever perplexity, sorrow, guilt, may weigh upon their souls, they can fling down the dark burden at the foot of the cross, and go forth—to sin no more, nor be any longer disquieted; but to live again in the freshness and elasticity of innocence.

"Do not these inestimable advantages," thought Hilda, "or some of them at least, belong to Christianity itself? Are they not a part of the blessings which the system was meant to bestow upon mankind? Can the faith in which I was born and bred be perfect, if it leave a weak girl like me to wander, desolate, with this great trouble crushing me down?"

A poignant anguish thrilled within her breast; it was like a thing that had life, and was struggling to get out.

"O help! O help!" cried Hilda; "I cannot, cannot bear it!"

Only by the reverberations that followed—arch echoing the sound to arch, and a pope of bronze repeating it to a pope of marble, as each sat enthroned over his tomb—did Hilda become aware that she had really spoken above her breath. But, in that great space, there is no need to hush up the heart within one's own bosom, so carefully as elsewhere; and if the cry reached any distant auditor, it came broken into many fragments, and from various quarters of the church.

Approaching one of the confessionals, she saw a woman kneeling within. Just as Hilda drew near, the penitent rose, came forth, and kissed the hand of the priest, who regarded her with a look of paternal benignity, and appeared to be giving her some spiritual counsel, in a low voice. She then knelt to receive his blessing, which was fervently bestowed. Hilda was so struck with the peace and joy in the woman's face, that, as the latter retired, she could not help speaking to her.

"You look very happy!" said she. "Is it so sweet, then, to go to the confessional?"

"O, very sweet, my dear signorina!" answered the woman, with moistened eyes and an affectionate smile; for she was so thoroughly softened with what she had been doing, that she felt as if Hilda were her younger sister. "My heart is at rest now. Thanks be to the Saviour, and the Blessed Virgin and the saints, and this good father, there is no more trouble for poor Teresa!"

"I am glad for your sake," said Hilda, sighing for her own. "I am a poor heretic, but a human sister; and I rejoice for you!"

She went from one to another of the confessionals, and, looking at each, perceived that they were inscribed with gilt letters: on one, Pro Italica Lingua; on another, Pro Flandrica Lingua; on a third, Pro Polonica Lingua; on a fourth, Pro Illyrica Lingua; on a fifth, Pro Hispanica Lingua. In this vast and hospitable cathedral, worthy to be the religious heart of the whole world, there was room for all nations; there was access to the Divine Grace for every Christian soul; there was an ear for what the overburdened heart might have to murmur, speak in what native tongue it would.

When Hilda had almost completed the circuit of the transept, she came to a confessional—the central part was closed, but a mystic room protruded from it, indicating the presence of a priest within—on which was inscribed, Pro Anglica Lingua.

It was the word in season! If she had heard her mother's voice from within the tabernacle, calling her, in her own mother-tongue, to come and lay her poor head in her lap, and sob out all her troubles, Hilda could not have responded with a more inevitable obedience. She did not think; she only felt. Within her heart was a great need. Close at hand, within the veil of the confessional, was the relief. She flung herself down in the penitent's place; and, tremulously, passionately, with sobs, tears, and the turbulent overflow of emotion too long repressed, she poured out the dark story which had infused its poison into her innocent life.

Hilda had not seen, nor could she now see, the visage of the priest. But, at intervals, in the pauses of that strange confession, half choked by the struggle of her feelings toward an outlet, she heard a mild, calm voice, somewhat mellowed by age. It spoke soothingly; it encouraged her; it led her on by apposite questions that seemed to be suggested by a great and tender interest, and acted like magnetism in attracting the girl's confidence to this unseen friend. The priest's share in the interview, indeed, resembled that of one who removes the stones, clustered branches, or whatever entanglements impede the current of a swollen stream. Hilda could have imagined—so much to the purpose were his inquiries—that he was already acquainted with some outline of what she strove to tell him.

129

Thus assisted, she revealed the whole of her terrible secret! The whole, except that no name escaped her lips.

And, ah, what a relief! When the hysteric gasp, the strife between words and sobs, had subsided, what a torture had passed away from her soul! It was all gone; her bosom was as pure now as in her childhood. She was a girl again; she was Hilda of the dove-cote; not that doubtful creature whom her own doves had hardly recognized as their mistress and playmate, by reason of the death-scent that clung to her garments!

After she had ceased to speak, Hilda heard the priest bestir himself with an old man's reluctant movement. He stepped out of the confessional; and as the girl was still kneeling in the penitential corner, he summoned her forth.

"Stand up, my daughter," said the mild voice of the confessor; "what we have further to say must be spoken face to face."

Hilda did his bidding, and stood before him with a downcast visage, which flushed and grew pale again. But it had the wonderful beauty which we may often observe in those who have recently gone through a great struggle, and won the peace that lies just on the other side. We see it in a new mother's face; we see it in the faces of the dead; and in Hilda's countenance—which had always a rare natural charm for her friends—this glory of peace made her as lovely as an angel.

On her part, Hilda beheld a venerable figure with hair as white as snow, and a face strikingly characterized by benevolence. It bore marks of thought, however, and penetrative insight; although the keen glances of the eyes were now somewhat bedimmed with tears, which the aged shed, or almost shed, on lighter stress of emotion than would elicit them from younger men.

"It has not escaped my observation, daughter," said the priest, "that this is your first acquaintance with the confessional. How is this?"

"Father," replied Hilda, raising her eyes, and again letting them fall, "I am of New Eng land birth, and was bred as what you call a heretic."

130

"From New England!" exclaimed the priest. "It was my own birthplace, likewise; nor have fifty years of absence made me cease to love it. But a heretic! And are you reconciled to the Church?"

"Never, father," said Hilda.

"And, that being the case," demanded the old man, "on what ground, my daughter, have you sought to avail yourself of these blessed privileges, confined exclusively to members of the one true Church, of confession and absolution?"

"Absolution, father?" exclaimed Hilda, shrinking back. "O no, no! I never dreamed of that! Only our Heavenly Father can forgive my sins; and it is only by sincere repentance of whatever wrong I may have done, and by my own best efforts towards a higher life, that I can hope for his forgiveness! God forbid that I should ask absolution from mortal man!"

"Then wherefore," rejoined the priest, with somewhat less mildness in his tone,—"wherefore, I ask again, have you taken possession, as I may term it, of this holy ordinance; being a heretic, and neither seeking to share, nor having faith in, the unspeakable advantages which the Church offers to its penitents?"

"Father," answered Hilda, trying to tell the old man the simple truth, "I am a motherless girl, and a stranger here in Italy. I had only God to take care of me, and be my closest friend; and the terrible, terrible crime, which I have revealed to you, thrust itself between him and me; so that I groped for him in the darkness, as it were, and found him not,—found nothing but a dreadful solitude, and this crime in the midst of it! I could not bear it. It seemed as if I made the awful guilt my own, by keeping it hidden in my heart. I grew a fearful thing to myself. I was going mad!"

"It was a grievous trial, my poor child!" observed the confessor. "Your relief, I trust, will prove to be greater than you yet know!"

"I feel already how immense it is!" said Hilda, looking gratefully in his face. "Surely, father, it was the hand of Providence that led me hither, and made me feel that this vast temple of Christianity, this great home of religion, must needs contain some cure, some ease, at least, for my unutterable anguish. And it has proved so. I have told the hideous secret; told it under the sacred seal of the confessional; and now it will burn my poor heart no more!"

"But, daughter," answered the venerable priest, not unmoved by what Hilda said, "you forget! you mistake!—you claim a privilege to which you have not entitled yourself! The seal of the confessional, do you say? God forbid that it should ever be broken where it has been fairly impressed; but it applies only to matters that have been confided to its keeping in a certain prescribed method, and by persons, moreover, who have faith in the sanctity of the ordinance. I hold myself, and any learned casuist of the Church would hold me, as free to disclose all the particulars of what you term your confession, as if they had come to my knowledge in a secular way."

"This is not right, father!" said Hilda, fixing her eyes on the old man's.

"Do not you see, child," he rejoined, with some little heat, "with all your nicety of conscience, cannot you recognize it as my duty to make the story known to the proper authorities; a great crime against public justice being involved, and further evil consequences likely to ensue?"

"No, father, no!" answered Hilda, courageously, her cheeks flushing and her eyes brightening as she spoke. "Trust a girl's simple heart sooner than any casuist of your Church, however learned he may be. Trust your own heart, too! I came to your confessional, father, as I devoutly believe, by the direct impulse of Heaven, which also brought you hither to-day, in its mercy and love, to relieve me of a torture that I could no longer bear. I trusted in the pledge which your Church has always held sacred between the priest and the human soul, which, through his medium, is struggling towards its Father above. What I have confided to you lies sacredly between God and yourself. Let it rest there, father; for this is right, and if you do otherwise, you will perpetrate a great wrong, both as a priest and a man! And believe me, no question, no torture, shall ever force my lips to utter what would be necessary, in order to make my confession available towards the punishment of the guilty ones. Leave Providence to deal with them!"

"My quiet little countrywoman," said the priest, with half a smile on his kindly old face, "you can pluck up a spirit, I perceive, when you fancy an occasion for one."

132

"I have spirit only to do what I think right," replied Hilda simply. "In other respects I am timorous."

"But you confuse yourself between right feelings and very foolish inferences," continued the priest, "as is the wont of women,—so much I have learnt by long experience in the confessional,—be they young or old. However, to set your heart at rest, there is no probable need for me to reveal the matter. What you have told, if I mistake not, and perhaps more, is already known in the quarter which it most concerns."

"Known!" exclaimed Hilda. "Known to the authorities of Rome! And what will be the consequence?"

"Hush!" answered the confessor, laying his finger on his lips. "I tell you my supposition—mind, it is no assertion of the fact—in order that you may go the more cheerfully on your way, not deeming yourself burdened with any responsibility as concerns this dark deed. And now, daughter, what have you to give in return for an old man's kindness and sympathy?"

"My grateful remembrance," said Hilda, fervently, "as long as I live!"

"And nothing more?" the priest inquired, with a persuasive smile. "Will you not reward him with a great joy; one of the last joys that he may know on earth, and a fit one to take with him into the better world? In a word, will you not allow me to bring you as a stray lamb into the true fold? You have experienced some little taste of the relief and comfort which the Church keeps abundantly in store for all its faithful children. Come home, dear child,—poor wanderer, who hast caught a glimpse of the heavenly light,— come home, and be at rest."

"Father," said Hilda, much moved by his kindly earnestness, in which, however, genuine as it was, there might still be a leaven of professional craft, "I dare not come a step farther than Providence shall guide me. Do not let it grieve you, therefore, if I never return to the confessional; never dip my fingers in holy water; never sign my bosom with the cross. I am a daughter of the Puritans. But, in spite of my heresy," she added with a sweet, tearful smile, "you may one day see the poor girl, to whom you have done this great

133

Christian kindness, coming to remind you of it, and thank you for it, in the Better Land."

The old priest shook his head. But, as he stretched out his hands at the same moment, in the act of benediction, Hilda knelt down and received the blessing with as devout a simplicity as any Catholic of them all.

CHAPTER XL. HILDA AND A FRIEND

When Hilda knelt to receive the priest's benediction, the act was witnessed by a person who stood leaning against the marble balustrade that surrounds the hundred golden lights, before the high altar. He had stood there, indeed, from the moment of the girl's entrance into the confessional. His start of surprise, at first beholding her, and the anxious gloom that afterwards settled on his face, sufficiently betokened that he felt a deep and sad interest in what was going forward.

After Hilda had bidden the priest farewell, she came slowly towards the high altar. The individual to whom we have alluded seemed irresolute whether to advance or retire. His hesitation lasted so long that the maiden, straying through a happy reverie, had crossed the wide extent of the pavement between the confessional and the altar, before he had decided whether to meet her. At last, when within a pace or two, she raised her eyes and recognized Kenyon.

"It is you!" she exclaimed, with joyful surprise. "I am so happy."

In truth, the sculptor had never before seen, nor hardly imagined, such a figure of peaceful beatitude as Hilda now presented. While coming towards him in the solemn radiance which, at that period of the day, is diffused through the transept, and showered down beneath the dome, she seemed of the same substance as the atmosphere that enveloped her. He could scarcely tell whether she was imbued with sunshine, or whether it was a glow of happiness that shone out of her.

At all events, it was a marvellous change from the sad girl, who had entered the confessional bewildered with anguish, to this bright, yet softened image of religious consolation that emerged from it. It was as if one of the throng of angelic people, who might be hovering in the sunny depths of the dome, had alighted on the pavement. Indeed, this capability of transfiguration, which we often see wrought by inward delight on persons far less capable of it than Hilda, suggests how angels come by their beauty, it grows out of their happiness, and lasts forever only because that is immortal.

She held out her hand, and Kenyon was glad to take it in his own, if only to assure himself that she was made of earthly material.

"Yes, Hilda, I see that you are very happy," he replied gloomily, and withdrawing his hand after a single pressure. "For me, I never was less so than at this moment."

"Has any misfortune befallen you?" asked Hilda with earnestness. "Pray tell me, and you shall have my sympathy, though I must still be very happy. Now I know how it is that the saints above are touched by the sorrows of distressed people on earth, and yet are never made wretched by them. Not that I profess to be a saint, you know," she added, smiling radiantly. "But the heart grows so large, and so rich, and so variously endowed, when it has a great sense of bliss, that it can give smiles to some, and tears to others, with equal sincerity, and enjoy its own peace throughout all."

"Do not say you are no saint!" answered Kenyon with a smile, though he felt that the tears stood in his eyes. "You will still be Saint Hilda, whatever church may canonize you."

"Ah! you would not have said so, had you seen me but an hour ago!" murmured she. "I was so wretched, that there seemed a grievous sin in it."

"And what has made you so suddenly happy?" inquired the sculptor. "But first, Hilda, will you not tell me why you were so wretched?"

"Had I met you yesterday, I might have told you that," she replied. "To-day, there is no need."

"Your happiness, then?" said the sculptor, as sadly as before. "Whence comes it?"

"A great burden has been lifted from my heart—from my conscience, I had almost said,"—answered Hilda, without shunning the glance that he fixed upon her. "I am a new creature, since this morning, Heaven be praised for it! It was a blessed hour—a blessed impulse—that brought me to this beautiful and glorious cathedral. I shall hold it in loving remembrance while I live, as the spot where I found infinite peace after infinite trouble."

Her heart seemed so full, that it spilt its new gush of happiness, as it were, like rich and sunny wine out of an over-brimming goblet. Kenyon saw that she was in one of those moods of elevated feeling, when the soul is upheld by a strange tranquility, which is really more passionate and less controllable than emotions far exceeding it in violence. He felt that there would be indelicacy, if he ought not rather to call it impiety, in his stealing upon Hilda, while she was thus beyond her own guardianship, and surprising her out of secrets which she might afterwards bitterly regret betraying to him. Therefore, though yearning to know what had happened, he resolved to forbear further question.

Simple and earnest people, however, being accustomed to speak from their genuine impulses, cannot easily, as craftier men do, avoid the subject which they have at heart. As often as the sculptor unclosed his lips, such words as these were ready to burst out:—"Hilda, have you flung your angelic purity into that mass of unspeakable corruption, the Roman Church?"

"What were you saying?" she asked, as Kenyon forced back an almost uttered exclamation of this kind.

"I was thinking of what you have just remarked about the cathedral," said he, looking up into the mighty hollow of the dome. "It is indeed a magnificent structure, and an adequate expression of the Faith which built it. When I behold it in a proper mood,—that is to say, when I bring my mind into a fair relation with the minds and purposes of its spiritual and material architects,—I see but one or two criticisms to make. One is, that it needs painted windows."

"O, no!" said Hilda. "They would be quite inconsistent with so much richness of color in the interior of the church. Besides, it is a Gothic ornament, and only suited to that style of architecture, which requires a gorgeous dimness."

"Nevertheless," continued the sculptor, "yonder square apertures, filled with ordinary panes of glass, are quite out of keeping with the superabundant splendor of everything about them. They remind me of that portion of Aladdin's palace which he left unfinished, in order that his royal father-in-law might put the finishing touch. Daylight, in its natural state, ought not to be admitted here. It should stream through a brilliant illusion of saints and hierarchies, and old scriptural images, and symbolized dogmas, purple, blue, golden, and a broad flame of scarlet. Then, it would be just such an illumination as the Catholic faith allows to its believers. But, give me—to live and die in—the pure, white light of heaven!"

"Why do you look so sorrowfully at me?" asked Hilda, quietly meeting his disturbed gaze. "What would you say to me? I love the white light too!"

"I fancied so," answered Kenyon. "Forgive me, Hilda; but I must needs speak. You seemed to me a rare mixture of impressibility, sympathy, sensitiveness to many influences, with a certain quality of common sense;—no, not that, but a higher and finer attribute, for which I find no better word. However tremulously you might vibrate, this quality, I supposed, would always bring you back to the equipoise. You were a creature of imagination, and yet as truly a New England girl as any with whom you grew up in your native village. If there were one person in the world whose native rectitude of thought, and something deeper, more reliable, than thought, I would have trusted against all the arts of a priesthood,—whose taste alone, so exquisite and sincere that it rose to be a moral virtue, I would have rested upon as a sufficient safeguard,—it was yourself!"

"I am conscious of no such high and delicate qualities as you allow me," answered Hilda. "But what have I done that a girl of New England birth and culture, with the right sense that her mother taught her, and the conscience that she developed in her, should not do?"

"Hilda, I saw you at the confessional!" said Kenyon.

"Ah well, my dear friend," replied Hilda, casting down her eyes, and looking somewhat confused, yet not ashamed, "you must try to forgive me for that,—if you deem it wrong, because it has saved my reason, and made me very happy. Had you been here yesterday, I would have confessed to you."

"Would to Heaven I had!" ejaculated Kenyon.

"I think," Hilda resumed, "I shall never go to the confessional again; for there can scarcely come such a sore trial twice in my life. If I had been a wiser girl, a stronger, and a more sensible, very likely I might not have gone to the confessional at all. It was the sin of others that drove me thither; not my own, though it almost seemed so. Being what I am, I must either have done what you saw me doing, or have gone mad. Would that have been better?"

"Then you are not a Catholic?" asked the sculptor earnestly.

"Really, I do not quite know what I am," replied Hilda, encountering his eyes with a frank and simple gaze. "I have a great deal of faith, and Catholicism seems to have a great deal of good. Why should not I be a Catholic, if I find there what I need, and what I cannot find elsewhere? The more I see of this worship, the more I wonder at the exuberance with which it adapts itself to all the demands of human infirmity. If its ministers were but a little more than human, above all error, pure from all iniquity, what a religion would it be!"

"I need not fear your conversion to the Catholic faith," remarked Kenyon, "if you are at all aware of the bitter sarcasm implied in your last observation. It is very just. Only the exceeding ingenuity of the system stamps it as the contrivance of man, or some worse author; not an emanation of the broad and simple wisdom from on high."

"It may be so," said Hilda; "but I meant no sarcasm."

Thus conversing, the two friends went together down the grand extent of the nave. Before leaving the church, they turned to admire again its mighty breadth, the remoteness of the glory behind the altar, and the effect of visionary splendor and magnificence imparted by the long bars of smoky sunshine, which travelled so far before arriving at a place of rest.

"Thank Heaven for having brought me hither!" said Hilda fervently.

Kenyon's mind was deeply disturbed by his idea of her Catholic propensities; and now what he deemed her disproportionate and misapplied veneration for the sublime edifice stung him into irreverence.

"The best thing I know of St. Peter's," observed he, "is its equable temperature. We are now enjoying the coolness of last winter, which, a few months hence, will be the warmth of the present summer. It has no cure, I suspect, in all its length and breadth, for a sick soul, but it would make an admirable atmospheric hospital for sick bodies. What a delightful shelter would it be for the invalids who throng to Rome, where the sirocco steals away their strength, and the tramontana stabs them through and through, like cold steel with a poisoned point! But within these walls, the thermometer never varies. Winter and summer are married at the high altar, and dwell together in perfect harmony."

"Yes," said Hilda; "and I have always felt this soft, unchanging climate of St. Peter's to be another manifestation of its sanctity."

"That is not precisely my idea," replied Kenyon. "But what a delicious life it would be, if a colony of people with delicate lungs or merely with delicate fancies—could take up their abode in this ever-mild and tranquil air. These architectural tombs of the popes might serve for dwellings, and each brazen sepulchral doorway would become a domestic threshold. Then the lover, if he dared, might say to his mistress, 'Will you share my tomb with me?' and, winning her soft consent, he would lead her to the altar, and thence to yonder sepulchre of Pope Gregory, which should be their nuptial home. What a life would be theirs, Hilda, in their marble Eden!"

"It is not kind, nor like yourself," said Hilda gently, "to throw ridicule on emotions which are genuine. I revere this glorious church for itself and its purposes; and love it, moreover, because here I have found sweet peace, after' a great anguish."

"Forgive me," answered the sculptor, "and I will do so no more. My heart is not so irreverent as my words."

They went through the piazza of St. Peter's and the adjacent streets, silently at first; but, before reaching the bridge of St. Angelo, Hilda's flow of spirits began to bubble forth, like the gush of a streamlet that has been shut up by frost, or by a heavy stone over its source. Kenyon had never found her so delightful as now; so softened out of the chillness of her virgin pride; so full of fresh thoughts, at which he was often moved to smile, although, on turning them over a little more, he sometimes discovered that they looked fanciful only because so absolutely true.

But, indeed, she was not quite in a normal state. Emerging from gloom into sudden cheerfulness, the effect upon Hilda was as if she were just now created. After long torpor, receiving back her intellectual activity, she derived an exquisite pleasure from the use of her faculties, which were set in motion by causes that seemed inadequate. She continually brought to Kenyon's mind the image of a child, making its plaything of every object, but sporting in good faith, and with a kind of seriousness. Looking up, for example, at the statue of St. Michael, on the top of Hadrian's castellated tomb, Hilda fancied an interview between the Archangel and the old emperor's ghost, who was naturally displeased at finding his mausoleum, which he had ordained for the stately and solemn repose of his ashes, converted to its present purposes.

"But St. Michael, no doubt," she thoughtfully remarked, "would finally convince the Emperor Hadrian that where a warlike despot is sown as the seed, a fortress and a prison are the only possible crop."

They stopped on the bridge to look into the swift eddying flow of the yellow Tiber, a mud puddle in strenuous motion; and Hilda wondered whether the seven-branched golden candlestick,—the holy candlestick of the Jews, which was lost at the Ponte Molle, in Constantine's time, had yet been swept as far down the river as this.

"It probably stuck where it fell," said the sculptor; "and, by this time, is imbedded thirty feet deep in the mud of the Tiber. Nothing will ever bring it to light again."

"I fancy you are mistaken," replied Hilda, smiling. "There was a meaning and purpose in each of its seven branches, and such a candlestick cannot be lost forever. When it is found again, and seven lights are kindled and burning in it, the whole world will gain the illumination which it needs. Would not this be an admirable idea for a mystic story or parable, or seven-branched allegory, full of poetry, art, philosophy, and religion? It shall be called 'The Recovery of the Sacred Candlestick.' As each branch is lighted, it shall have a differently colored lustre from the other six; and when all the seven are kindled, their radiance shall combine into the intense white light of truth."

141

"Positively, Hilda, this is a magnificent conception," cried Kenyon. "The more I look at it, the brighter it burns."

"I think so too," said Hilda, enjoying a childlike pleasure in her own idea. "The theme is better suited for verse than prose; and when I go home to America, I will suggest it to one of our poets. Or seven poets might write the poem together, each lighting a separate branch of the Sacred Candlestick."

"Then you think of going home?" Kenyon asked.

"Only yesterday," she replied, "I longed to flee away. Now, all is changed, and, being happy again, I should feel deep regret at leaving the Pictorial Land. But I cannot tell. In Rome, there is something dreary and awful, which we can never quite escape. At least, I thought so yesterday."

When they reached the Via Portoghese, and approached Hilda's tower, the doves, who were waiting aloft, flung themselves upon the air, and came floating down about her head. The girl caressed them, and responded to their cooings with similar sounds from her own lips, and with words of endearment; and their joyful flutterings and airy little flights, evidently impelled by pure exuberance of spirits, seemed to show that the doves had a real sympathy with their mistress's state of mind. For peace had descended upon her like a dove.

Bidding the sculptor farewell, Hilda climbed her tower, and came forth upon its summit to trim the Virgin's lamp. The doves, well knowing her custom, had flown up thither to meet her, and again hovered about her head; and very lovely was her aspect, in the evening Sunlight, which had little further to do with the world just then, save to fling a golden glory on Hilda's hair, and vanish.

Turning her eyes down into the dusky street which she had just quitted, Hilda saw the sculptor still there, and waved her hand to him.

"How sad and dim he looks, down there in that dreary street!" she said to herself. "Something weighs upon his spirits. Would I could comfort him!"

"How like a spirit she looks, aloft there, with the evening glory round her head, and those winged creatures claiming her as akin to them!" thought

Kenyon, on his part. "How far above me! how unattainable! Ah, if I could lift myself to her region! Or—if it be not a sin to wish it—would that I might draw her down to an earthly fireside!"

What a sweet reverence is that, when a young man deems his mistress a little more than mortal, and almost chides himself for longing to bring her close to his heart! A trifling circumstance, but such as lovers make much of, gave him hope. One of the doves, which had been resting on Hilda's shoulder, suddenly flew downward, as if recognizing him as its mistress's dear friend; and, perhaps commissioned with an errand of regard, brushed his upturned face with its wings, and again soared aloft.

The sculptor watched the bird's return, and saw Hilda greet it with a smile.

CHAPTER XLI. SNOWDROPS AND MAIDENLY DELIGHTS

It being still considerably earlier than the period at which artists and tourists are accustomed to assemble in Rome, the sculptor and Hilda found themselves comparatively alone there. The dense mass of native Roman life, in the midst of which they were, served to press them near one another. It was as if they had been thrown together on a desert island. Or they seemed to have wandered, by some strange chance, out of the common world, and encountered each other in a depopulated city, where there were streets of lonely palaces, and unreckonable treasures of beautiful and admirable things, of which they two became the sole inheritors.

In such circumstances, Hilda's gentle reserve must have been stronger than her kindly disposition permitted, if the friendship between Kenyon and herself had not grown as warm as a maiden's friendship can ever be, without absolutely and avowedly blooming into love. On the sculptor's side, the amaranthine flower was already in full blow. But it is very beautiful, though the lover's heart may grow chill at the perception, to see how the snow will sometimes linger in a virgin's breast, even after the spring is well advanced. In such alpine soils, the summer will not be anticipated; we seek vainly for passionate flowers, and blossoms of fervid hue and spicy fragrance, finding only snowdrops and sunless violets, when it is almost the full season for the crimson rose.

With so much tenderness as Hilda had in her nature, it was strange that she so reluctantly admitted the idea of love; especially as, in the sculptor, she found both congeniality and variety of taste, and likenesses and differences of character; these being as essential as those to any poignancy of mutual emotion.

So Hilda, as far as Kenyon could discern, still did not love him, though she admitted him within the quiet circle of her affections as a dear friend and trusty counsellor. If we knew what is best for us, or could be content with what is reasonably good, the sculptor might well have been satisfied, for a season, with this calm intimacy, which so sweetly kept him a stranger in her heart, and a ceremonious guest; and yet allowed him the free enjoyment of all but its deeper recesses. The flowers that grow outside of those minor sanctities have a wild, hasty charm, which it is well to prove; there may be sweeter ones within the sacred precinct, but none that will die while you are handling them, and bequeath you a delicious legacy, as these do, in the perception of their evanescence and unreality.

And this may be the reason, after all, why Hilda, like so many other maidens, lingered on the hither side of passion; her finer instinct and keener sensibility made her enjoy those pale delights in a degree of which men are incapable. She hesitated to grasp a richer happiness, as possessing already such measure of it as her heart could hold, and of a quality most agreeable to her virgin tastes.

Certainly, they both were very happy. Kenyon's genius, unconsciously wrought upon by Hilda's influence, took a more delicate character than heretofore. He modelled, among other things, a beautiful little statue of maidenhood gathering a snowdrop. It was never put into marble, however, because the sculptor soon recognized it as one of those fragile creations which are true only to the moment that produces them, and are wronged if we try to imprison their airy excellence in a permanent material.

On her part, Hilda returned to her customary Occupations with a fresh love for them, and yet with a deeper look into the heart of things; such as those necessarily acquire who have passed from picture galleries into dungeon gloom, and thence come back to the picture gallery again. It is questionable whether she was ever so perfect a copyist thenceforth. She could not yield herself up to the painter so unreservedly as in times past; her character had developed a sturdier quality, which made her less pliable to the influence of other minds. She saw into the picture as profoundly as ever, and perhaps more so, but not with the devout sympathy that had formerly given her entire possession of the old master's idea. She had known such a reality, that it taught her to distinguish inevitably the large portion that is unreal, in every work of art. Instructed by sorrow, she felt that there is something beyond almost all which pictorial genius has produced; and she never forgot those sad wanderings from gallery to gallery, and from church to church, where she had vainly sought a type of the Virgin Mother, or the Saviour, or saint, or martyr, which a soul in extreme need might recognize as the adequate one.

How, indeed, should she have found such? How could holiness be revealed to the artist of an age when the greatest of them put genius and imagination in the place of spiritual insight, and when, from the pope downward, all Christendom was corrupt?

Meanwhile, months wore away, and Rome received back that large portion of its life-blood which runs in the veins of its foreign and temporary population. English visitors established themselves in the hotels, and in all the sunny suites of apartments, in the streets convenient to the Piazza di Spagna; the English tongue was heard familiarly along the Corso, and English children sported in the Pincian Gardens.

The native Romans, on the other hand, like the butterflies and grasshoppers, resigned themselves to the short, sharp misery which winter brings to a people whose arrangements are made almost exclusively with a view to summer. Keeping no fire within-doors, except possibly a spark or two in the kitchen, they crept out of their cheerless houses into the narrow, sunless, sepulchral streets, bringing their firesides along with them, in the shape of little earthen pots, vases, or pipkins, full of lighted charcoal and warm ashes, over which they held their tingling finger-ends. Even in this half-torpid wretchedness, they still seemed to dread a pestilence in the sunshine, and kept on the shady side of the piazzas, as scrupulously as in summer. Through the open doorways w no need to shut them when the weather within was bleaker than without—a glimpse into the interior of their dwellings showed the uncarpeted brick floors, as dismal as the pavement of a tomb.

They drew their old cloaks about them, nevertheless, and threw the corners over their shoulders, with the dignity of attitude and action that have come down to these modern citizens, as their sole inheritance from the togated nation. Somehow or other, they managed to keep up their poor, frost-bitten hearts against the pitiless atmosphere with a quiet and uncomplaining endurance that really seems the most respectable point in the present Roman character. For in New England, or in Russia, or scarcely in a hut of the Esquimaux, there is no such discomfort to be borne as by Romans in wintry weather, when the orange-trees bear icy fruit in the gardens; and when the rims of all the fountains are shaggy with icicles, and the Fountain of Trevi skimmed almost across with a glassy surface; and when there is a slide in the piazza of St. Peter's, and a fringe of brown, frozen foam along the eastern shore of the Tiber, and sometimes a fall of great snowflakes into the dreary lanes and alleys of the miserable city. Cold blasts, that bring death with them, now blow upon the shivering invalids, who came hither in the hope of breathing balmy airs.

Wherever we pass our summers, may all our inclement months, from November to April, henceforth be spent in some country that recognizes winter as an integral portion of its year!

Now, too, there was especial discomfort in the stately picture galleries, where nobody, indeed,—not the princely or priestly founders, nor any who have inherited their cheerless magnificence,—ever dreamed of such an impossibility as fireside warmth, since those great palaces were built. Hilda, therefore, finding her fingers so much benumbed that the spiritual influence could not be transmitted to them, was persuaded to leave her easel before a picture, on one of these wintry days, and pay a visit to Kenyon's studio. But neither was the studio anything better than a dismal den, with its marble shapes shivering around the walls, cold as the snow images which the sculptor used to model in his boyhood, and sadly behold them weep themselves away at the first thaw.

Kenyon's Roman artisans, all this while, had been at work on the Cleopatra. The fierce Egyptian queen had now struggled almost out of the imprisoning stone; or, rather, the workmen had found her within the mass of marble, imprisoned there by magic, but still fervid to the touch with fiery life, the fossil woman of an age that produced statelier, stronger, and more passionate creatures than our own. You already felt her compressed heat, and were aware of a tiger-like character even in her repose. If Octavius should make his appearance, though the marble still held her within its embrace, it was evident that she would tear herself forth in a twinkling, either to spring enraged at his throat, or, sinking into his arms, to make one more proof of her rich blandishments, or, falling lowly at his feet, to try the efficacy of a woman's tears.

"I am ashamed to tell you how much I admire this statue," said Hilda. "No other sculptor could have done it."

"This is very sweet for me to hear," replied Kenyon; "and since your reserve keeps you from saying more, I shall imagine you expressing everything that an artist would wish to hear said about his work."

"You will not easily go beyond my genuine opinion," answered Hilda, with a smile.

"Ah, your kind word makes me very happy," said the sculptor, "and I need it, just now, on behalf of my Cleopatra. That inevitable period has come,—for I have found it inevitable, in regard to all my works,—when I look at what I fancied to be a statue, lacking only breath to make it live, and find it a mere lump of senseless stone, into which I have not really succeeded in moulding the spiritual part of my idea. I should like, now,—only it would be such shameful treatment for a discrowned queen, and my own offspring too,—I should like to hit poor Cleopatra a bitter blow on her Egyptian nose with this mallet."

"That is a blow which all statues seem doomed to receive, sooner or later, though seldom from the hand that sculptured them," said Hilda, laughing. "But you must not let yourself be too much disheartened by the decay of your faith in what you produce. I have heard a poet express similar distaste for his own most exquisite poem, and I am afraid that this final despair, and sense of short-coming, must always be the reward and punishment of those who try to grapple with a great or beautiful idea. It only proves that you have been able to imagine things too high for mortal faculties to execute. The idea leaves you an imperfect image of itself, which you at first mistake for the ethereal reality, but soon find that the latter has escaped out of your closest embrace."

"And the only consolation is," remarked Kenyon, "that the blurred and imperfect image may still make a very respectable appearance in the eyes of those who have not seen the original."

"More than that," rejoined Hilda; "for there is a class of spectators whose sympathy will help them to see the perfect through a mist of imperfection. Nobody, I think, ought to read poetry, or look at pictures or statues, who cannot find a great deal more in them than the poet or artist has actually expressed. Their highest merit is suggestiveness."

"You, Hilda, are yourself the only critic in whom I have much faith," said Kenyon. "Had you condemned Cleopatra, nothing should have saved her."

"You invest me with such an awful responsibility," she replied, "that I shall not dare to say a single word about your other works."

"At least," said the sculptor, "tell me whether you recognize this bust?"

He pointed to a bust of Donatello. It was not the one which Kenyon had begun to model at Monte Beni, but a reminiscence of the Count's face, wrought under the influence of all the sculptor's knowledge of his history, and of his personal and hereditary character. It stood on a wooden pedestal, not nearly finished, but with fine white dust and small chips of marble scattered about it, and itself incrusted all round with the white, shapeless substance of the block. In the midst appeared the features, lacking sharpness, and very much resembling a fossil countenance,—but we have already used this simile, in reference to Cleopatra, with the accumulations of long-past ages clinging to it.

And yet, strange to say, the face had an expression, and a more recognizable one than Kenyon had succeeded in putting into the clay model at Monte Beni. The reader is probably acquainted with Thorwaldsen's three-fold analogy,—the clay model, the Life; the plaster cast, the Death; and the sculptured marble, the Resurrection,—and it seemed to be made good by the spirit that was kindling up these imperfect features, like a lambent flame.

"I was not quite sure, at first glance, that I knew the face," observed Hilda; "the likeness surely is not a striking one. There is a good deal of external resemblance, still, to the features of the Faun of Praxiteles, between whom and Donatello, you know, we once insisted that there was a perfect twin-brotherhood. But the expression is now so very different!"

"What do you take it to be?" asked the sculptor.

"I hardly know how to define it," she answered. "But it has an effect as if I could see this countenance gradually brightening while I look at it. It gives the impression of a growing intellectual power and moral sense. Donatello's face used to evince little more than a genial, pleasurable sort of vivacity, and capability of enjoyment. But here, a soul is being breathed into him; it is the Faun, but advancing towards a state of higher development."

"Hilda, do you see all this?" exclaimed Kenyon, in considerable surprise. "I may have had such an idea in my mind, but was quite unaware that I had succeeded in conveying it into the marble."

"Forgive me," said Hilda, "but I question whether this striking effect has been brought about by any skill or purpose on the sculptor's part. Is it not, perhaps, the chance result of the bust being just so far shaped out, in the marble, as the process of moral growth had advanced in the original? A few more strokes of the chisel might change the whole expression, and so spoil it for what it is now worth."

"I believe you are right," answered Kenyon, thoughtfully examining his work; "and, strangely enough, it was the very expression that I tried unsuccessfully to produce in the clay model. Well; not another chip shall be struck from the marble."

And, accordingly, Donatello's bust (like that rude, rough mass of the head of Brutus, by Michael Angelo, at Florence) has ever since remained in an unfinished state. Most spectators mistake it for an unsuccessful attempt towards copying the features of the Faun of Praxiteles. One observer in a thousand is conscious of something more, and lingers long over this mysterious face, departing from it reluctantly, and with many a glance thrown backward. What perplexes him is the riddle that he sees propounded there; the riddle of the soul's growth, taking its first impulse amid remorse and pain, and struggling through the incrustations of the senses. It was the contemplation of this imperfect portrait of Donatello that originally interested us in his history, and impelled us to elicit from Kenyon what he knew of his friend's adventures.

CHAPTER XLII. REMINISCENCES OF MIRIAM

When Hilda and himself turned away from the unfinished bust, the sculptor's mind still dwelt upon the reminiscences which it suggested. "You have not seen Donatello recently," he remarked, "and therefore cannot be aware how sadly he is changed."

"No wonder!" exclaimed Hilda, growing pale.

The terrible scene which she had witnessed, when Donatello's face gleamed out in so fierce a light, came back upon her memory, almost for the first time since she knelt at the confessional. Hilda, as is sometimes the case with persons whose delicate organization requires a peculiar safeguard, had an elastic faculty of throwing off such recollections as would be too painful for endurance. The first shock of Donatello's and Miriam's crime had, indeed, broken through the frail defence of this voluntary forgetfulness; but, once enabled to relieve herself of the ponderous anguish over which she had so long brooded, she had practised a subtle watchfulness in preventing its return.

"No wonder, do you say?" repeated the sculptor, looking at her with interest, but not exactly with surprise; for he had long suspected that Hilda had a painful knowledge of events which he himself little more than surmised. "Then you know!—you have heard! But what can you possibly have heard, and through what channel?"

"Nothing!" replied Hilda faintly. "Not one word has reached my ears from the lips of any human being. Let us never speak of it again! No, no! never again!"

"And Miriam!" said Kenyon, with irrepressible interest. "Is it also forbidden to speak of her?"

"Hush! do not even utter her name! Try not to think of it!" Hilda whispered. "It may bring terrible consequences!"

"My dear Hilda!" exclaimed Kenyon, regarding her with wonder and deep sympathy. "My sweet friend, have you had this secret hidden in your

The Marble Faun Vol. 2

delicate, maidenly heart, through all these many months! No wonder that your life was withering out of you."

"It was so, indeed!" said Hilda, shuddering. "Even now, I sicken at the recollection."

"And how could it have come to your knowledge?" continued the sculptor. "But no matter! Do not torture yourself with referring to the subject. Only, if at any time it should be a relief to you, remember that we can speak freely together, for Miriam has herself suggested a confidence between us."

"Miriam has suggested this!" exclaimed Hilda. "Yes, I remember, now, her advising that the secret should be shared with you. But I have survived the death struggle that it cost me, and need make no further revelations. And Miriam has spoken to you! What manner of woman can she be, who, after sharing in such a deed, can make it a topic of conversation with her friends?"

"Ah, Hilda," replied Kenyon, "you do not know, for you could never learn it from your own heart, which is all purity and rectitude, what a mixture of good there may be in things evil; and how the greatest criminal, if you look at his conduct from his own point of view, or from any side point, may seem not so unquestionably guilty, after all. So with Miriam; so with Donatello. They are, perhaps, partners in what we must call awful guilt; and yet, I will own to you,—when I think of the original cause, the motives, the feelings, the sudden concurrence of circumstances thrusting them onward, the urgency of the moment, and the sublime unselfishness on either part,—I know not well how to distinguish it from much that the world calls heroism. Might we not render some such verdict as this?—'Worthy of Death, but not unworthy of Love!'"

"Never!" answered Hilda, looking at the matter through the clear crystal medium of her own integrity. "This thing, as regards its causes, is all a mystery to me, and must remain so. But there is, I believe, only one right and one wrong; and I do not understand, and may God keep me from ever understanding, how two things so totally unlike can be mistaken for one another; nor how two mortal foes, as Right and Wrong surely are, can work together in the same deed. This is my faith; and I should be led astray, if you could persuade me to give it up."

"Alas for poor human nature, then!" said Kenyon sadly, and yet half smiling at Hilda's unworldly and impracticable theory. "I always felt you, my dear friend, a terribly severe judge, and have been perplexed to conceive how such tender sympathy could coexist with the remorselessness of a steel blade. You need no mercy, and therefore know not how to show any."

"That sounds like a bitter gibe," said Hilda, with the tears springing into her eyes. "But I cannot help it. It does not alter my perception of the truth. If there be any such dreadful mixture of good and evil as you affirm,—and which appears to me almost more shocking than pure evil,—then the good is turned to poison, not the evil to wholesomeness."

The sculptor seemed disposed to say something more, but yielded to the gentle steadfastness with which Hilda declined to listen. She grew very sad; for a reference to this one dismal topic had set, as it were, a prison door ajar, and allowed a throng of torturing recollections to escape from their dungeons into the pure air and white radiance of her soul. She bade Kenyon a briefer farewell than ordinary, and went homeward to her tower.

In spite of her efforts to withdraw them to other subjects, her thoughts dwelt upon Miriam; and, as had not heretofore happened, they brought with them a painful doubt whether a wrong had not been committed on Hilda's part, towards the friend once so beloved. Something that Miriam had said, in their final conversation, recurred to her memory, and seemed now to deserve more weight than Hilda had assigned to it, in her horror at the crime just perpetrated. It was not that the deed looked less wicked and terrible in the retrospect; but she asked herself whether there were not other questions to be considered, aside from that single one of Miriam's guilt or innocence; as, for example, whether a close bond of friendship, in which we once voluntarily engage, ought to be severed on account of any unworthiness, which we subsequently detect in our friend. For, in these unions of hearts,—call them marriage, or whatever else,—we take each other for better for worse. Availing ourselves of our friend's intimate affection, we pledge our own, as to be relied upon in every emergency. And what sadder, more desperate emergency could there be, than had befallen Miriam? Who more need the tender succor of the innocent, than wretches stained with guilt! And must a selfish care for the spotlessness of our own garments keep us from pressing the guilty ones close to our hearts, wherein, for the very reason that we are innocent, lies their securest refuge from further ill?

It was a sad thing for Hilda to find this moral enigma propounded to her conscience; and to feel that, whichever way she might settle it, there would be a cry of wrong on the other side. Still, the idea stubbornly came back, that the tie between Miriam and herself had been real, the affection true, and that therefore the implied compact was not to be shaken off.

"Miriam loved me well," thought Hilda remorsefully, "and I failed her at her sorest need."

Miriam loved her well; and not less ardent had been the affection which Miriam's warm, tender, and generous characteristics had excited in Hilda's more reserved and quiet nature. It had never been extinguished; for, in part, the wretchedness which Hilda had since endured was but the struggle and writhing of her sensibility, still yearning towards her friend. And now, at the earliest encouragement, it awoke again, and cried out piteously, complaining of the violence that had been done it.

Recurring to the delinquencies of which she fancied (we say "fancied," because we do not unhesitatingly adopt Hilda's present view, but rather suppose her misled by her feelings)—of which she fancied herself guilty towards her friend, she suddenly remembered a sealed packet that Miriam had confided to her. It had been put into her hands with earnest injunctions of secrecy and care, and if unclaimed after a certain period, was to be delivered according to its address. Hilda had forgotten it; or, rather, she had kept the thought of this commission in the background of her consciousness, with all other thoughts referring to Miriam.

But now the recollection of this packet, and the evident stress which Miriam laid upon its delivery at the specified time, impelled Hilda to hurry up the staircase of her tower, dreading lest the period should already have elapsed.

154

No; the hour had not gone by, but was on the very point of passing. Hilda read the brief note of instruction, on a corner of the envelope, and discovered, that, in case of Miriam's absence from Rome, the packet was to be taken to its destination that very day.

"How nearly I had violated my promise!" said Hilda. "And, since we are separated forever, it has the sacredness of an injunction from a dead friend. There is no time to be lost."

So Hilda set forth in the decline of the afternoon, and pursued her way towards the quarter of the city in which stands the Palazzo Cenci. Her habit of self-reliance was so simply strong, so natural, and now so well established by long use, that the idea of peril seldom or never occurred to Hilda, in her lonely life.

She differed, in this particular, from the generality of her sex, — although the customs and character of her native land often produce women who meet the world with gentle fearlessness, and discover that its terrors have been absurdly exaggerated by the tradition of mankind. In ninety-nine cases out of a hundred, the apprehensiveness of women is quite gratuitous. Even as matters now stand, they are really safer in perilous situations and emergencies than men; and might be still more so, if they trusted themselves more confidingly to the chivalry of manhood. In all her wanderings about Rome, Hilda had gone and returned as securely as she had been accustomed to tread the familiar street of her New England village, where every face wore a look of recognition. With respect to whatever was evil, foul, and ugly, in this populous and corrupt city, she trod as if invisible, and not only so, but blind. She was altogether unconscious of anything wicked that went along the same pathway, but without jostling or impeding her, any more than gross substance hinders the wanderings of a spirit. Thus it is, that, bad as the world is said to have grown, innocence continues to make a paradise around itself, and keep it still unfallen.

Hilda's present expedition led her into what was—physically, at least— the foulest and ugliest part of Rome. In that vicinity lies the Ghetto, where thousands of Jews are crowded within a narrow compass, and lead a close, unclean, and multitudinous life, resembling that of maggots when they over-populate a decaying cheese.

Hilda passed on the borders of this region, but had no occasion to step within it. Its neighborhood, however, naturally partook of characteristics 'like its own. There was a confusion of black and hideous houses, piled massively out of the ruins of former ages; rude and destitute of plan, as a pauper would build his hovel, and yet displaying here and there an arched gateway, a cornice, a pillar, or a broken arcade, that might have adorned a palace. Many of the houses, indeed, as they stood, might once have been palaces, and possessed still a squalid kind of grandeur. Dirt was everywhere, strewing the narrow streets, and incrusting the tall shabbiness of the edifices, from the foundations to the roofs; it lay upon the thresholds, and looked out of the windows, and assumed the guise of human life in the children that Seemed to be engendered out of it. Their father was the sun, and their mother—a heap of Roman mud.

It is a question of speculative interest, whether the ancient Romans were as unclean a people as we everywhere find those who have succeeded them. There appears to be a kind of malignant spell in the spots that have been inhabited by these masters of the world, or made famous in their history; an inherited and inalienable curse, impelling their successors to fling dirt and defilement upon whatever temple, column, mined palace, or triumphal arch may be nearest at hand, and on every monument that the old Romans built. It is most probably a classic trait, regularly transmitted downward, and perhaps a little modified by the better civilization of Christianity; so that Caesar may have trod narrower and filthier ways in his path to the Capitol, than even those of modern Rome.

As the paternal abode of Beatrice, the gloomy old palace of the Cencis had an interest for Hilda, although not sufficiently strong, hitherto, to overcome the disheartening effect of the exterior, and draw her over its threshold. The adjacent piazza, of poor aspect, contained only an old woman selling roasted chestnuts and baked squash-seeds; she looked sharply at Hilda, and inquired whether she had lost her way.

"No," said Hilda; "I seek the Palazzo Cenci."

"Yonder it is, fair signorina," replied the Roman matron. "If you wish that packet delivered, which I see in your hand, my grandson Pietro shall run with it for a baiocco. The Cenci palace is a spot of ill omen for young maidens."

Hilda thanked the old dame, but alleged the necessity of doing her errand in person. She approached the front of the palace, which, with all its immensity, had but a mean appearance, and seemed an abode which the lovely shade of Beatrice would not be apt to haunt, unless her doom made it inevitable. Some soldiers stood about the portal, and gazed at the brown-haired, fair-cheeked Anglo-Saxon girl, with approving glances, but not indecorously. Hilda began to ascend the staircase, three lofty flights of which were to be surmounted, before reaching the door whither she was bound.

CHAPTER XLIII. THE EXTINCTION OF A LAMP

Between Hilda and the sculptor there had been a kind of half-expressed understanding, that both were to visit the galleries of the Vatican the day subsequent to their meeting at the studio. Kenyon, accordingly, failed not to be there, and wandered through the vast ranges of apartments, but saw nothing of his expected friend. The marble faces, which stand innumerable along the walls, and have kept themselves so calm through the vicissitudes of twenty centuries, had no sympathy for his disappointment; and he, on the other hand, strode past these treasures and marvels of antique art, with the indifference which any preoccupation of the feelings is apt to produce, in reference to objects of sculpture. Being of so cold and pure a substance, and mostly deriving their vitality more from thought than passion, they require to be seen through a perfectly transparent medium.

And, moreover, Kenyon had counted so much upon Hilda's delicate perceptions in enabling him to look at two or three of the statues, about which they had talked together, that the entire purpose of his visit was defeated by her absence. It is a delicious sort of mutual aid, when the united power of two sympathetic, yet dissimilar, intelligences is brought to bear upon a poem by reading it aloud, or upon a picture or statue by viewing it in each other's company. Even if not a word of criticism be uttered, the insight of either party is wonderfully deepened, and the comprehension broadened; so that the inner mystery of a work of genius, hidden from one, will often reveal itself to two. Missing such help, Kenyon saw nothing at the Vatican which he had not seen a thousand times before, and more perfectly than now.

In the chili of his disappointment, he suspected that it was a very cold art to which he had devoted himself. He questioned, at that moment, whether sculpture really ever softens and warms the material which it handles; whether carved marble is anything but limestone, after all; and whether the Apollo Belvedere itself possesses any merit above its physical beauty, or is beyond criticism even in that generally acknowledged excellence. In flitting glances, heretofore, he had seemed to behold this statue, as something ethereal and godlike, but not now.

Nothing pleased him, unless it were the group of the Laocoon, which, in its immortal agony, impressed Kenyon as a type of the long, fierce struggle of man, involved in the knotted entanglements of Error and Evil, those two snakes, which, if no divine help intervene, will be sure to strangle him and his children in the end. What he most admired was the strange calmness diffused through this bitter strife; so that it resembled the rage of the sea made calm by its immensity,' or the tumult of Niagara which ceases to be tumult because it lasts forever. Thus, in the Laocoon, the horror of a moment grew to be the fate of interminable ages. Kenyon looked upon the group as the one triumph of sculpture, creating the repose, which is essential to it, in the very acme of turbulent effort; but, in truth, it was his mood of unwonted despondency that made him so sensitive to the terrible magnificence, as well as to the sad moral, of this work. Hilda herself could not have helped him to see it with nearly such intelligence.

A good deal more depressed than the nature of the disappointment warranted, Kenyon went to his studio, and took in hand a great lump of clay. He soon found, however, that his plastic cunning had departed from him for the time. So he wandered forth again into the uneasy streets of Rome, and walked up and down the Corso, where, at that period of the day, a throng of passers-by and loiterers choked up the narrow sidewalk. A penitent was thus brought in contact with the sculptor.

It was a figure in a white robe, with a kind of featureless mask over the face, through the apertures of which the eyes threw an unintelligible light. Such odd, questionable shapes are often seen gliding through the streets of Italian cities, and are understood to be usually persons of rank, who quit their palaces, their gayeties, their pomp and pride, and assume the penitential garb for a season, with a view of thus expiating some crime, or atoning for the aggregate of petty sins that make up a worldly life. It is their custom to ask alms, and perhaps to measure the duration of their penance by the time requisite to accumulate a sum of money out of the little droppings of individual charity. The avails are devoted to some beneficent or religious

159

purpose; so that the benefit accruing to their own souls is, in a manner, linked with a good done, or intended, to their fellow-men. These figures have a ghastly and startling effect, not so much from any very impressive peculiarity in the garb, as from the mystery which they bear about with them, and the sense that there is an acknowledged sinfulness as the nucleus of it.

In the present instance, however, the penitent asked no alms of Kenyon; although, for the space of a minute or two, they stood face to face, the hollow eyes of the mask encountering the sculptor's gaze. But, just as the crowd was about to separate them, the former spoke, in a voice not unfamiliar to Kenyon, though rendered remote and strange by the guilty veil through which it penetrated.

"Is all well with you, Signore?" inquired the penitent, out of the cloud in which he walked.

"All is well," answered Kenyon. "And with you?"

But the masked penitent returned no answer, being borne away by the pressure of the throng.

The sculptor stood watching the figure, and was almost of a mind to hurry after him and follow up the conversation that had been begun; but it occurred to him that there is a sanctity (or, as we might rather term it, an inviolable etiquette) which prohibits the recognition of persons who choose to walk under the veil of penitence.

"How strange!" thought Kenyon to himself. "It was surely Donatello! What can bring him to Rome, where his recollections must be so painful, and his presence not without peril? And Miriam! Can she have accompanied him?"

He walked on, thinking of the vast change in Donatello, since those days of gayety and innocence, when the young Italian was new in Rome, and was just beginning to be sensible of a more poignant felicity than he had yet experienced, in the sunny warmth of Miriam's smile. The growth of a soul, which the sculptor half imagined that he had witnessed in his friend, seemed hardly worth the heavy price that it had cost, in the sacrifice of those simple enjoyments that were gone forever. A creature of antique healthfulness had vanished from the earth; and, in his stead, there was only one other morbid and remorseful man, among millions that were cast in the same indistinguishable mould.

The accident of thus meeting Donatello the glad Faun of his imagination and memory, now transformed into a gloomy penitent—contributed to deepen the cloud that had fallen over Kenyon's spirits. It caused him to fancy, as we generally do, in the petty troubles which extend not a hand's-breadth beyond our own sphere, that the whole world was saddening around him. It took the sinister aspect of an omen, although he could not distinctly see what trouble it might forebode.

If it had not been for a peculiar sort of pique, with which lovers are much conversant, a preposterous kind of resentment which endeavors to wreak itself on the beloved object, and on one's own heart, in requital of mishaps for which neither are in fault, Kenyon might at once have betaken himself to Hilda's studio, and asked why the appointment was not kept. But the interview of to-day was to have been so rich in present joy, and its results so important to his future life, that the bleak failure was too much for his equanimity. He was angry with poor Hilda, and censured her without a hearing; angry with himself, too, and therefore inflicted on this latter criminal the severest penalty in his power; angry with the day that was passing over him, and would not permit its latter hours to redeem the disappointment of the morning.

To confess the truth, it had been the sculptor's purpose to stake all his hopes on that interview in the galleries of the Vatican. Straying with Hilda through those long vistas of ideal beauty, he meant, at last, to utter himself upon that theme which lovers are fain to discuss in village lanes, in wood paths, on seaside sands, in crowded streets; it little matters where, indeed, since roses are sure to blush along the way, and daisies and violets to spring beneath the feet, if the spoken word be graciously received. He was resolved to make proof whether the kindness that Hilda evinced for him was the precious token of an individual preference, or merely the sweet fragrance of her disposition, which other friends might share as largely as himself. He would try if it were possible to take this shy, yet frank, and innocently fearless creature captive, and imprison her in his heart, and make her sensible of a wider freedom there, than in all the world besides.

It was hard, we must allow, to see the shadow of a wintry sunset falling upon a day that was to have been so bright, and to find himself just where yesterday had left him, only with a sense of being drearily balked, and defeated without an opportunity for struggle. So much had been anticipated from these now vanished hours, that it seemed as if no other day could bring back the same golden hopes.

In a case like this, it is doubtful whether Kenyon could have done a much better thing than he actually did, by going to dine at the Cafe Nuovo, and drinking a flask of Montefiascone; longing, the while, for a beaker or two of Donatello's Sunshine. It would have been just the wine to cure a lover's melancholy, by illuminating his heart with tender light and warmth, and suggestions of undefined hopes, too ethereal for his morbid humor to examine and reject them.

No decided improvement resulting from the draught of Montefiascone, he went to the Teatro Argentino, and sat gloomily to see an Italian comedy, which ought to have cheered him somewhat, being full of glancing merriment, and effective over everybody's disabilities except his own. The sculptor came out, however, before the close of the performance, as disconsolate as he went in.

As he made his way through the complication of narrow streets, which perplex that portion of the city, a carriage passed him. It was driven rapidly, but not too fast for the light of a gas-lamp to flare upon a face within—especially as it was bent forward, appearing to recognize him, while a beckoning hand was protruded from the window. On his part, Kenyon at once knew the face, and hastened to the carriage, which had now stopped.

"Miriam! you in Rome?" he exclaimed, "And your friends know nothing of it?"

"Is all well with you?" she asked.

This inquiry, in the identical words which Donatello had so recently addressed to him from beneath the penitent's mask, startled the sculptor. Either the previous disquietude of his mind, or some tone in Miriam's voice, or the unaccountableness of beholding her there at all, made it seem ominous.

"All is well, I believe," answered he doubtfully. "I am aware of no misfortune. Have you any to announce'?"

He looked still more earnestly at Miriam, and felt a dreamy uncertainty whether it was really herself to whom he spoke. True; there were those beautiful features, the contour of which he had studied too often, and with a sculptor's accuracy of perception, to be in any doubt that it was Miriam's identical face. But he was conscious of a change, the nature of which he could not satisfactorily define; it might be merely her dress, which, imperfect as the light was, he saw to be richer than the simple garb that she had usually worn. The effect, he fancied, was partly owing to a gem which she had on her bosom; not a diamond, but something that glimmered with a clear, red lustre, like the stars in a southern sky. Somehow or other, this colored light seemed an emanation of herself, as if all that was passionate and glowing in her native disposition had crystallized upon her breast, and were just now scintillating more brilliantly than ever, in sympathy with some emotion of her heart.

Of course there could be no real doubt that it was Miriam, his artist friend, with whom and Hilda he had spent so many pleasant and familiar hours, and whom he had last seen at Perugia, bending with Donatello beneath the bronze pope's benediction. It must be that selfsame Miriam; but the sensitive sculptor felt a difference of manner, which impressed him more than he conceived it possible to be affected by so external a thing. He remembered the gossip so prevalent in Rome on Miriam's first appearance; how that she was no real artist, but the daughter of an illustrious or golden lineage, who was merely playing at necessity; mingling with human struggle for her pastime; stepping out of her native sphere only for an interlude, just as a princess might alight from her gilded equipage to go on foot through a rustic lane. And now, after a mask in which love and death had performed their several parts, she had resumed her proper character.

"Have you anything to tell me?" cried he impatiently; for nothing causes a more disagreeable vibration of the nerves than this perception of ambiguousness in familiar persons or affairs. "Speak; for my spirits and patience have been much tried to-day."

Miriam put her finger on her lips, and seemed desirous that Kenyon should know of the presence of a third person. He now saw, indeed, that, there was some one beside her in the carriage, hitherto concealed by her attitude; a man, it appeared, with a sallow Italian face, which the sculptor distinguished but imperfectly, and did not recognize.

"I can tell you nothing," she replied; and leaning towards him, she whispered,—appearing then more like the Miriam whom he knew than in what had before passed,—"Only, when the lamp goes out do not despair."

The carriage drove on, leaving Kenyon to muse over this unsatisfactory interview, which seemed to have served no better purpose than to fill his mind with more ominous forebodings than before. Why were Donatello and Miriam in Rome, where both, in all likelihood, might have much to dread? And why had one and the other addressed him with a question that seemed prompted by a knowledge of some calamity, either already fallen on his unconscious head, or impending closely over him?

"I am sluggish," muttered Kenyon, to himself; "a weak, nerveless fool, devoid of energy and promptitude; or neither Donatello nor Miriam could have escaped me thus! They are aware of some misfortune that concerns me deeply. How soon am I to know it too?"

There seemed but a single calamity possible to happen within so narrow a sphere as that with which the sculptor was connected; and even to that one mode of evil he could assign no definite shape, but only felt that it must have some reference to Hilda.

Flinging aside the morbid hesitation, and the dallyings with his own wishes, which he had permitted to influence his mind throughout the day, he now hastened to the Via Portoghese. Soon the old palace stood before him, with its massive tower rising into the clouded night; obscured from view at its midmost elevation, but revealed again, higher upward, by the Virgin's lamp that twinkled on the summit. Feeble as it was, in the broad, surrounding gloom, that little ray made no inconsiderable illumination among Kenyon's sombre thoughts; for; remembering Miriam's last words, a fantasy had seized him that he should find the sacred lamp extinguished.

And even while he stood gazing, as a mariner at the star in which he put his trust, the light quivered, sank, gleamed up again, and finally went out, leaving the battlements of Hilda's tower in utter darkness. For the first time in centuries, the consecrated and legendary flame before the loftiest shrine in Rome had ceased to burn.

CHAPTER XLIV. THE DESERTED SHRINE

Kenyon knew the sanctity which Hilda (faithful Protestant, and daughter of the Puritans, as the girl was) imputed to this shrine. He was aware of the profound feeling of responsibility, as well earthly as religious, with which her conscience had been impressed, when she became the occupant of her aerial chamber, and undertook the task of keeping the consecrated lamp alight. There was an accuracy and a certainty about Hilda's movements, as regarded all matters that lay deep enough to have their roots in right or wrong, which made it as possible and safe to rely upon the timely and careful trimming of this lamp (if she were in life, and able to creep up the steps), as upon the rising of to-morrow's sun, with lustre-undiminished from to-day.

The sculptor could scarcely believe his eyes, therefore, when he saw the flame flicker and expire. His sight had surely deceived him. And now, since the light did not reappear, there must be some smoke wreath or impenetrable mist brooding about the tower's gray old head, and obscuring it from the lower world. But no! For right over the dim battlements, as the wind chased away a mass of clouds, he beheld a star, and moreover, by an earnest concentration of his sight, was soon able to discern even the darkened shrine itself. There was no obscurity around the tower; no infirmity of his own vision. The flame had exhausted its supply of oil, and become extinct. But where was Hilda?

A man in a cloak happened to be passing; and Kenyon—anxious to distrust the testimony of his senses, if he could get more acceptable evidence on the other side—appealed to him.

"Do me the favor, Signore," said he, "to look at the top of yonder tower, and tell me whether you see the lamp burning at the Virgin's shrine."

"The lamp, Signore?" answered the man, without at first troubling himself to look up. "The lamp that has burned these four hundred years! How is it possible, Signore, that it should not be burning now?" "But look!" said the sculptor impatiently. With good-natured indulgence for what he seemed to consider as the whim of an eccentric Forestiero, the Italian carelessly threw his eyes upwards; but, as soon as he perceived that there was really no light, he lifted his hands with a vivid expression of wonder and alarm.

"The lamp is extinguished!" cried he. "The lamp that has been burning these four hundred years! This surely must portend some great misfortune; and, by my advice, Signore, you will hasten hence, lest the tower tumble on our heads. A priest once told me that, if the Virgin withdrew her blessing and the light went out, the old Palazzo del Torte would sink into the earth, with all that dwell in it. There will be a terrible crash before morning!"

The stranger made the best of his way from the doomed premises; while Kenyon—who would willingly have seen the tower crumble down before his eyes, on condition of Hilda's safety—determined, late as it was, to attempt ascertaining if she were in her dove-cote.

Passing through the arched entrance,—which, as is often the case with Roman entrances, was as accessible at midnight as at noon,—he groped his way to the broad staircase, and, lighting his wax taper, went glimmering up the multitude of steps that led to Hilda's door. The hour being so unseasonable, he intended merely to knock, and, as soon as her voice from within should reassure him, to retire, keeping his explanations and apologies for a fitter time. Accordingly, reaching the lofty height where the maiden, as he trusted, lay asleep, with angels watching over her, though the Virgin seemed to have suspended her care, he tapped lightly at the door panels,—then knocked more forcibly,—then thundered an impatient summons. No answer came; Hilda, evidently, was not there.

After assuring himself that this must be the fact, Kenyon descended the stairs, but made a pause at every successive stage, and knocked at the door of its apartment, regardless whose slumbers he might disturb, in his anxiety to learn where the girl had last been seen. But, at each closed entrance, there came those hollow echoes, which a chamber, or any dwelling, great or small, never sends out, in response to human knuckles or iron hammer, as long as there is life within to keep its heart from getting dreary.

Once indeed, on the lower landing-place, the sculptor fancied that there was a momentary stir inside the door, as if somebody were listening at the threshold. He hoped, at least, that the small iron-barred aperture would be unclosed, through which Roman housekeepers are wont to take careful cognizance of applicants for admission, from a traditionary dread, perhaps, of letting in a robber or assassin. But it remained shut; neither was the sound repeated; and Kenyon concluded that his excited nerves had played a trick upon his senses, as they are apt to do when we most wish for the clear evidence of the latter.

There was nothing to be done, save to go heavily away, and await whatever good or ill to-morrow's daylight might disclose.

Betimes in the morning, therefore, Kenyon went back to the Via Portoghese, before the slant rays of the sun had descended halfway down the gray front of Hilda's tower. As he drew near its base, he saw the doves perched in full session, on the sunny height of the battlements, and a pair of them—who were probably their mistress's especial pets, and the confidants of her bosom secrets, if Hilda had any—came shooting down, and made a feint of alighting on his shoulder. But, though they evidently recognized him, their shyness would not yet allow so decided a demonstration. Kenyon's eyes followed them as they flew upward, hoping that they might have come as joyful messengers of the girl's safety, and that he should discern her slender form, half hidden by the parapet, trimming the extinguished lamp at the Virgin's shrine, just as other maidens set about the little duties of a household. Or, perhaps, he might see her gentle and sweet face smiling down upon him, midway towards heaven, as if she had flown thither for a day or two, just to visit her kindred, but had been drawn earthward again by the spell of unacknowledged love.

But his eyes were blessed by no such fair vision or reality; nor, in truth, were the eager, unquiet flutterings of the doves indicative of any joyful intelligence, which they longed to share with Hilda's friend, but of anxious inquiries that they knew not how to utter. They could not tell, any more than he, whither their lost companion had withdrawn herself, but were in the same void despondency with him, feeling their sunny and airy lives darkened and grown imperfect, now that her sweet society was taken out of it.

In the brisk morning air, Kenyon found it much easier to pursue his researches than at the preceding midnight, when, if any slumberers heard the clamor that he made, they had responded only with sullen and drowsy maledictions, and turned to sleep again. It must be a very dear and intimate reality for which people will be content to give up a dream. When the sun was fairly up, however, it was quite another thing. The heterogeneous population, inhabiting the lower floor of the old tower, and the other extensive regions of the palace, were now willing to tell all they knew, and imagine a great deal more. The amiability of these Italians, assisted by their sharp and nimble wits, caused them to overflow with plausible suggestions, and to be very bounteous in their avowals of interest for the lost Hilda. In a less demonstrative people, such expressions would have implied an eagerness to search land and sea, and never rest till she were found. In the mouths that uttered them they meant good wishes, and were, so far, better than indifference. There was little doubt that many of them felt a genuine kindness for the shy, brown-haired, delicate young foreign maiden, who had flown from some distant land to alight upon their tower, where she consorted only with the doves. But their energy expended itself in exclamation, and they were content to leave all more active measures to Kenyon, and to the Virgin, whose affair it was to see that the faithful votary of her lamp received no harm.

In a great Parisian domicile, multifarious as its inhabitants might be, the concierge under the archway would be cognizant of all their incomings and issuings forth. But except in rare cases, the general entrance and main staircase of a Roman house are left as free as the street, of which they form a sort of by-lane. The sculptor, therefore, could hope to find information about Hilda's movements only from casual observers.

On probing the knowledge of these people to the bottom, there was various testimony as to the period when the girl had last been seen. Some said that it was four days since there had been a trace of her; but an English lady, in the second piano of the palace, was rather of opinion that she had met her, the morning before, with a drawing-book in her hand. Having no acquaintance with the young person, she had taken little notice and might have been mistaken. A count, on the piano next above, was very certain that he had lifted his hat to Hilda, under the archway, two afternoons ago. An old woman, who had formerly tended the shrine, threw some light upon the matter, by testifying that the lamp required to be replenished once, at least, in three days, though its reservoir of oil was exceedingly capacious.

On the whole, though there was other evidence enough to create some perplexity, Kenyon could not satisfy himself that she had been visible since the afternoon of the third preceding day, when a fruit seller remembered her coming out of the arched passage, with a sealed packet in her hand. As nearly as he could ascertain, this was within an hour after Hilda had taken leave of the sculptor at his own studio, with the understanding that they were to meet at the Vatican the next day. Two nights, therefore, had intervened, during which the lost maiden was unaccounted for.

The door of Hilda's apartments was still locked, as on the preceding night; but Kenyon sought out the wife of the person who sublet them, and prevailed on her to give him admittance by means of the duplicate key which the good woman had in her possession. On entering, the maidenly neatness and simple grace, recognizable in all the arrangements, made him visibly sensible that this was the daily haunt of a pure soul, in whom religion and the love of beauty were at one.

Thence, the sturdy Roman matron led the sculptor across a narrow passage, and threw open the door of a small chamber, on the threshold of which he reverently paused. Within, there was a bed, covered with white drapery, enclosed with snowy curtains like a tent, and of barely width enough for a slender figure to repose upon it. The sight of this cool, airy, and secluded bower caused the lover's heart to stir as if enough of Hilda's gentle dreams were lingering there to make him happy for a single instant. But then came the closer consciousness of her loss, bringing along with it a sharp sting of anguish.

"Behold, Signore," said the matron; "here is the little staircase by which the signorina used to ascend and trim the Blessed Virgin's lamp. She was worthy to be a Catholic, such pains the good child bestowed to keep it burning; and doubtless the Blessed Mary will intercede for her, in consideration of her pious offices, heretic though she was. What will become of the old palazzo, now that the lamp is extinguished, the saints above us only know! Will you mount, Signore, to the battlements, and see if she have left any trace of herself there?"

The sculptor stepped across the chamber and ascended the little staircase, which gave him access to the breezy summit of the tower. It affected him inexpressibly to see a bouquet of beautiful flowers beneath the shrine, and to recognize in them an offering of his own to Hilda, who had put them in a vase of water, and dedicated them to the Virgin, in a spirit partly fanciful, perhaps, but still partaking of the religious sentiment which so profoundly influenced her character. One rosebud, indeed, she had selected for herself from the rich mass of flowers; for Kenyon well remembered recognizing it in her bosom when he last saw her at his studio.

"That little part of my great love she took," said he to himself. "The remainder she would have devoted to Heaven; but has left it withering in the sun and wind. Ah! Hilda, Hilda, had you given me a right to watch over you, this evil had not come!"

"Be not downcast, signorino mio," said the Roman matron, in response to the deep sigh which struggled out of Kenyon's breast. "The dear little maiden, as we see, has decked yonder blessed shrine as devoutly as I myself, or any Other good Catholic woman, could have done. It is a religious act, and has more than the efficacy of a prayer. The signorina will as surely come back as the sun will fall through the window to-morrow no less than to-day. Her own doves have often been missing for a day or two, but they were sure to come fluttering about her head again, when she least expected them. So will it be with this dove-like child."

"It might be so," thought Kenyon, with yearning anxiety, "if a pure maiden were as safe as a dove, in this evil world of ours."

As they returned through the studio, with the furniture and arrangements of which the sculptor was familiar, he missed a small ebony writing-desk that he remembered as having always been placed on a table there. He knew that it was Hilda's custom to deposit her letters in this desk, as well as other little objects of which she wished to be specially careful.

"What has become of it?" he suddenly inquired, laying his hand on the table.

"Become of what, pray?" exclaimed the woman, a little disturbed. "Does the Signore suspect a robbery, then?"

"The signorina's writing-desk is gone," replied Kenyon; "it always stood on this table, and I myself saw it there only a few days ago."

"Ah, well!" said the woman, recovering her composure, which she seemed partly to have lost. "The signorina has doubtless taken it away with her. The fact is of good omen; for it proves that she did not go unexpectedly, and is likely to return when it may best suit her convenience."

"This is very singular," observed Kenyon. "Have the rooms been entered by yourself, or any other person, since the signorina's disappearance?"

"Not by me, Signore, so help me Heaven and the saints!" said the matron. "And I question whether there are more than two keys in Rome that will suit this strange old lock. Here is one; and as for the other, the signorina carlies it in her pocket."

The sculptor had no reason to doubt the word of this respectable dame. She appeared to be well meaning and kind hearted, as Roman matrons generally are; except when a fit of passion incites them to shower horrible curses on an obnoxious individual, or perhaps to stab him with the steel stiletto that serves them for a hairpin. But Italian asseverations of any questionable fact, however true they may chance to be, have no witness of their truth in the faces of those who utter them. Their words are spoken with strange earnestness, and yet do not vouch for themselves as coming from any depth, like roots drawn out of the substance of the soul, with some of the soil clinging to them. There is always a something inscrutable, instead of frankness, in their eyes. In short, they lie so much like truth, and speak truth so much as if they were telling a lie, that their auditor suspects himself in the wrong, whether he believes or disbelieves them; it being the one thing certain, that falsehood is seldom an intolerable burden to the tenderest of Italian consciences.

"It is very strange what can have become of the desk!" repeated Kenyon, looking the woman in the face.

"Very strange, indeed, Signore," she replied meekly, without turning away her eyes in the least, but checking his insight of them at about half an inch below the surface. "I think the signorina must have taken it with her."

It seemed idle to linger here any longer. Kenyon therefore departed, after making an arrangement with the woman, by the terms of which she was to allow the apartments to remain in their present state, on his assuming the responsibility for the rent.

He spent the day in making such further search and investigation as he found practicable; and, though at first trammelled by an unwillingness to draw public attention to Hilda's affairs, the urgency of the circumstances soon compelled him to be thoroughly in earnest. In the course of a week, he tried all conceivable modes of fathoming the mystery, not merely by his personal efforts and those of his brother artists and friends, but through the police, who readily undertook the task, and expressed strong confidence of success. But the Roman police has very little efficiency, except in the interest of the despotism of which it is a tool. With their cocked hats, shoulder belts, and swords, they wear a sufficiently imposing aspect, and doubtless keep their eyes open wide enough to track a political offender, but are too often blind to private outrage, be it murder or any lesser crime. Kenyon counted little upon their assistance, and profited by it not at all.

Remembering the mystic words which Miriam had addressed to him, he was anxious to meet her, but knew not whither she had gone, nor how to obtain an interview either with herself or Donatello. The days wore away, and still there were no tidings of the lost one; no lamp rekindled before the Virgin's shrine; no light shining into the lover's heart; no star of Hope— he was ready to say, as he turned his eyes almost reproachfully upward—in heaven itself!

CHAPTER XLV. THE FLIGHT OF HILDA'S DOVES

Along with the lamp on Hilda's tower, the sculptor now felt that a light had gone out, or, at least, was ominously obscured, to which he owed whatever cheerfulness had heretofore illuminated his cold, artistic life. The idea of this girl had been like a taper of virgin wax, burning with a pure and steady flame, and chasing away the evil spirits out of the magic circle of its beams. It had darted its rays afar, and modified the whole sphere in which Kenyon had his being. Beholding it no more, he at once found himself in darkness and astray.

This was the time, perhaps, when Kenyon first became sensible what a dreary city is Rome, and what a terrible weight is there imposed on human life, when any gloom within the heart corresponds to the spell of ruin that has been thrown over the site of ancient empire. He wandered, as it were, and stumbled over the fallen columns, and among the tombs, and groped his way into the sepulchral darkness of the catacombs, and found no path emerging from them. The happy may well enough continue to be such, beneath the brilliant sky of Rome. But, if you go thither in melancholy mood, if you go with a ruin in your heart, or with a vacant site there, where once stood the airy fabric of happiness, now vanished,—all the ponderous gloom of the Roman Past will pile itself upon that spot, and crush you down as with the heaped-up marble and granite, the earth-mounds, and multitudinous bricks of its material decay.

It might be supposed that a melancholy man would here make acquaintance with a grim philosophy. He should learn to bear patiently his individual griefs, that endure only for one little lifetime, when here are the tokens of such infinite misfortune on an imperial scale, and when so many far landmarks of time, all around him, are bringing the remoteness of a thousand years ago into the sphere of yesterday. But it is in vain that you seek this shrub of bitter sweetness among the plants that root themselves on the roughness of massive walls, or trail downward from the capitals of pillars, or spring out of the green turf in the palace of the Caesars. It does not grow in Rome; not even among the five hundred various weeds which deck the grassy arches of the Coliseum. You look through a vista of century beyond century,—through much shadow, and a little sunshine,—through barbarism and civilization, alternating with one another like actors that have prearranged their parts: through a broad pathway of progressive generations bordered by palaces and temples, and bestridden by old, triumphal arches, until, in the distance, you behold the obelisks, with their unintelligible inscriptions, hinting at a past infinitely more remote than history can define. Your own life is as nothing, when compared with that immeasurable distance; but still you demand, none the less earnestly, a gleam of sunshine, instead of a speck of shadow, on the step or two that will bring you to your quiet rest.

How exceedingly absurd! All men, from the date of the earliest obelisk,— and of the whole world, moreover, since that far epoch, and before,—have made a similar demand, and seldom had their wish. If they had it, what are they the better now? But, even while you taunt yourself with this sad lesson, your heart cries out obstreperously for its small share of earthly happiness, and will not be appeased by the myriads of dead hopes that lie crushed into the soil of Rome. How wonderful that this our narrow foothold of the Present should hold its own so constantly, and, while every moment changing, should still be like a rock betwixt the encountering tides of the long Past and the infinite To-come!

Man of marble though he was, the sculptor grieved for the Irrevocable. Looking back upon Hilda's way of life, he marvelled at his own blind stupidity, which had kept him from remonstrating as a friend, if with no stronger right against the risks that she continually encountered. Being so innocent, she had no means of estimating those risks, nor even a possibility of suspecting their existence. But he—who had spent years in Rome, with a man's far wider scope of observation and experience—knew things that made him shudder. It seemed to Kenyon, looking through the darkly colored medium of his fears, that all modes of crime were crowded into the close intricacy of Roman streets, and that there was no redeeming element, such as exists in other dissolute and wicked cities.

For here was a priesthood, pampered, sensual, with red and bloated cheeks, and carnal eyes. With apparently a grosser development of animal life than most men, they were placed in an unnatural relation with woman, and thereby lost the healthy, human conscience that pertains to other human beings, who own the sweet household ties connecting them with wife and daughter. And here was an indolent nobility, with no high aims or opportunities, but cultivating a vicious way of life, as if it were an art, and the only one which they cared to learn. Here was a population, high and low, that had no genuine belief in virtue; and if they recognized any act as criminal, they might throw off all care, remorse, and memory of it, by kneeling a little while at the confessional, and rising unburdened, active, elastic, and incited by fresh appetite for the next ensuing sin. Here was a soldiery who felt Rome to be their conquered city, and doubtless considered themselves the legal inheritors of the foul license which Gaul, Goth, and Vandal have here exercised in days gone by.

And what localities for new crime existed in those guilty sites, where the crime of departed ages used to be at home, and had its long, hereditary haunt! What street in Rome, what ancient ruin, what one place where man had standing-room, what fallen stone was there, unstained with one or another kind of guilt! In some of the vicissitudes of the city's pride or its calamity, the dark tide of human evil had swelled over it, far higher than the Tiber ever rose against the acclivities of the seven hills. To Kenyon's morbid view, there appeared to be a contagious element, rising fog-like from the ancient depravity of Rome, and brooding over the dead and half-rotten city, as nowhere else on earth. It prolonged the tendency to crime, and developed an instantaneous growth of it, whenever an opportunity was found; And where could it be found so readily as here! In those vast palaces, there were a hundred remote nooks where Innocence might shriek in vain. Beneath meaner houses there were unsuspected dungeons that had once been princely chambers, and open to the daylight; but, on account of some wickedness there perpetrated, each passing age had thrown its handful of dust upon the spot, and buried it from sight. Only ruffians knew of its existence, and kept it for murder, and worse crime.

Such was the city through which Hilda, for three years past, had been wandering without a protector or a guide. She had trodden lightly over the crumble of old crimes; she had taken her way amid the grime and corruption which Paganism had left there, and a perverted Christianity had made more noisome; walking saint-like through it all, with white, innocent feet; until, in some dark pitfall that lay right across her path, she had vanished out of sight. It was terrible to imagine what hideous outrage might have thrust her into that abyss!

Then the lover tried to comfort himself with the idea that Hilda's sanctity was a sufficient safeguard. Ah, yes; she was so pure! The angels, that were of the same sisterhood, would never let Hilda come to harm. A miracle would be wrought on her behalf, as naturally as a father would stretch out his hand to save a best-beloved child. Providence would keep a little area and atmosphere about her as safe and wholesome as heaven itself, although the flood of perilous iniquity might hem her round, and its black waves hang curling above her head! But these reflections were of slight avail. No doubt they were the religious truth. Yet the ways of Providence are utterly inscrutable; and many a murder has been done, and many an innocent virgin has lifted her white arms, beseeching its aid in her extremity, and all in vain; so that, though Providence is infinitely good and wise, and perhaps for that very reason, it may be half an eternity before the great circle of its scheme shall bring us the superabundant recompense for all these sorrows! But what the lover asked was such prompt consolation as might consist with the brief span of mortal life; the assurance of Hilda's present safety, and her restoration within that very hour.

An imaginative man, he suffered the penalty of his endowment in the hundred-fold variety of gloomily tinted scenes that it presented to him, in which Hilda was always a central figure. The sculptor forgot his marble. Rome ceased to be anything, for him, but a labyrinth of dismal streets, in one or another of which the lost girl had disappeared. He was haunted with the idea that some circumstance, most important to be known, and perhaps easily discoverable, had hitherto been overlooked, and that, if he could lay hold of this one clew, it would guide him directly in the track of Hilda's footsteps.

With this purpose in view, he went, every morning, to the Via Portoghese, and made it the starting-point of fresh investigations. After nightfall, too, he invariably returned thither, with a faint hope fluttering at his heart that the lamp might again be shining on the summit of the tower, and would dispel this ugly mystery out of the circle consecrated by its rays. There being no point of which he could take firm hold, his mind was filled with unsubstantial hopes and fears. Once Kenyon had seemed to cut his life in marble; now he vaguely clutched at it, and found it vapor.

In his unstrung and despondent mood, one trifling circumstance affected him with an idle pang. The doves had at first been faithful to their lost mistress. They failed not to sit in a row upon her window-sill, or to alight on the shrine, or the church-angels, and on the roofs and portals of the neighboring houses, in evident expectation of her reappearance. After the second week, however, they began to take flight, and dropping off by pairs, betook themselves to other dove-cotes. Only a single dove remained, and brooded drearily beneath the shrine. The flock that had departed were like the many hopes that had vanished from Kenyon's heart; the one that still lingered, and looked so wretched,—was it a Hope, or already a Despair?

In the street, one day, the sculptor met a priest of mild and venerable aspect; and as his mind dwelt continually upon Hilda, and was especially active in bringing up all incidents that had ever been connected with her, it immediately struck him that this was the very father with whom he had seen her at the confessional. Such trust did Hilda inspire in him, that Kenyon had never asked what was the subject of the communication between herself and this old priest. He had no reason for imagining that it could have any relation with her disappearance, so long subsequently; but, being thus brought face to face with a personage, mysteriously associated, as he now remembered, with her whom he had lost, an impulse ran before his thoughts and led the sculptor to address him.

It might be that the reverend kindliness of the old man's expression took Kenyon's heart by surprise; at all events, he spoke as if there were a recognized acquaintanceship, and an object of mutual interest between them.

"She has gone from me, father," said he.

"Of whom do you speak, my son?" inquired the priest.

"Of that sweet girl," answered Kenyon, "who knelt to you at the confessional. Surely you remember her, among all the mortals to whose confessions you have listened! For she alone could have had no sins to reveal."

"Yes; I remember," said the priest, with a gleam of recollection in his eyes. "She was made to bear a miraculous testimony to the efficacy of the divine ordinances of the Church, by seizing forcibly upon one of them, and finding immediate relief from it, heretic though she was. It is my purpose to publish a brief narrative of this miracle, for the edification of mankind, in Latin, Italian, and English, from the printing press of the Propaganda. Poor child! Setting apart her heresy, she was spotless, as you say. And is she dead?"

"Heaven forbid, father!" exclaimed Kenyon, shrinking back. "But she has gone from me, I know not whither. It may be—yes, the idea seizes upon my mind—that what she revealed to you will suggest some clew to the mystery of her disappearance.'"

"None, my son, none," answered the priest, shaking his head; "nevertheless, I bid you be of good cheer. That young maiden is not doomed to die a heretic. Who knows what the Blessed Virgin may at this moment be doing for her soul! Perhaps, when you next behold her, she will be clad in the shining white robe of the true faith."

This latter suggestion did not convey all the comfort which the old priest possibly intended by it; but he imparted it to the sculptor, along with his blessing, as the two best things that he could bestow, and said nothing further, except to bid him farewell.

When they had parted, however, the idea of Hilda's conversion to Catholicism recurred to her lover's mind, bringing with it certain reflections, that gave a new turn to his surmises about the mystery into which she had vanished. Not that he seriously apprehended—although the superabundance of her religious sentiment might mislead her for a moment—that the New England girl would permanently succumb to the scarlet superstitions which surrounded her in Italy. But the incident of the confessional if known, as probably it was, to the eager propagandists who prowl about for souls, as cats to catch a mouse—would surely inspire the most confident expectations of bringing her over to the faith. With so pious an end in view, would Jesuitical morality be shocked at the thought of kidnapping the mortal body, for the sake of the immortal spirit that might otherwise be lost forever? Would not the kind old priest, himself, deem this to be infinitely the kindest service that he could perform for the stray lamb, who had so strangely sought his aid?

If these suppositions were well founded, Hilda was most likely a prisoner in one of the religious establishments that are so numerous in Rome. The idea, according to the aspect in which it was viewed, brought now a degree of comfort, and now an additional perplexity. On the one hand, Hilda was safe from any but spiritual assaults; on the other, where was the possibility of breaking through all those barred portals, and searching a thousand convent cells, to set her free?

Kenyon, however, as it happened, was prevented from endeavoring to follow out this surmise, which only the state of hopeless uncertainty, that almost bewildered his reason, could have led him for a moment to entertain. A communication reached him by an unknown hand, in consequence of which, and within an hour after receiving it, he took his way through one of the gates of Rome.

CHAPTER XLVI. A WALK ON THE CAMPAGNA

It was a bright forenoon of February; a month in which the brief severity of a Roman winter is already past, and when violets and daisies begin to show themselves in spots favored by the sun. The sculptor came out of the city by the gate of San Sebastiano, and walked briskly along the Appian Way.

For the space of a mile or two beyond the gate, this ancient and famous road is as desolate and disagreeable as most of the other Roman avenues. It extends over small, uncomfortable paving-stones, between brick and plastered walls, which are very solidly constructed, and so high as almost to exclude a view of the surrounding country. The houses are of most uninviting aspect, neither picturesque, nor homelike and social; they have seldom or never a door opening on the wayside, but are accessible only from the rear, and frown inhospitably upon the traveller through iron-grated windows. Here and there appears a dreary inn or a wine-shop, designated by the withered bush beside the entrance, within which you discern a stone-built and sepulchral interior, where guests refresh themselves with sour bread and goats'-milk cheese, washed down with wine of dolorous acerbity.

At frequent intervals along the roadside up-rises the ruin of an ancient tomb. As they stand now, these structures are immensely high and broken mounds of conglomerated brick, stone, pebbles, and earth, all molten by time into a mass as solid and indestructible as if each tomb were composed of a single boulder of granite. When first erected, they were cased externally, no doubt, with slabs of polished marble, artfully wrought bas-reliefs, and all such suitable adornments, and were rendered majestically beautiful by grand architectural designs. This antique splendor has long since been stolen from the dead, to decorate the palaces and churches of the living. Nothing remains to the dishonored sepulchres, except their massiveness.

Even the pyramids form hardly a stranger spectacle, or are more alien from human sympathies, than the tombs of the Appian Way, with their gigantic height, breadth, and solidity, defying time and the elements, and far too mighty to be demolished by an ordinary earthquake. Here you may see a modern dwelling, and a garden with its vines and olive-trees, perched on the lofty dilapidation of a tomb, which forms a precipice of fifty feet in depth on each of the four sides. There is a home on that funereal mound, where generations of children have been born, and successive lives been spent, undisturbed by the ghost of the stern Roman whose ashes were so preposterously burdened. Other sepulchres wear a crown of grass, shrubbery, and forest-trees, which throw out a broad sweep of branches, having had time, twice over, to be a thousand years of age. On one of them stands a tower, which, though immemorially more modern than the tomb, was itself built by immemorial hands, and is now rifted quite from top to bottom by a vast fissure of decay; the tomb-hillock, its foundation, being still as firm as ever, and likely to endure until the last trump shall rend it wide asunder, and summon forth its unknown dead.

Yes; its unknown dead! For, except in one or two doubtful instances, these mountainous sepulchral edifices have not availed to keep so much as the bare name of an individual or a family from oblivion. Ambitious of everlasting remembrance, as they were, the slumberers might just as well have gone quietly to rest, each in his pigeon-hole of a columbarium, or under his little green hillock in a graveyard, without a headstone to mark the spot. It is rather satisfactory than otherwise, to think that all these idle pains have turned out so utterly abortive.

About two miles, or more, from the city gate, and right upon the roadside, Kenyon passed an immense round pile, sepulchral in its original purposes, like those already mentioned. It was built of great blocks of hewn stone, on a vast, square foundation of rough, agglomerated material, such as composes the mass of all the other ruinous tombs. But whatever might be the cause, it was in a far better state of preservation than they. On its broad summit rose the battlements of a mediaeval fortress, out of the midst of which (so long since had time begun to crumble the supplemental structure, and cover it with soil, by means of wayside dust) grew trees, bushes, and thick festoons of ivy. This tomb of a woman had become the citadel and donjon-keep of a castle; and all the care that Cecilia Metella's husband could bestow, to secure endless peace for her beloved relics, had only sufficed to make that handful of precious ashes the nucleus of battles, long ages after her death.

A little beyond this point, the sculptor turned aside from the Appian Way, and directed his course across the Campagna, guided by tokens that were obvious only to himself. On one side of him, but at a distance, the Claudian aqueduct was striding over fields and watercourses. Before him, many miles away, with a blue atmosphere between, rose the Alban hills, brilliantly silvered with snow and sunshine.

He was not without a companion. A buffalo-calf, that seemed shy and sociable by the selfsame impulse, had begun to make acquaintance with him, from the moment when he left the road. This frolicsome creature gambolled along, now before, now behind; standing a moment to gaze at him, with wild, curious eyes, he leaped aside and shook his shaggy head, as Kenyon advanced too nigh; then, after loitering in the rear, he came galloping up, like a charge of cavalry, but halted, all of a sudden, when the sculptor turned to look, and bolted across the Campagna at the slightest signal of nearer approach. The young, sportive thing, Kenyon half fancied, was serving him as a guide, like the heifer that led Cadmus to the site of his destined city; for, in spite of a hundred vagaries, his general course was in the right direction, and along by several objects which the sculptor had noted as landmarks of his way.

In this natural intercourse with a rude and healthy form of animal life, there was something that wonderfully revived Kenyon's spirits. The warm rays of the sun, too, were wholesome for him in body and soul; and so was a breeze that bestirred itself occasionally, as if for the sole purpose of breathing upon his cheek and dying softly away, when he would fain have felt a little more decided kiss. This shy but loving breeze reminded him strangely of what Hilda's deportment had sometimes been towards himself.

The weather had very much to do, no doubt, with these genial and delightful sensations, that made the sculptor so happy with mere life, in spite of a head and heart full of doleful thoughts, anxieties, and fears, which ought in all reason to have depressed him. It was like no weather that exists anywhere, save in Paradise and in Italy; certainly not in America, where it is always too strenuous on the side either of heat or cold. Young as the season was, and wintry, as it would have been under a more rigid sky, it resembled summer rather than what we New Englanders recognize in our idea of spring. But there was an indescribable something, sweet, fresh, and remotely affectionate, which the matronly summer loses, and which thrilled, and, as it were, tickled Kenyon's heart with a feeling partly of the senses, yet far more a spiritual delight. In a word, it was as if Hilda's delicate breath were on his cheek.

After walking at a brisk pace for about half an hour, he reached a spot where an excavation appeared to have been begun, at some not very distant period. There was a hollow space in the earth, looking exceedingly like a deserted cellar, being enclosed within old subterranean walls, constructed of thin Roman bricks, and made accessible by a narrow flight of stone steps. A suburban villa had probably stood over this site, in the imperial days of Rome, and these might have been the ruins of a bathroom, or some other apartment that was required to be wholly or partly under ground. A spade can scarcely be put into that soil, so rich in lost and forgotten things, without hitting upon some discovery which would attract all eyes, in any other land. If you dig but a little way, you gather bits of precious marble, coins, rings, and engraved gems; if you go deeper, you break into columbaria, or into sculptured and richly frescoed apartments that look like festive halls, but were only sepulchres.

The sculptor descended into the cellar-like cavity, and sat down on a block of stone. His eagerness had brought him thither sooner than the appointed hour. The sunshine fell slantwise into the hollow, and happened to be resting on what Kenyon at first took to be a shapeless fragment of stone, possibly marble, which was partly concealed by the crumbling down of earth.

But his practised eye was soon aware of something artistic in this rude object. To relieve the anxious tedium of his situation, he cleared away some of the soil, which seemed to have fallen very recently, and discovered a headless figure of marble. It was earth stained, as well it might be, and had a slightly corroded surface, but at once impressed the sculptor as a Greek production, and wonderfully delicate and beautiful. The head was gone; both arms were broken off at the elbow. Protruding from the loose earth, however, Kenyon

184

beheld the fingers of a marble hand; it was still appended to its arm, and a little further search enabled him to find the other. Placing these limbs in what the nice adjustment of the fractures proved to be their true position, the poor, fragmentary woman forthwith showed that she retained her modest instincts to the last. She had perished with them, and snatched them back at the moment of revival. For these long-buried hands immediately disposed themselves in the manner that nature prompts, as the antique artist knew, and as all the world has seen, in the Venus de' Medici.

"What a discovery is here!" thought Kenyon to himself. "I seek for Hilda, and find a marble woman! Is the omen good or ill?"

In a corner of the excavation lay a small round block of stone, much incrusted with earth that had dried and hardened upon it. So, at least, you would have described this object, until the sculptor lifted it, turned it hither and thither in his hands, brushed off the clinging soil, and finally placed it on the slender neck of the newly discovered statue. The effect was magical. It immediately lighted up and vivified the whole figure, endowing it with personality, soul, and intelligence. The beautiful Idea at once asserted its immortality, and converted that heap of forlorn fragments into a whole, as perfect to the mind, if not to the eye, as when the new marble gleamed with snowy lustre; nor was the impression marred by the earth that still hung upon the exquisitely graceful limbs, and even filled the lovely crevice of the lips. Kenyon cleared it away from between them, and almost deemed himself rewarded with a living smile.

It was either the prototype or a better repetition of the Venus of the Tribune. But those who have been dissatisfied with the small head, the narrow, soulless face, the button-hole eyelids, of that famous statue, and its mouth such as nature never moulded, should see the genial breadth of this far nobler and sweeter countenance. It is one of the few works of antique sculpture in which we recognize womanhood, and that, moreover, without prejudice to its divinity.

Here, then, was a treasure for the sculptor to have found! How happened it to be lying there, beside its grave of twenty centuries? Why were not the

185

tidings of its discovery already noised abroad? The world was richer than yesterday, by something far more precious than gold. Forgotten beauty had come back, as beautiful as ever; a goddess had risen from her long slumber, and was a goddess still. Another cabinet in the Vatican was destined to shine as lustrously as that of the Apollo Belvedere; or, if the aged pope should resign his claim, an emperor would woo this tender marble, and win her as proudly as an imperial bride!

Such were the thoughts with which Kenyon exaggerated to himself the importance of the newly discovered statue, and strove to feel at least a portion of the interest which this event would have inspired in him a little while before. But, in reality, he found it difficult to fix his mind upon the subject. He could hardly, we fear, be reckoned a consummate artist, because there was something dearer to him than his art; and, by the greater strength of a human affection, the divine statue seemed to fall asunder again, and become only a heap of worthless fragments.

While the sculptor sat listlessly gazing at it, there was a sound of small hoofs, clumsily galloping on the Campagna; and soon his frisky acquaintance, the buffalo-calf, came and peeped over the edge of the excavation. Almost at the same moment he heard voices, which approached nearer and nearer; a man's voice, and a feminine one, talking the musical tongue of Italy. Besides the hairy visage of his four footed friend, Kenyon now saw the figures of a peasant and a contadina, making gestures of salutation to him, on the opposite verge of the hollow space.

CHAPTER XLVII. THE PEASANT AND CONTADINA

They descended into the excavation: a young peasant, in the short blue jacket, the small-clothes buttoned at the knee, and buckled shoes, that compose one of the ugliest dresses ever worn by man, except the wearer's form have a grace which any garb, or the nudity of an antique statue, would equally set off; and, hand in hand with him, a village girl, in one of those brilliant costumes largely kindled up with scarlet, and decorated with gold embroidery, in which the contadinas array themselves on feast-days. But Kenyon was not deceived; he had recognized the voices of his friends, indeed, even before their disguised figures came between him and the sunlight. Donatello was the peasant; the contadina, with the airy smile, half mirthful, though it shone out of melancholy eyes,—was Miriam.

They both greeted the sculptor with a familiar kindness which reminded him of the days when Hilda and they and he had lived so happily together, before the mysterious adventure of the catacomb. What a succession of sinister events had followed one spectral figure out of that gloomy labyrinth.

"It is carnival time, you know," said Miriam, as if in explanation of Donatello's and her own costume. "Do you remember how merrily we spent the Carnival, last year?"

"It seems many years ago," replied Kenyon. "We are all so changed!"

When individuals approach one another with deep purposes on both sides, they seldom come at once to the matter which they have most at heart. They dread the electric shock of a too sudden contact with it. A natural impulse leads them to steal gradually onward, hiding themselves, as it were, behind a closer, and still a closer topic, until they stand face to face with the true point of interest. Miriam was conscious of this impulse, and partially obeyed it.

"So your instincts as a sculptor have brought you into the presence of our newly discovered statue," she observed. "Is it not beautiful? A far truer image of immortal womanhood than the poor little damsel at Florence, world famous though she be."

"Most beautiful," said Kenyon, casting an indifferent glance at the Venus. "The time has been when the sight of this statue would have been enough to make the day memorable."

"And will it not do so now?" Miriam asked.

"I fancied so, indeed, when we discovered it two days ago. It is Donatello's prize. We were sitting here together, planning an interview with you, when his keen eyes detected the fallen goddess, almost entirely buried under that heap of earth, which the clumsy excavators showered down upon her, I suppose. We congratulated ourselves, chiefly for your sake. The eyes of us three are the only ones to which she has yet revealed herself. Does it not frighten you a little, like the apparition of a lovely woman that lived of old, and has long lain in the grave?"

"Ah, Miriam! I cannot respond to you," said the sculptor, with irrepressible impatience. "Imagination and the love of art have both died out of me."

"Miriam," interposed Donatello with gentle gravity, "why should we keep our friend in suspense? We know what anxiety he feels. Let us give him what intelligence we can."

"You are so direct and immediate, my beloved friend!" answered Miriam with an unquiet smile. "There are several reasons why I should like to play round this matter a little while, and cover it with fanciful thoughts, as we strew a grave with flowers."

"A grave!" exclaimed the sculptor.

"No grave in which your heart need be buried," she replied; "you have no such calamity to dread. But I linger and hesitate, because every word I speak brings me nearer to a crisis from which I shrink. Ah, Donatello! let us live a little longer the life of these last few days! It is so bright, so airy, so childlike, so without either past or future! Here, on the wild Campagna, you seem to have found, both for yourself and me, the life that belonged to you in early youth; the sweet irresponsible life which you inherited from your mythic ancestry, the Fauns of Monte Beni. Our stern and black reality will come upon us speedily enough. But, first, a brief time more of this strange happiness."

"I dare not linger upon it," answered Donatello, with an expression that reminded the sculptor of the gloomiest days of his remorse at Monte Beni. "I dare to be so happy as you have seen me, only because I have felt the time to be so brief."

"One day, then!" pleaded Miriam. "One more day in the wild freedom of this sweet-scented air."

"Well, one more day," said Donatello, smiling; and his smile touched Kenyon with a pathos beyond words, there being gayety and sadness both melted into it; "but here is Hilda's friend, and our own. Comfort him, at least, and set his heart at rest, since you have it partly in your power."

"Ah, surely he might endure his pangs a little longer!" cried Miriam, turning to Kenyon with a tricksy, fitful kind of mirth, that served to hide some solemn necessity, too sad and serious to be looked at in its naked aspect. "You love us both, I think, and will be content to suffer for our sakes, one other day. Do I ask too much?"

"Tell me of Hilda," replied the sculptor; "tell me only that she is safe, and keep back what else you will."

"Hilda is safe," said Miriam. "There is a Providence purposely for Hilda, as I remember to have told you long ago. But a great trouble—an evil deed, let us acknowledge it has spread out its dark branches so widely, that the shadow falls on innocence as well as guilt. There was one slight link that connected your sweet Hilda with a crime which it was her unhappy fortune to witness, but of which I need not say she was as guiltless as the angels that looked out of heaven, and saw it too. No matter, now, what the consequence has been. You shall have your lost Hilda back, and—who knows?—perhaps tenderer than she was."

"But when will she return?" persisted the sculptor; "tell me the when, and where, and how!"

"A little patience. Do not press me so," said Miriam; and again Kenyon was struck by the sprite-like, fitful characteristic of her manner, and a sort of hysteric gayety, which seemed to be a will-o'-the-wisp from a sorrow stagnant at her heart. "You have more time to spare than I. First, listen to something that I have to tell. We will talk of Hilda by and by."

Then Miriam spoke of her own life, and told facts that threw a gleam of light over many things which had perplexed the sculptor in all his previous knowledge of her. She described herself as springing from English parentage, on the mother's side, but with a vein, likewise, of Jewish blood; yet connected, through her father, with one of those few princely families of Southern Italy, which still retain great wealth and influence. And she revealed a name at which her auditor started and grew pale; for it was one that, only a few years before, had been familiar to the world in connection with a mysterious and terrible event. The reader, if he think it worth while to recall some of the strange incidents which have been talked of, and forgotten, within no long time past, will remember Miriam's name.

"You shudder at me, I perceive," said Miriam, suddenly interrupting her narrative.

"No; you were innocent," replied the sculptor. "I shudder at the fatality that seems to haunt your footsteps, and throws a shadow of crime about your path, you being guiltless."

"There was such a fatality," said Miriam; "yes; the shadow fell upon me, innocent, but I went astray in it, and wandered—as Hilda could tell you—into crime."

She went on to say that, while yet a child, she had lost her English mother. From a very early period of her life, there had been a contract of betrothal between herself and a certain marchese, the representative of another branch of her paternal house,—a family arrangement between two persons of disproportioned ages, and in which feeling went for nothing. Most

Italian girls of noble rank would have yielded themselves to such a marriage as an affair of course. But there was something in Miriam's blood, in her mixed race, in her recollections of her mother,—some characteristic, finally, in her own nature,—which had given her freedom of thought, and force of will, and made this prearranged connection odious to her. Moreover, the character of her destined husband would have been a sufficient and insuperable objection; for it betrayed traits so evil, so treacherous, so vile, and yet so strangely subtle, as could only be accounted for by the insanity which often develops itself in old, close-kept races of men, when long unmixed with newer blood. Reaching the age when the marriage contract should have been fulfilled, Miriam had utterly repudiated it.

Some time afterwards had occurred that terrible event to which Miriam had alluded when she revealed her name; an event, the frightful and mysterious circumstances of which will recur to many minds, but of which few or none can have found for themselves a satisfactory explanation. It only concerns the present narrative, inasmuch as the suspicion of being at least an accomplice in the crime fell darkly and directly upon Miriam herself.

"But you know that I am innocent!" she cried, interrupting herself again, and looking Kenyon in the face.

"I know it by my deepest consciousness," he answered; "and I know it by Hilda's trust and entire affection, which you never could have won had you been capable of guilt."

"That is sure ground, indeed, for pronouncing me innocent," said Miriam, with the tears gushing into her eyes. "Yet I have since become a horror to your saint-like Hilda, by a crime which she herself saw me help to perpetrate!"

She proceeded with her story. The great influence of her family connections had shielded her from some of the consequences of her imputed guilt. But, in her despair, she had fled from home, and had surrounded her flight with such circumstances as rendered it the most probable conclusion that she had committed suicide. Miriam, however, was not of the feeble nature which takes advantage of that obvious and poor resource in earthly difficulties. She flung herself upon the world, and speedily created a new sphere, in which Hilda's gentle purity, the sculptor's sensibility, clear thought, and genius, and Donatello's genial simplicity had given her almost her first experience of happiness. Then came that ill-omened adventure of the catacomb, The spectral figure which she encountered there was the evil fate that had haunted her through life.

Looking back upon what had happened, Miriam observed, she now considered him a madman. Insanity must have been mixed up with his original composition, and developed by those very acts of depravity which it suggested, and still more intensified, by the remorse that ultimately followed them. Nothing was stranger in his dark career than the penitence which often seemed to go hand in hand with crime. Since his death she had ascertained that it finally led him to a convent, where his severe and self-inflicted penance had even acquired him the reputation of unusual sanctity, and had been the cause of his enjoying greater freedom than is commonly allowed to monks.

"Need I tell you more?" asked Miriam, after proceeding thus far. "It is still a dim and dreary mystery, a gloomy twilight into which I guide you; but possibly you may catch a glimpse of much that I myself can explain only by conjecture. At all events, you can comprehend what my situation must have been, after that fatal interview in the catacomb. My persecutor had gone thither for penance, but followed me forth with fresh impulses to crime. He had me in his power. Mad as he was, and wicked as he was, with one word he could have blasted me in the belief of all the world. In your belief too, and Hilda's! Even Donatello would have shrunk from me with horror!"

"Never," said Donatello, "my instinct would have known you innocent."

"Hilda and Donatello and myself,—we three would have acquitted you," said Kenyon, "let the world say what it might. Ah, Miriam, you should have told us this sad story sooner!"

"I thought often of revealing it to you," answered Miriam; "on one occasion, especially,—it was after you had shown me your Cleopatra; it seemed to leap out of my heart, and got as far as my very lips. But finding you cold to accept my confidence, I thrust it back again. Had I obeyed my first impulse, all would have turned out differently."

"And Hilda!" resumed the sculptor. "What can have been her connection with these dark incidents?"

"She will, doubtless, tell you with her own lips," replied Miriam. "Through sources of information which I possess in Rome, I can assure you of her safety. In two days more—by the help of the special Providence that, as I love to tell you, watches over Hilda—she shall rejoin you."

"Still two days more!" murmured the sculptor.

"Ah, you are cruel now! More cruel than you know!" exclaimed Miriam, with another gleam of that fantastic, fitful gayety, which had more than once marked her manner during this interview. "Spare your poor friends!"

"I know not what you mean, Miriam," said Kenyon.

"No matter," she replied; "you will understand hereafter. But could you think it? Here is Donatello haunted with strange remorse, and an unmitigable resolve to obtain what he deems justice upon himself. He fancies, with a kind of direct simplicity, which I have vainly tried to combat, that, when a wrong has been done, the doer is bound to submit himself to whatsoever tribunal takes cognizance of such things, and abide its judgment. I have assured him that there is no such thing as earthly justice, and especially none here, under the head of Christendom."

"We will not argue the point again," said Donatello, smiling. "I have no head for argument, but only a sense, an impulse, an instinct, I believe, which sometimes leads me right. But why do we talk now of what may make us sorrowful? There are still two days more. Let us be happy!"

It appeared to Kenyon that since he last saw Donatello, some of the sweet and delightful characteristics of the antique Faun had returned to him. There were slight, careless graces, pleasant and simple peculiarities, that had been obliterated by the heavy grief through which he was passing at Monte Beni, and out of which he had hardly emerged when the sculptor parted with Miriam and him beneath the bronze pontiff's outstretched hand. These happy blossoms had now reappeared. A playfulness came out of his heart, and glimmered like firelight in his actions, alternating, or even closely intermingled, with profound sympathy and serious thought.

"Is he not beautiful?" said Miriam, watching the sculptor's eye as it dwelt admiringly on Donatello. "So changed, yet still, in a deeper sense, so much the same! He has travelled in a circle, as all things heavenly and earthly do, and now comes back to his original self, with an inestimable treasure of improvement won from an experience of pain. How wonderful is this! I tremble at my own thoughts, yet must needs probe them to their depths. Was the crime—in which he and I were wedded—was it a blessing, in that strange disguise? Was it a means of education, bringing a simple and imperfect nature to a point of feeling and intelligence which it could have reached under no other discipline?"

"You stir up deep and perilous matter, Miriam," replied Kenyon. "I dare not follow you into the unfathomable abysses whither you are tending."

"Yet there is a pleasure in them! I delight to brood on the verge of this great mystery," returned she. "The story of the fall of man! Is it not repeated in our romance of Monte Beni? And may we follow the analogy yet further? Was that very sin,—into which Adam precipitated himself and all his race, was it the destined means by which, over a long pathway of toil and sorrow, we are to attain a higher, brighter, and profounder happiness, than our lost birthright gave? Will not this idea account for the permitted existence of sin, as no other theory can?"

"It is too dangerous, Miriam! I cannot follow you!" repeated the sculptor. "Mortal man has no right to tread on the ground where you now set your feet."

"Ask Hilda what she thinks of it," said Miriam, with a thoughtful smile. "At least, she might conclude that sin—which man chose instead of good—has been so beneficently handled by omniscience and omnipotence, that, whereas our dark enemy sought to destroy us by it, it has really become an instrument most effective in the education of intellect and soul."

Miriam paused a little longer among these meditations, which the sculptor rightly felt to be so perilous; she then pressed his hand, in token of farewell.

"The day after to-morrow," said she, "an hour before sunset, go to the Corso, and stand in front of the fifth house on your left, beyond the Antonine column. You will learn tidings of a friend."

Kenyon would have besought her for more definite intelligence, but she shook her head, put her finger on her lips, and turned away with an illusive smile. The fancy impressed him that she too, like Donatello, had reached a wayside paradise, in their mysterious life journey, where they both threw down the burden of the before and after, and, except for this interview with himself, were happy in the flitting moment. To-day Donatello was the sylvan Faun; to-day Miriam was his fit companion, a Nymph of grove or fountain; to-morrow—a remorseful man and woman, linked by a marriage bond of crime—they would set forth towards an inevitable goal.

CHAPTER XLVIII. A SCENE IN THE CORSO

On the appointed afternoon, Kenyon failed not to make his appearance in the Corso, and at an hour much earlier than Miriam had named.

It was carnival time. The merriment of this famous festival was in full progress; and the stately avenue of the Corso was peopled with hundreds of fantastic shapes, some of which probably represented the mirth of ancient times, surviving through all manner of calamity, ever since the days of the Roman Empire. For a few afternoons of early spring, this mouldy gayety strays into the sunshine; all the remainder of the year, it seems to be shut up in the catacombs or some other sepulchral storehouse of the past.

Besides these hereditary forms, at which a hundred generations have laughed, there were others of modern date, the humorous effluence of the day that was now passing. It is a day, however, and an age, that appears to be remarkably barren, when compared with the prolific originality of former times, in productions of a scenic and ceremonial character, whether grave or gay. To own the truth, the Carnival is alive, this present year, only because it has existed through centuries gone by. It is traditionary, not actual. If decrepit and melancholy Rome smiles, and laughs broadly, indeed, at carnival time, it is not in the old simplicity of real mirth, but with a half-conscious effort, like our self-deceptive pretence of jollity at a threadbare joke. Whatever it may once have been, it is now but a narrow stream of merriment, noisy of set purpose, running along the middle of the Corso, through the solemn heart of the decayed city, without extending its shallow influence on either side. Nor, even within its own limits, does it affect the mass of spectators, but only a comparatively few, in street and balcony, who carry on the warfare of nosegays and counterfeit sugar plums. The populace look on with staid composure; the nobility and priesthood take little or no part in the matter; and, but for the hordes of Anglo-Saxons who annually take up the flagging mirth, the Carnival might long ago have been swept away, with the snowdrifts of confetti that whiten all the pavement.

No doubt, however, the worn-out festival is still new to the youthful and light hearted, who make the worn-out world itself as fresh as Adam found it on his first forenoon in Paradise. It may be only age and care that chill the life out of its grotesque and airy riot, with the impertinence of their cold criticism.

Kenyon, though young, had care enough within his breast to render the Carnival the emptiest of mockeries. Contrasting the stern anxiety of his present mood with the frolic spirit of the preceding year, he fancied that so much trouble had, at all events, brought wisdom in its train. But there is a wisdom that looks grave, and sneers at merriment; and again a deeper wisdom, that stoops to be gay as often as occasion serves, and oftenest avails itself of shallow and trifling grounds of mirth; because, if we wait for more substantial ones, we seldom can be gay at all. Therefore, had it been possible, Kenyon would have done well to mask himself in some wild, hairy visage, and plunge into the throng of other maskers, as at the Carnival before. Then Donatello had danced along the Corso in all the equipment of a Faun, doing the part with wonderful felicity of execution, and revealing furry ears, which looked absolutely real; and Miriam had been alternately a lady of the antique regime, in powder and brocade, and the prettiest peasant girl of the Campagna, in the gayest of costumes; while Hilda, sitting demurely in a balcony, had hit the sculptor with a single rosebud,—so sweet and fresh a bud that he knew at once whose hand had flung it.

These were all gone; all those dear friends whose sympathetic mirth had made him gay. Kenyon felt as if an interval of many years had passed since the last Carnival. He had grown old, the nimble jollity was tame, and the maskers dull and heavy; the Corso was but a narrow and shabby street of decaying palaces; and even the long, blue streamer of Italian sky, above it, not half so brightly blue as formerly.

Yet, if he could have beheld the scene with his clear, natural eyesight, he might still have found both merriment and splendor in it. Everywhere, and all day long, there had been tokens of the festival, in the baskets brimming over with bouquets, for sale at the street corners, or borne about on people's heads; while bushels upon bushels of variously colored confetti were displayed, looking just like veritable sugar plums; so that a stranger would have imagined that the whole commerce and business of stern old Rome lay in flowers and sweets. And now, in the sunny afternoon, there could hardly be a spectacle more picturesque than the vista of that noble street, stretching into the interminable distance between two rows of lofty edifices, from every window of which, and many a balcony, flaunted gay and gorgeous carpets, bright silks, scarlet cloths with rich golden fringes, and Gobelin tapestry, still lustrous with varied hues, though the product of antique looms. Each separate palace had put on a gala dress, and looked festive for the occasion, whatever sad or guilty secret it might hide within. Every window, moreover, was alive with the faces of women, rosy girls, and children, all kindled into brisk and mirthful expression, by the incidents in the street below. In the balconies that projected along the palace fronts stood groups of ladies, some beautiful, all richly dressed, scattering forth their laughter, shrill, yet sweet, and the musical babble of their voices, to thicken into an airy tumult over the heads of common mortals.

All these innumerable eyes looked down into the street, the whole capacity of which was thronged with festal figures, in such fantastic variety that it had taken centuries to contrive them; and through the midst of the mad, merry stream of human life rolled slowly onward a never-ending procession of all the vehicles in Rome, from the ducal carriage, with the powdered coachman high in front, and the three golden lackeys clinging in the rear, down to the rustic cart drawn by its single donkey. Among this various crowd, at windows and in balconies, in cart, cab, barouche, or gorgeous equipage, or bustling to and fro afoot, there was a sympathy of nonsense; a true and genial brotherhood and sisterhood, based on the honest purpose—and a wise one, too—of being foolish, all together. The sport of mankind, like its deepest earnest, is a battle; so these festive people fought one another with an ammunition of sugar plums and flowers.

Not that they were veritable sugar plums, however, but something that resembled them only as the apples of Sodom look like better fruit. They were concocted mostly of lime, with a grain of oat, or some other worthless kernel, in the midst. Besides the hailstorm of confetti, the combatants threw handfuls of flour or lime into the air, where it hung like smoke over a battlefield, or, descending, whitened a black coat or priestly robe, and made the curly locks of youth irreverently hoary.

At the same time with this acrid contest of quicklime, which caused much effusion of tears from suffering eyes, a gentler warfare of flowers was carried on, principally between knights and ladies. Originally, no doubt, when this pretty custom was first instituted, it may have had a sincere and modest import. Each youth and damsel, gathering bouquets of field flowers, or the sweetest and fairest that grew in their own gardens, all fresh and virgin blossoms, flung them with true aim at the one, or few, whom they regarded with a sentiment of shy partiality at least, if not with love. Often, the lover in the Corso may thus have received from his bright mistress, in her father's princely balcony, the first sweet intimation that his passionate glances had not struck against a heart of marble. What more appropriate mode of suggesting her tender secret could a maiden find than by the soft hit of a rosebud against a young man's cheek?

This was the pastime and the earnest of a more innocent and homelier age. Nowadays the nosegays are gathered and tied up by sordid hands, chiefly of the most ordinary flowers, and are sold along the Corso, at mean price, yet more than such Venal things are worth. Buying a basketful, you find them miserably wilted, as if they had flown hither and thither through two or three carnival days already; muddy, too, having been fished up from the pavement, where a hundred feet have trampled on them. You may see throngs of men and boys who thrust themselves beneath the horses' hoofs to gather up bouquets that were aimed amiss from balcony and carriage; these they sell again, and yet once more, and ten times over, defiled as they all are with the wicked filth of Rome.

Such are the flowery favors—the fragrant bunches of sentiment—that fly between cavalier and dame, and back again, from one end of the Corso to the other. Perhaps they may symbolize, more aptly than was intended, the poor, battered, wilted hearts of those who fling them; hearts which—crumpled and crushed by former possessors, and stained with various mishap—have been passed from hand to hand along the muddy street-way of life, instead of being treasured in one faithful bosom.

These venal and polluted flowers, therefore, and those deceptive bonbons, are types of the small reality that still subsists in the observance of the Carnival. Yet the government seemed to imagine that there might be excitement enough,—wild mirth, perchance, following its antics beyond law, and frisking from frolic into earnest,—to render it expedient to guard the Corso with an imposing show of military power. Besides the ordinary force of gendarmes, a strong patrol of papal dragoons, in steel helmets and white cloaks, were stationed at all the street corners. Detachments of French infantry stood by their stacked muskets in the Piazza del Popolo, at one extremity of the course, and before the palace of the Austrian embassy, at the other, and by the column of Antoninus, midway between. Had that chained tiger-cat, the Roman populace, shown only so much as the tip of his claws, the sabres would have been flashing and the bullets whistling, in right earnest, among the combatants who now pelted one another with mock sugar plums and wilted flowers.

But, to do the Roman people justice, they were restrained by a better safeguard than the sabre or the bayonet; it was their own gentle courtesy, which imparted a sort of sacredness to the hereditary festival. At first sight of a spectacle so fantastic and extravagant, a cool observer might have imagined the whole town gone mad; but, in the end, he would see that all this apparently unbounded license is kept strictly within a limit of its own; he would admire a people who can so freely let loose their mirthful propensities, while muzzling those fiercer ones that tend to mischief. Everybody seemed lawless; nobody was rude. If any reveller overstepped the mark, it was sure to be no Roman, but an Englishman or an American; and even the rougher play of this Gothic race was still softened by the insensible influence of a moral atmosphere more delicate, in some respects, than we breathe at home. Not that, after all, we like the fine Italian spirit better than our own; popular rudeness is sometimes the symptom of rude moral health. But, where a Carnival is in question, it would probably pass off more decorously, as well as more airily and delightfully, in Rome, than in any Anglo-Saxon city.

When Kenyon emerged from a side lane into the Corso, the mirth was at its height. Out of the seclusion of his own feelings, he looked forth at the tapestried and damask-curtained palaces, the slow-moving double line of carriages, and the motley maskers that swarmed on foot, as if he were gazing through the iron lattice of a prison window. So remote from the scene were his sympathies, that it affected him like a thin dream, through the dim, extravagant material of which he could discern more substantial objects, while too much under its control to start forth broad awake. Just at that moment, too, there came another spectacle, making its way right through the masquerading throng.

It was, first and foremost, a full band of martial music, reverberating, in that narrow and confined though stately avenue, between the walls of the lofty palaces, and roaring upward to the sky with melody so powerful that it almost grew to discord. Next came a body of cavalry and mounted gendarmes, with great display of military pomp. They were escorting a long train of equipages, each and all of which shone as gorgeously as Cinderella's coach, with paint and gilding. Like that, too, they were provided with coachmen of mighty breadth, and enormously tall footmen, in immense powdered wigs, and all the splendor of gold-laced, three cornered hats, and embroidered silk coats and breeches. By the old-fashioned magnificence of this procession, it might worthily have included his Holiness in person, with a suite of attendant Cardinals, if those sacred dignitaries would kindly have lent their aid to heighten the frolic of the Carnival. But, for all its show of a martial escort, and its antique splendor of costume, it was but a train of the municipal authorities of Rome,—illusive shadows, every one, and among them a phantom, styled the Roman Senator,—proceeding to the Capitol.

The riotous interchange of nosegays and confetti was partially suspended, while the procession passed. One well-directed shot, however,—it was a double handful of powdered lime, flung by an impious New Englander,— hit the coachman of the Roman Senator full in the face, and hurt his dignity amazingly. It appeared to be his opinion that the Republic was again crumbling into ruin, and that the dust of it now filled his nostrils; though, in fact, it would hardly be distinguished from the official powder with which he was already plentifully bestrewn.

While the sculptor, with his dreamy eyes, was taking idle note of this trifling circumstance, two figures passed before him, hand in hand. The countenance of each was covered with an impenetrable black mask; but one seemed a peasant of the Campagna; the other, a contadina in her holiday costume.

CHAPTER XLIX. A FROLIC OF THE CARNIVAL

The crowd and confusion, just at that moment, hindered the sculptor from pursuing these figures,—the peasant and contadina,—who, indeed, were but two of a numerous tribe that thronged the Corso, in similar costume. As soon as he could squeeze a passage, Kenyon tried to follow in their footsteps, but quickly lost sight of them, and was thrown off the track by stopping to examine various groups of masqueraders, in which he fancied the objects of his search to be included. He found many a sallow peasant or herdsman of the Campagna, in such a dress as Donatello wore; many a contadina, too, brown, broad, and sturdy, in her finery of scarlet, and decked out with gold or coral beads, a pair of heavy earrings, a curiously wrought cameo or mosaic brooch, and a silver comb or long stiletto among her glossy hair. But those shapes of grace and beauty which he sought had vanished.

As soon as the procession of the Senator had passed, the merry-makers resumed their antics with fresh spirit, and the artillery of bouquets and sugar plums, suspended for a moment, began anew. The sculptor himself, being probably the most anxious and unquiet spectator there, was especially a mark for missiles from all quarters, and for the practical jokes which the license of the Carnival permits. In fact, his sad and contracted brow so ill accorded with the scene, that the revellers might be pardoned for thus using him as the butt of their idle mirth, since he evidently could not otherwise contribute to it.

Fantastic figures, with bulbous heads, the circumference of a bushel, grinned enormously in his face. Harlequins struck him with their wooden swords, and appeared to expect his immediate transformation into some jollier shape. A little, long-tailed, horned fiend sidled up to him and suddenly blew at him through a tube, enveloping our poor friend in a whole harvest of winged seeds. A biped, with an ass's snout, brayed close to his ear, ending his discordant uproar with a peal of human laughter. Five strapping damsels—so, at least, their petticoats bespoke them, in spite of an awful freedom in the flourish of their legs—joined hands, and danced around him, inviting him by their gestures to perform a hornpipe in the midst. Released from these gay persecutors, a clown in motley rapped him on the back with a blown bladder, in which a handful of dried peas rattled horribly.

Unquestionably, a care-stricken mortal has no business abroad, when the rest of mankind are at high carnival; they must either pelt him and absolutely martyr him with jests, and finally bury him beneath the aggregate heap; or else the potency of his darker mood, because the tissue of human life takes a sad dye more readily than a gay one, will quell their holiday humors, like the aspect of a death's-head at a banquet. Only that we know Kenyon's errand, we could hardly forgive him for venturing into the Corso with that troubled face.

Even yet, his merry martyrdom was not half over. There came along a gigantic female figure, seven feet high, at least, and taking up a third of the street's breadth with the preposterously swelling sphere of her crinoline skirts. Singling out the sculptor, she began to make a ponderous assault upon his heart, throwing amorous glances at him out of her great goggle eyes, offering him a vast bouquet of sunflowers and nettles, and soliciting his pity by all sorts of pathetic and passionate dumb-show. Her suit meeting no favor, the rejected Titaness made a gesture of despair and rage; then suddenly drawing a huge pistol, she took aim right at the obdurate sculptor's breast, and pulled the trigger. The shot took effect, for the abominable plaything went off by a spring, like a boy's popgun, covering Kenyon with a cloud of lime dust, under shelter of which the revengeful damsel strode away.

Hereupon, a whole host of absurd figures surrounded him, pretending to sympathize in his mishap. Clowns and party-colored harlequins; orang-outangs; bear-headed, bull-headed, and dog-headed individuals; faces that would have been human, but for their enormous noses; one terrific creature, with a visage right in the centre of his breast; and all other imaginable kinds of monstrosity and exaggeration. These apparitions appeared to be investigating the case, after the fashion of a coroner's jury, poking their pasteboard countenances close to the sculptor's with an unchangeable grin, that gave still more ludicrous effect to the comic alarm and sorrow of their gestures. Just then, a figure came by, in a gray wig and rusty gown, with an inkhorn at his buttonhole and a pen behind his ear; he announced himself as a notary, and offered to make the last will and testament of the assassinated man. This solemn duty, however, was interrupted by a surgeon, who brandished a lancet, three feet long, and proposed to him to let him take blood.

The affair was so like a feverish dream, that Kenyon resigned himself to let it take its course. Fortunately the humors of the Carnival pass from one absurdity to another, without lingering long enough on any, to wear out even the slightest of them. The passiveness of his demeanor afforded too little scope for such broad merriment as the masqueraders sought. In a few moments they vanished from him, as dreams and spectres do, leaving him at liberty to pursue his quest, with no impediment except the crowd that blocked up the footway.

He had not gone far when the peasant and the contadina met him. They were still hand in hand, and appeared to be straying through the grotesque and animated scene, taking as little part in it as himself. It might be because he recognized them, and knew their solemn secret, that the sculptor fancied a melancholy emotion to be expressed by the very movement and attitudes of these two figures; and even the grasp of their hands, uniting them so closely, seemed to set them in a sad remoteness from the world at which they gazed.

"I rejoice to meet you," said Kenyon. But they looked at him through the eye-holes of their black masks, without answering a word.

"Pray give me a little light on the matter which I have so much at heart," said he; "if you know anything of Hilda, for Heaven's sake, speak!"

Still they were silent; and the sculptor began to imagine that he must have mistaken the identity of these figures, there being such a multitude in similar costume. Yet there was no other Donatello, no other Miriam. He felt, too, that spiritual certainty which impresses us with the presence of our friends, apart from any testimony of the senses.

"You are unkind," resumed he,—"knowing the anxiety which oppresses me, —not to relieve it, if in your power."

The reproach evidently had its effect; for the contadina now spoke, and it was Miriam's voice.

"We gave you all the light we could," said she. "You are yourself unkind, though you little think how much so, to come between us at this hour. There may be a sacred hour, even in carnival time."

In another state of mind, Kenyon could have been amused by the impulsiveness of this response, and a sort of vivacity that he had often noted in Miriam's conversation. But he was conscious of a profound sadness in her tone, overpowering its momentary irritation, and assuring him that a pale, tear-stained face was hidden behind her mask.

"Forgive me!" said he.

Donatello here extended his hand,—not that which was clasping Miriam's,—and she, too, put her free one into the sculptor's left; so that they were a linked circle of three, with many reminiscences and forebodings flashing through their hearts. Kenyon knew intuitively that these once familiar friends were parting with him now.

"Farewell!" they all three said, in the same breath.

No sooner was the word spoken, than they loosed their hands; and the uproar of the Carnival swept like a tempestuous sea over the spot which they had included within their small circle of isolated feeling.

By this interview, the sculptor had learned nothing in reference to Hilda; but he understood that he was to adhere to the instructions already received, and await a solution of the mystery in some mode that he could not yet anticipate. Passing his hands over his eyes, and looking about him,—for the event just described had made the scene even more dreamlike than before,— he now found himself approaching that broad piazza bordering on the Corso, which has for its central object the sculptured column of Antoninus. It was not far from this vicinity that Miriam had bid him wait. Struggling onward as fast as the tide of merrymakers, setting strong against him, would permit, he was now beyond the Palazzo Colonna, and began to count the houses. The fifth was a palace, with a long front upon the Corso, and of stately height, but somewhat grim with age.

Over its arched and pillared entrance there was a balcony, richly hung with tapestry and damask, and tenanted, for the time, by a gentleman of venerable aspect and a group of ladies. The white hair and whiskers of the former, and the winter roses in his cheeks, had an English look; the ladies, too, showed a fair-haired Saxon bloom, and seemed to taste the mirth of the Carnival with the freshness of spectators to whom the scene was new. All the party, the old gentleman with grave earnestness, as if he were defending a rampart, and his young companions with exuberance of frolic, showered confetti inexhaustibly upon the passers-by.

In the rear of the balcony, a broad-brimmed, ecclesiastical beaver was visible. An abbate, probably an acquaintance and cicerone of the English family, was sitting there, and enjoying the scene, though partially withdrawn from view, as the decorum for his order dictated.

There seemed no better nor other course for Kenyon than to keep watch at this appointed spot, waiting for whatever should happen next. Clasping his arm round a lamp-post, to prevent being carried away by the turbulent stream of wayfarers, he scrutinized every face, with the idea that some one of them might meet his eyes with a glance of intelligence. He looked at each mask,—harlequin, ape, bulbous-headed monster, or anything that was absurdest,—not knowing but that the messenger might come, even in such fantastic guise. Or perhaps one of those quaint figures, in the stately ruff, the cloak, tunic, and trunk-hose of three centuries ago, might bring him tidings of Hilda, out of that long-past age. At times his disquietude took a hopeful aspect; and he fancied that Hilda might come by, her own sweet self, in some shy disguise which the instinct Of his love would be sure to penetrate. Or, she might be borne past on a triumphal car, like the one just now approaching, its slow-moving wheels encircled and spoked with foliage, and drawn by horses, that were harnessed and wreathed with flowers. Being, at best, so far beyond the bounds of reasonable conjecture, he might anticipate the wildest event, or find either his hopes or fears disappointed in what appeared most probable.

The old Englishman and his daughters, in the opposite balcony, must have seen something unutterably absurd in the sculptor's deportment, poring into this whirlpool of nonsense so earnestly, in quest of what was to make his life dark or bright. Earnest people, who try to get a reality out of human existence, are necessarily absurd in the view of the revellers and masqueraders. At all events, after a good deal of mirth at the expense of his melancholy visage, the fair occupants of the balcony favored Kenyon with a salvo of confetti, which came rattling about him like a hailstorm. Looking up instinctively, he was surprised to see the abbate in the background lean forward and give a courteous sign of recognition.

It was the same old priest with whom he had seen Hilda, at the confessional; the same with whom he had talked of her disappearance on meeting him in the street.

Yet, whatever might be the reason, Kenyon did not now associate this ecclesiastical personage with the idea of Hilda. His eyes lighted on the old man, just for an instant, and then returned to the eddying throng of the Corso, on his minute scrutiny of which depended, for aught he knew, the sole chance of ever finding any trace of her. There was, about this moment, a bustle on the other side of the street, the cause of which Kenyon did not see, nor exert himself to discover. A small party of soldiers or gendarmes appeared to be concerned in it; they were perhaps arresting some disorderly character, who, under the influence of an extra flask of wine, might have reeled across the mystic limitation of carnival proprieties.

The sculptor heard some people near him talking of the incident.

"That contadina, in a black mask, was a fine figure of a woman."

"She was not amiss," replied a female voice; "but her companion was far the handsomer figure of the two. Could they be really a peasant and a contadina, do you imagine?"

"No, no," said the other. "It is some frolic of the Carnival, carried a little too far."

This conversation might have excited Kenyon's interest; only that, just as the last words were spoken, he was hit by two missiles, both of a kind that were flying abundantly on that gay battlefield. One, we are ashamed to say, was a cauliflower, which, flung by a young man from a passing carriage, came with a prodigious thump against his shoulder; the other was a single rosebud, so fresh that it seemed that moment gathered. It flew from the opposite balcony, smote gently on his lips, and fell into his hand. He looked upward, and beheld the face of his lost Hilda!

She was dressed in a white domino, and looked pale and bewildered, and yet full of tender joy. Moreover, there was a gleam of delicate mirthfulness in her eyes, which the sculptor had seen there only two or three times in the course of their acquaintance, but thought it the most bewitching and fairylike of all Hilda's expressions. That soft, mirthful smile caused her to melt, as it were, into the wild frolic of the Carnival, and become not so strange and alien to the scene, as her unexpected apparition must otherwise have made her.

Meanwhile, the venerable Englishman and his daughters were staring at poor Hilda in a way that proved them altogether astonished, as well as inexpressibly shocked, by her sudden intrusion into their private balcony. They looked,—as, indeed, English people of respectability would, if an angel were to alight in their circle, without due introduction from somebody whom they knew, in the court above,—they looked as if an unpardonable liberty had been taken, and a suitable apology must be made; after which, the intruder would be expected to withdraw.

The abbate, however, drew the old gentleman aside, and whispered a few words that served to mollify him; he bestowed on Hilda a sufficiently benignant, though still a perplexed and questioning regard, and invited her, in dumb-show, to put herself at her ease.

But, whoever was in fault, our shy and gentle Hilda had dreamed of no intrusion. Whence she had come, or where she had been hidden, during this mysterious interval, we can but imperfectly surmise, and do not mean, at present, to make it a matter of formal explanation with the reader. It is better, perhaps, to fancy that she had been snatched away to a land of picture; that she had been straying with Claude in the golden light which he used to shed over his landscapes, but which he could never have beheld with his waking eyes till he awoke in the better clime. We will imagine that, for the sake of the true simplicity with which she loved them, Hilda had been permitted, for a season, to converse with the great, departed masters of the pencil, and behold the diviner works which they have painted in heavenly colors. Guido had shown her another portrait of Beatrice Cenci, done from the celestial life, in which that forlorn mystery of the earthly countenance was exchanged for a radiant joy. Perugino had allowed her a glimpse at his easel, on which she discerned what seemed a woman's face, but so divine, by the very depth and softness of its womanhood, that a gush of happy tears blinded the maiden's eyes before she had time to look. Raphael had taken Hilda by the hand, that fine, forcible hand which Kenyon sculptured,—and drawn aside the curtain of gold-fringed cloud that hung before his latest masterpiece. On earth, Raphael painted the Transfiguration. What higher scene may he have since depicted, not from imagination, but as revealed to his actual sight!

Neither will we retrace the steps by which she returned to the actual world. For the present, be it enough to say that Hilda had been summoned forth from a secret place, and led we know not through what mysterious passages, to a point where the tumult of life burst suddenly upon her ears. She heard the tramp of footsteps, the rattle of wheels, and the mingled hum of a multitude of voices, with strains of music and loud laughter breaking through. Emerging into a great, gloomy hall, a curtain was drawn aside; she found herself gently propelled into an open balcony, whence she looked out upon the festal street, with gay tapestries flaunting over all the palace fronts, the windows thronged with merry faces, and a crowd of maskers rioting upon the pavement below.

Immediately she seemed to become a portion of the scene. Her pale, large-eyed, fragile beauty, her wondering aspect and bewildered grace, attracted the gaze of many; and there fell around her a shower of bouquets and bonbons—freshest blossoms and sweetest sugar plums, sweets to the sweet—such as the revellers of the Carnival reserve as tributes to especial loveliness. Hilda pressed her hand across her brow; she let her eyelids fall, and, lifting them again, looked through the grotesque and gorgeous show, the chaos of mad jollity, in quest of some object by which she might assure herself that the whole spectacle was not an illusion.

Beneath the balcony, she recognized a familiar and fondly remembered face. The spirit of the hour and the scene exercised its influence over her quick and sensitive nature; she caught up one of the rosebuds that had been showered upon her, and aimed it at the sculptor; It hit the mark; he turned his sad eyes upward, and there was Hilda, in whose gentle presence his own secret sorrow and the obtrusive uproar of the Carnival alike died away from his perception.

That night, the lamp beneath the Virgin's shrine burned as brightly as if it had never been extinguished; and though the one faithful dove had gone to her melancholy perch, she greeted Hilda rapturously the next morning, and summoned her less constant companions, whithersoever they had flown, to renew their homage.

CHAPTER L. MIRIAM, HILDA, KENYON, DONATELLO

The gentle reader, we trust, would not thank us for one of those minute elucidations, which are so tedious, and, after all, so unsatisfactory, in clearing up the romantic mysteries of a story. He is too wise to insist upon looking closely at the wrong side of the tapestry, after the right one has been sufficiently displayed to him, woven with the best of the artist's skill, and cunningly arranged with a view to the harmonious exhibition of its colors. If any brilliant, or beautiful, or even tolerable effect have been produced, this pattern of kindly readers will accept it at its worth, without tearing its web apart, with the idle purpose of discovering how the threads have been knit together; for the sagacity by which he is distinguished will long ago have taught him that any narrative of human action and adventure whether we call it history or romance—is certain to be a fragile handiwork, more easily rent than mended. The actual experience of even the most ordinary life is full of events that never explain themselves, either as regards their origin or their tendency.

It would be easy, from conversations which we have held with the sculptor, to suggest a clew to the mystery of Hilda's disappearance; although, as long as she remained in Italy, there was a remarkable reserve in her communications upon this subject, even to her most intimate friends. Either a pledge of secrecy had been exacted, or a prudential motive warned her not to reveal the stratagems of a religious body, or the secret acts of a despotic government—whichever might be responsible in the present instance—while still within the scope of their jurisdiction. Possibly, she might not herself be fully aware what power had laid its grasp upon her person. What has chiefly perplexed us, however, among Hilda's adventures, is the mode of her release, in which some inscrutable tyranny or other seemed to take part in the frolic of the Carnival. We can only account for it, by supposing that the fitful and fantastic imagination of a woman—sportive, because she must otherwise be desperate—had arranged this incident, and made it the condition of a step which her conscience, or the conscience of another, required her to take.

A few days after Hilda's reappearance, she and the sculptor were straying together through the streets of Rome. Being deep in talk, it so happened that they found themselves near the majestic, pillared portico, and huge, black rotundity of the Pantheon. It stands almost at the central point of the labyrinthine intricacies of the modern city, and often presents itself before the bewildered stranger, when he is in search of other objects. Hilda, looking up, proposed that they should enter.

"I never pass it without going in," she said, "to pay my homage at the tomb of Raphael."

"Nor I," said Kenyon, "without stopping to admire the noblest edifice which the barbarism of the early ages, and the more barbarous pontiffs and princes of later ones, have spared to us."

They went in accordingly, and stood in the free space of that great circle, around which are ranged the arched recesses and stately altars, formerly dedicated to heathen gods, but Christianized through twelve centuries gone by. The world has nothing else like the Pantheon. So grand it is, that the pasteboard statues over the lofty cornice do not disturb the effect, any more than the tin crowns and hearts, the dusty artificial flowers, and all manner of trumpery gew-gaws, hanging at the saintly shrines. The rust and dinginess that have dimmed the precious marble on the walls; the pavement, with its great squares and rounds of porphyry and granite, cracked crosswise and in a hundred directions, showing how roughly the troublesome ages have trampled here; the gray dome above, with its opening to the sky, as if heaven were looking down into the interior of this place of worship, left unimpeded for prayers to ascend the more freely; all these things make an impression of solemnity, which St. Peter's itself fails to produce.

"I think," said the sculptor, "it is to the aperture in the dome—that great Eye, gazing heavenward that the Pantheon owes the peculiarity of its effect. It is so heathenish, as it were,—so unlike all the snugness of our modern civilization! Look, too, at the pavement, directly beneath the open space! So much rain has fallen there, in the last two thousand years, that it is green with small, fine moss, such as grows over tombstones in a damp English churchyard."

213

"I like better," replied Hilda, "to look at the bright, blue sky, roofing the edifice where the builders left it open. It is very delightful, in a breezy day, to see the masses of white cloud float over the opening, and then the sunshine fall through it again, fitfully, as it does now. Would it be any wonder if we were to see angels hovering there, partly in and partly out, with genial, heavenly faces, not intercepting the light, but only transmuting it into beautiful colors? Look at that broad, golden beam—a sloping cataract of sunlight—which comes down from the aperture and rests upon the shrine, at the right hand of the entrance!"

"There is a dusky picture over that altar," observed the sculptor. "Let us go and see if this strong illumination brings out any merit in it."

Approaching the shrine, they found the picture little worth looking at, but could not forbear smiling, to see that a very plump and comfortable tabby-cat—whom we ourselves have often observed haunting the Pantheon—had established herself on the altar, in the genial sunbeam, and was fast asleep among the holy tapers. Their footsteps disturbing her, she awoke, raised herself, and sat blinking in the sun, yet with a certain dignity and self-possession, as if conscious of representing a saint.

"I presume," remarked Kenyon, "that this is the first of the feline race that has ever set herself up as an object of worship, in the Pantheon or elsewhere, since the days of ancient Egypt. See; there is a peasant from the neighboring market, actually kneeling to her! She seems a gracious and benignant saint enough."

"Do not make me laugh," said Hilda reproachfully, "but help me to drive the creature away. It distresses me to see that poor man, or any human being, directing his prayers so much amiss."

"Then, Hilda," answered the sculptor more seriously, "the only Place in the Pantheon for you and me to kneel is on the pavement beneath the central aperture. If we pray at a saint's shrine, we shall give utterance to earthly wishes; but if we pray face to face with the Deity, we shall feel it impious to petition for aught that is narrow and selfish. Methinks it is this that makes the Catholics so delight in the worship of saints; they can bring up all their little worldly wants and whims, their individualities and human weaknesses, not as things to be repented of, but to be humored by the canonized humanity to which they pray. Indeed, it is very tempting!"

What Hilda might have answered must be left to conjecture; for as she turned from the shrine, her eyes were attracted to the figure of a female penitent, kneeling on the pavement just beneath the great central eye, in the very spot which Kenyon had designated as the only one whence prayers should ascend. The upturned face was invisible, behind a veil or mask, which formed a part of the garb.

"It cannot be!" whispered Hilda, with emotion. "No; it cannot be!"

"What disturbs you?" asked Kenyon. "Why do you tremble so?"

"If it were possible," she replied, "I should fancy that kneeling figure to be Miriam!"

"As you say, it is impossible," rejoined the sculptor; "We know too well what has befallen both her and Donatello." "Yes; it is impossible!" repeated Hilda. Her voice was still tremulous, however, and she seemed unable to withdraw her attention from the kneeling figure. Suddenly, and as if the idea of Miriam had opened the whole volume of Hilda's reminiscences, she put this question to the sculptor: "Was Donatello really a Faun?"

"If you had ever studied the pedigree of the far-descended heir of Monte Beni, as I did," answered Kenyon, with an irrepressible smile, "you would have retained few doubts on that point. Faun or not, he had a genial nature, which, had the rest of mankind been in accordance with it, would have made earth a paradise to our poor friend. It seems the moral of his story, that human beings of Donatello's character, compounded especially for happiness, have no longer any business on earth, or elsewhere. Life has grown so sadly serious, that such men must change their nature, or else perish, like the antediluvian creatures that required, as the condition of their existence, a more summer-like atmosphere than ours."

"I will not accept your moral!" replied the hopeful and happy-natured Hilda.

"Then here is another; take your choice!" said the sculptor, remembering what Miriam had recently suggested, in reference to the same point. "He perpetrated a great crime; and his remorse, gnawing into his soul, has awakened it; developing a thousand high capabilities, moral and intellectual, which we never should have dreamed of asking for, within the scanty compass of the Donatello whom we knew."

"I know not whether this is so," said Hilda. "But what then?"

"Here comes my perplexity," continued Kenyon. "Sin has educated Donatello, and elevated him. Is sin, then,—which we deem such a dreadful blackness in the universe,—is it, like sorrow, merely an element of human education, through which we struggle to a higher and purer state than we could otherwise have attained? Did Adam fall, that we might ultimately rise to a far loftier paradise than his?" "O hush!" cried Hilda, shrinking from him with an expression of horror which wounded the poor, speculative sculptor to the soul. "This is terrible; and I could weep for you, if you indeed believe it. Do not you perceive what a mockery your creed makes, not only of all religious sentiments, but of moral law? And how it annuls and obliterates whatever precepts of Heaven are written deepest within us? You have shocked me beyond words!"

"Forgive me, Hilda!" exclaimed the sculptor, startled by her agitation; "I never did believe it! But the mind wanders wild and wide; and, so lonely as I live and work, I have neither pole-star above nor light of cottage windows here below, to bring me home. Were you my guide, my counsellor, my inmost friend, with that white wisdom which clothes you as a celestial garment, all would go well. O Hilda, guide me home!"

"We are both lonely; both far from home!" said Hilda, her eyes filling with tears. "I am a poor, weak girl, and have no such wisdom as you fancy in me."

What further may have passed between these lovers, while standing before the pillared shrine, and the marble Madonna that marks Raphael's tomb; whither they had now wandered, we are unable to record. But when the kneeling figure beneath the open eye of the Pantheon arose, she looked towards the pair and extended her hands with a gesture of benediction. Then they knew that it was Miriam. They suffered her to glide out of the portal, however, without a greeting; for those extended hands, even while they blessed, seemed to repel, as if Miriam stood on the other side of a fathomless abyss, and warned them from its verge.

So Kenyon won the gentle Hilda's shy affection, and her consent to be his bride. Another hand must henceforth trim the lamp before the Virgin's shrine; for Hilda was coming down from her old tower, to be herself enshrined and worshipped as a household saint, in the light of her husband's fireside. And, now that life had so much human promise in it, they resolved to go back to their own land; because the years, after all, have a kind of emptiness, when we spend too many of them on a foreign shore. We defer the reality of life, in such cases, until a future moment, when we shall again breathe our native air; but, by and by, there are no future moments; or, if we do return, we find that the native air has lost its invigorating quality, and that life has shifted its reality to the spot where we have deemed ourselves only temporary residents. Thus, between two countries, we have none at all, or only that little space of either in which we finally lay down our discontented bones. It is wise, therefore, to come back betimes, or never.

Before they quitted Rome, a bridal gift was laid on Hilda's table. It was a bracelet, evidently of great cost, being composed of seven ancient Etruscan gems, dug out of seven sepulchres, and each one of them the signet of some princely personage, who had lived an immemorial time ago. Hilda remembered this precious ornament. It had been Miriam's; and once, with the exuberance of fancy that distinguished her, she had amused herself with telling a mythical and magic legend for each gem, comprising the imaginary adventures and catastrophe of its former wearer. Thus the Etruscan bracelet became the connecting bond of a series of seven wondrous tales, all of which, as they were dug out of seven sepulchres, were characterized by a sevenfold sepulchral gloom; such as Miriam's imagination, shadowed by her own misfortunes, was wont to fling over its most sportive flights.

And now, happy as Hilda was, the bracelet brought the tears into her eyes, as being, in its entire circle, the symbol of as sad a mystery as any that

Miriam had attached to the separate gems. For, what was Miriam's life to be? And where was Donatello? But Hilda had a hopeful soul, and saw sunlight on the mountain-tops.

CONCLUSION

There comes to the author, from many readers of the foregoing pages, a demand for further elucidations respecting the mysteries of the story.

He reluctantly avails himself of the opportunity afforded by a new edition, to explain such incidents and passages as may have been left too much in the dark; reluctantly, he repeats, because the necessity makes him sensible that he can have succeeded but imperfectly, at best, in throwing about this Romance the kind of atmosphere essential to the effect at which he aimed.

He designed the story and the characters to bear, of course, a certain relation to human nature and human life, but still to be so artfully and airily removed from our mundane sphere, that some laws and proprieties of their own should be implicitly and insensibly acknowledged.

The idea of the modern Faun, for example, loses all the poetry and beauty which the Author fancied in it, and becomes nothing better than a grotesque absurdity, if we bring it into the actual light of day. He had hoped to mystify this anomalous creature between the Real and the Fantastic, in such a manner that the reader's sympathies might be excited to a certain pleasurable degree, without impelling him to ask how Cuvier would have classified poor Donatello, or to insist upon being told, in so many words, whether he had furry ears or no. As respects all who ask such questions, the book is, to that extent, a failure.

Nevertheless, the Author fortunately has it in his power to throw light upon several matters in which some of his readers appear to feel an interest. To confess the truth, he was himself troubled with a curiosity similar to that which he has just deprecated on the part of his readers, and once took occasion to cross-examine his friends, Hilda and the sculptor, and to pry into several dark recesses of the story, with which they had heretofore imperfectly acquainted him.

We three had climbed to the top of St. Peter's, and were looking down upon the Rome we were soon to leave, but which (having already sinned sufficiently in that way) it is not my purpose further to describe. It occurred to me, that, being so remote in the upper air, my friends might safely utter here the secrets which it would be perilous even to whisper on lower earth.

"Hilda," I began, "can you tell me the contents of that mysterious packet which Miriam entrusted to your charge, and which was addressed to Signore Luca Barboni, at the Palazzo Cenci?"

"I never had any further knowledge of it," replied Hilda, "nor felt it right to let myself be curious upon the subject."

"As to its precise contents," interposed Kenyon, "it is impossible to speak. But Miriam, isolated as she seemed, had family connections in Rome, one of whom, there is reason to believe, occupied a position in the papal government.

"This Signore Luca Barboni was either the assumed name of the personage in question, or the medium of communication between that individual and Miriam. Now, under such a government as that of Rome, it is obvious that Miriam's privacy and isolated life could only be maintained through the connivance and support of some influential person connected with the administration of affairs. Free and self-controlled as she appeared, her every movement was watched and investigated far more thoroughly by the priestly rulers than by her dearest friends.

"Miriam, if I mistake not, had a purpose to withdraw herself from this irksome scrutiny, and to seek real obscurity in another land; and the packet, to be delivered long after her departure, contained a reference to this design, besides certain family documents, which were to be imparted to her relative as from one dead and gone."

"Yes, it is clear as a London fog," I remarked. "On this head no further elucidation can be desired. But when Hilda went quietly to deliver the packet, why did she so mysteriously vanish?"

"You must recollect," replied Kenyon, with a glance of friendly commiseration at my obtuseness, "that Miriam had utterly disappeared, leaving no trace by which her whereabouts could be known. In the meantime, the municipal authorities had become aware of the murder of the Capuchin; and from many preceding circumstances, such as his persecution of Miriam, they must have seen an obvious connection between herself and that tragical event. Furthermore, there is reason to believe that Miriam was suspected of connection with some plot, or political intrigue, of which there may have been tokens in the packet. And when Hilda appeared as the bearer of this missive, it was really quite a matter of course, under a despotic government, that she should be detained."

"Ah, quite a matter of course, as you say," answered I. "How excessively stupid in me not to have seen it sooner! But there are other riddles. On the night of the extinction of the lamp, you met Donatello, in a penitent's garb, and afterwards saw and spoke to Miriam, in a coach, with a gem glowing on her bosom. What was the business of these two guilty ones in Rome, and who was Miriam's companion?"

"Who!" repeated Kenyon, "why, her official relative, to be sure; and as to their business, Donatello's still gnawing remorse had brought him hitherward, in spite of Miriam's entreaties, and kept him lingering in the neighborhood of Rome, with the ultimate purpose of delivering himself up to justice. Hilda's disappearance, which took place the day before, was known to them through a secret channel, and had brought them into the city, where Miriam, as I surmise, began to make arrangements, even then, for that sad frolic of the Carnival."

"And where was Hilda all that dreary time between?" inquired I.

"Where were you, Hilda?" asked Kenyon, smiling.

Hilda threw her eyes on all sides, and seeing that there was not even a bird of the air to fly away with the secret, nor any human being nearer than the loiterers by the obelisk in the piazza below, she told us about her mysterious abode.

221

"I was a prisoner in the Convent of the Sacre Coeur, in the Trinita de Monte," said she, "but in such kindly custody of pious maidens, and watched over by such a dear old priest, that—had it not been for one or two disturbing recollections, and also because I am a daughter of the Puritans I could willingly have dwelt there forever.

"My entanglement with Miriam's misfortunes, and the good abbate's mistaken hope of a proselyte, seem to me a sufficient clew to the whole mystery."

"The atmosphere is getting delightfully lucid," observed I, "but there are one or two things that still puzzle me. Could you tell me—and it shall be kept a profound secret, I assure you what were Miriam's real name and rank, and precisely the nature of the troubles that led to all those direful consequences?"

"Is it possible that you need an answer to those questions?" exclaimed Kenyon, with an aspect of vast surprise. "Have you not even surmised Miriam's name? Think awhile, and you will assuredly remember it. If not, I congratulate you most sincerely; for it indicates that your feelings have never been harrowed by one of the most dreadful and mysterious events that have occurred within the present century!"

"Well," resumed I, after an interval of deep consideration, "I have but few things more to ask. Where, at this moment, is Donatello?"

"The Castle of Saint Angelo," said Kenyon sadly, turning his face towards that sepulchral fortress, "is no longer a prison; but there are others which have dungeons as deep, and in one of them, I fear, lies our poor Faun."

"And why, then, is Miriam at large?" I asked.

"Call it cruelty if you like, not mercy," answered Kenyon. "But, after all, her crime lay merely in a glance. She did no murder!"

"Only one question more," said I, with intense earnestness. "Did Donatello's ears resemble those of the Faun of Praxiteles?"

"I know, but may not tell," replied Kenyon, smiling mysteriously. "On that point, at all events, there shall be not one word of explanation."

Leamington, March 14, 1860.

About Author

Nathaniel Hawthorne (**Hathorne**; July 4, 1804 – May 19, 1864) was an American novelist, dark romantic, and short story writer. His works often focus on history, morality, and religion.

He was born in 1804 in Salem, Massachusetts, to Nathaniel Hathorne and the former Elizabeth Clarke Manning. His ancestors include John Hathorne, the only judge involved in the Salem witch trials who never repented of his actions. He entered Bowdoin College in 1821, was elected to Phi Beta Kappa in 1824, and graduated in 1825. He published his first work in 1828, the novel Fanshawe; he later tried to suppress it, feeling that it was not equal to the standard of his later work. He published several short stories in periodicals, which he collected in 1837 as Twice-Told Tales. The next year, he became engaged to Sophia Peabody. He worked at the Boston Custom House and joined Brook Farm, a transcendentalist community, before marrying Peabody in 1842. The couple moved to The Old Manse in Concord, Massachusetts, later moving to Salem, the Berkshires, then to The Wayside in Concord. The Scarlet Letter was published in 1850, followed by a succession of other novels. A political appointment as consul took Hawthorne and family to Europe before their return to Concord in 1860. Hawthorne died on May 19, 1864, and was survived by his wife and their three children.

Much of Hawthorne's writing centers on New England, many works featuring moral metaphors with an anti-Puritan inspiration. His fiction works are considered part of the Romantic movement and, more specifically, dark romanticism. His themes often center on the inherent evil and sin of humanity, and his works often have moral messages and deep psychological complexity. His published works include novels, short stories, and a biography of his college friend Franklin Pierce, the 14th President of the United States.

Biography

Early life

Nathaniel Hawthorne was born on July 4, 1804, in Salem, Massachusetts;

his birthplace is preserved and open to the public. William Hathorne was the author's great-great-great-grandfather. He was a Puritan and was the first of the family to emigrate from England, settling in Dorchester, Massachusetts, before moving to Salem. There he became an important member of the Massachusetts Bay Colony and held many political positions, including magistrate and judge, becoming infamous for his harsh sentencing. William's son and the author's great-great-grandfather John Hathorne was one of the judges who oversaw the Salem witch trials. Hawthorne probably added the "w" to his surname in his early twenties, shortly after graduating from college, in an effort to dissociate himself from his notorious forebears. Hawthorne's father Nathaniel Hathorne Sr. was a sea captain who died in 1808 of yellow fever in Suriname; he had been a member of the East India Marine Society. After his death, his widow moved with young Nathaniel and two daughters to live with relatives named the Mannings in Salem, where they lived for 10 years. Young Hawthorne was hit on the leg while playing "bat and ball" on November 10, 1813, and he became lame and bedridden for a year, though several physicians could find nothing wrong with him.

In the summer of 1816, the family lived as boarders with farmers before moving to a home recently built specifically for them by Hawthorne's uncles Richard and Robert Manning in Raymond, Maine, near Sebago Lake. Years later, Hawthorne looked back at his time in Maine fondly: "Those were delightful days, for that part of the country was wild then, with only scattered clearings, and nine tenths of it primeval woods." In 1819, he was sent back to Salem for school and soon complained of homesickness and being too far from his mother and sisters. He distributed seven issues of The Spectator to his family in August and September 1820 for the sake of having fun. The homemade newspaper was written by hand and included essays, poems, and news featuring the young author's adolescent humor.

Hawthorne's uncle Robert Manning insisted that the boy attend college, despite Hawthorne's protests. With the financial support of his uncle, Hawthorne was sent to Bowdoin College in 1821, partly because of family connections in the area, and also because of its relatively inexpensive tuition rate. Hawthorne met future president Franklin Pierce on the way to

Bowdoin, at the stage stop in Portland, and the two became fast friends. Once at the school, he also met future poet Henry Wadsworth Longfellow, future congressman Jonathan Cilley, and future naval reformer Horatio Bridge. He graduated with the class of 1825, and later described his college experience to Richard Henry Stoddard:

> I was educated (as the phrase is) at Bowdoin College. I was an idle student, negligent of college rules and the Procrustean details of academic life, rather choosing to nurse my own fancies than to dig into Greek roots and be numbered among the learned Thebans.

Early career

In 1836, Hawthorne served as the editor of the American Magazine of Useful and Entertaining Knowledge. At the time, he boarded with poet Thomas Green Fessenden on Hancock Street in Beacon Hill in Boston. He was offered an appointment as weigher and gauger at the Boston Custom House at a salary of $1,500 a year, which he accepted on January 17, 1839. During his time there, he rented a room from George Stillman Hillard, business partner of Charles Sumner. Hawthorne wrote in the comparative obscurity of what he called his "owl's nest" in the family home. As he looked back on this period of his life, he wrote: "I have not lived, but only dreamed about living." He contributed short stories to various magazines and annuals, including "Young Goodman Brown" and "The Minister's Black Veil", though none drew major attention to him. Horatio Bridge offered to cover the risk of collecting these stories in the spring of 1837 into the volume Twice-Told Tales, which made Hawthorne known locally.

Marriage and family

While at Bowdoin, Hawthorne wagered a bottle of Madeira wine with his friend Jonathan Cilley that Cilley would get married before Hawthorne did. By 1836, he had won the bet, but he did not remain a bachelor for life. He had public flirtations with Mary Silsbee and Elizabeth Peabody, then he began pursuing Peabody's sister, illustrator and transcendentalist Sophia Peabody. He joined the transcendentalist Utopian community at Brook Farm in 1841, not because he agreed with the experiment but because it helped him save money to marry Sophia. He paid a $1,000 deposit and was put in charge of shoveling the hill of manure referred to as "the Gold Mine". He left later that year, though his Brook Farm adventure became an inspiration for his novel The Blithedale Romance. Hawthorne married Sophia Peabody on July 9, 1842, at a ceremony in the Peabody parlor on West Street in Boston. The couple moved to The Old Manse in Concord, Massachusetts, where they lived for three years. His neighbor Ralph Waldo Emerson invited him into his social circle, but Hawthorne was almost pathologically shy and stayed silent at gatherings. At the Old Manse, Hawthorne wrote most of the tales collected in Mosses from an Old Manse.

Like Hawthorne, Sophia was a reclusive person. Throughout her early life, she had frequent migraines and underwent several experimental medical treatments. She was mostly bedridden until her sister introduced her to Hawthorne, after which her headaches seem to have abated. The Hawthornes enjoyed a long and happy marriage. He referred to her as his "Dove" and wrote that she "is, in the strictest sense, my sole companion; and I need no other—there is no vacancy in my mind, any more than in my heart ... Thank God that I suffice for her boundless heart!" Sophia greatly admired her husband's work. She wrote in one of her journals:

> I am always so dazzled and bewildered with the richness, the depth, the ... jewels of beauty in his productions that I am always looking forward to a second reading where I can ponder and muse and fully take in the miraculous wealth of thoughts.

Poet Ellery Channing came to the Old Manse for help on the first anniversary of the Hawthornes' marriage. A local teenager named Martha Hunt had drowned herself in the river and Hawthorne's boat Pond Lily was needed to find her body. Hawthorne helped recover the corpse, which he described as "a spectacle of such perfect horror ... She was the very image of death-agony". The incident later inspired a scene in his novel The Blithedale Romance.

The Hawthornes had three children. Their first was daughter Una, born March 3, 1844; her name was a reference to The Faerie Queene, to the displeasure of family members. Hawthorne wrote to a friend, "I find it a very sober and serious kind of happiness that springs from the birth of a child ... There is no escaping it any longer. I have business on earth now, and must look about me for the means of doing it." In October 1845, the Hawthornes moved to Salem. In 1846, their son Julian was born. Hawthorne wrote to his sister Louisa on June 22, 1846: "A small troglodyte made his appearance here at ten minutes to six o'clock this morning, who claimed to be your nephew." Daughter Rose was born in May 1851, and Hawthorne called her his "autumnal flower".

Middle years

In April 1846, Hawthorne was officially appointed the Surveyor for the District of Salem and Beverly and Inspector of the Revenue for the Port of Salem at an annual salary of $1,200. He had difficulty writing during this period, as he admitted to Longfellow:

> I am trying to resume my pen ... Whenever I sit alone, or walk alone, I find myself dreaming about stories, as of old; but these forenoons in the Custom House undo all that the afternoons and evenings have done. I should be happier if I could write.

This employment, like his earlier appointment to the custom house in Boston, was vulnerable to the politics of the spoils system. Hawthorne was a Democrat and lost this job due to the change of administration in Washington after the presidential election of 1848. He wrote a letter of protest to the Boston Daily Advertiser which was attacked by the Whigs and supported by the Democrats, making Hawthorne's dismissal a much-talked about event in New England. He was deeply affected by the death of his mother in late July, calling it "the darkest hour I ever lived". He was appointed the corresponding secretary of the Salem Lyceum in 1848. Guests who came to speak that season included Emerson, Thoreau, Louis Agassiz, and Theodore Parker.

Hawthorne returned to writing and published The Scarlet Letter in mid-March 1850, including a preface that refers to his three-year tenure in the Custom House and makes several allusions to local politicians—who did not appreciate their treatment. It was one of the first mass-produced books in America, selling 2,500 volumes within ten days and earning Hawthorne $1,500 over 14 years. The book was pirated by booksellers in London and became a best-seller in the United States; it initiated his most lucrative period as a writer. Hawthorne's friend Edwin Percy Whipple objected to the novel's "morbid intensity" and its dense psychological details, writing that the book "is therefore apt to become, like Hawthorne, too painfully anatomical in his exhibition of them", though 20th-century writer D. H. Lawrence said that there could be no more perfect work of the American imagination than The Scarlet Letter.

Hawthorne and his family moved to a small red farmhouse near Lenox, Massachusetts, at the end of March 1850. He became friends with Herman Melville beginning on August 5, 1850, when the authors met at a picnic hosted by a mutual friend. Melville had just read Hawthorne's short story collection Mosses from an Old Manse, and his unsigned review of the collection was printed in The Literary World on August 17 and August 24 titled "Hawthorne and His Mosses". Melville wrote that these stories revealed a dark side to Hawthorne, "shrouded in blackness, ten times black". He was composing his novel Moby-Dick at the time, and dedicated the work in 1851 to Hawthorne: "In token of my admiration for his genius, this book is inscribed to Nathaniel Hawthorne."

Hawthorne's time in the Berkshires was very productive. While there, he wrote The House of the Seven Gables (1851), which poet and critic James Russell Lowell said was better than The Scarlet Letter and called "the most valuable contribution to New England history that has been made." He also wrote The Blithedale Romance (1852), his only work written in the first person. He also published A Wonder-Book for Girls and Boys in 1851, a collection of short stories retelling myths which he had been thinking about writing since 1846. Nevertheless, poet Ellery Channing reported that Hawthorne "has suffered much living in this place". The family enjoyed the scenery of the Berkshires, although Hawthorne did not enjoy the winters in their small house. They left on November 21, 1851. Hawthorne noted, "I am sick to death of Berkshire ... I have felt languid and dispirited, during almost my whole residence."

The Wayside and Europe

In May 1852, the Hawthornes returned to Concord where they lived until July 1853. In February, they bought The Hillside, a home previously inhabited by Amos Bronson Alcott and his family, and renamed it The Wayside. Their neighbors in Concord included Emerson and Henry David Thoreau. That year, Hawthorne wrote The Life of Franklin Pierce, the campaign biography of his friend which depicted him as "a man of peaceful pursuits". Horace Mann said, "If he makes out Pierce to be a great man or a brave man, it will be the greatest work of fiction he ever wrote." In the biography, Hawthorne depicts Pierce as a statesman and soldier who had accomplished no great feats because of his need to make "little noise" and so "withdrew into the background". He also left out Pierce's drinking habits, despite rumors of his alcoholism, and emphasized Pierce's belief that slavery could not "be remedied by human contrivances" but would, over time, "vanish like a dream".

With Pierce's election as President, Hawthorne was rewarded in 1853 with the position of United States consul in Liverpool shortly after the publication of Tanglewood Tales. The role was considered the most lucrative foreign service position at the time, described by Hawthorne's wife as "second in dignity to the Embassy in London". His appointment ended in 1857 at the close of the Pierce administration, and the Hawthorne family toured France and Italy. During his time in Italy, the previously clean-shaven Hawthorne grew a bushy mustache.

The family returned to The Wayside in 1860, and that year saw the publication of The Marble Faun, his first new book in seven years. Hawthorne admitted that he had aged considerably, referring to himself as "wrinkled with time and trouble".

Later years and death

At the outset of the American Civil War, Hawthorne traveled with William D. Ticknor to Washington, D.C., where he met Abraham Lincoln and other notable figures. He wrote about his experiences in the essay "Chiefly About War Matters" in 1862.

Failing health prevented him from completing several more romance novels. Hawthorne was suffering from pain in his stomach and insisted on a recuperative trip with his friend Franklin Pierce, though his neighbor Bronson Alcott was concerned that Hawthorne was too ill. While on a tour of the White Mountains, he died in his sleep on May 19, 1864, in Plymouth, New Hampshire. Pierce sent a telegram to Elizabeth Peabody asking her to inform Mrs. Hawthorne in person. Mrs. Hawthorne was too saddened by the news to handle the funeral arrangements herself. Hawthorne's son Julian was a freshman at Harvard College, and he learned of his father's death the next day; coincidentally, he was initiated into the Delta Kappa Epsilon fraternity on the same day by being blindfolded and placed in a coffin.Longfellow wrote a tribute poem to Hawthorne published in 1866 called "The Bells of Lynn". Hawthorne was buried on what is now known as "Authors' Ridge" in Sleepy Hollow Cemetery, Concord, Massachusetts. Pallbearers included Longfellow, Emerson, Alcott, Oliver Wendell Holmes Sr., James Thomas Fields, and Edwin Percy Whipple. Emerson wrote of the funeral: "I thought there was a tragic element in the event, that might be more fully rendered—in the painful solitude of the man, which, I suppose, could no longer be endured, & he died of it."

His wife Sophia and daughter Una were originally buried in England. However, in June 2006, they were reinterred in plots adjacent to Hawthorne.

Writings

Hawthorne had a particularly close relationship with his publishers William Ticknor and James Thomas Fields. Hawthorne once told Fields, "I care more for your good opinion than for that of a host of critics." In fact, it was Fields who convinced Hawthorne to turn The Scarlet Letter into a novel rather than a short story. Ticknor handled many of Hawthorne's personal matters, including the purchase of cigars, overseeing financial accounts, and even purchasing clothes. Ticknor died with Hawthorne at his side in Philadelphia in 1864; according to a friend, Hawthorne was left "apparently dazed".

Literary style and themes

232

Hawthorne's works belong to romanticism or, more specifically, dark romanticism, cautionary tales that suggest that guilt, sin, and evil are the most inherent natural qualities of humanity. Many of his works are inspired by Puritan New England, combining historical romance loaded with symbolism and deep psychological themes, bordering on surrealism. His depictions of the past are a version of historical fiction used only as a vehicle to express common themes of ancestral sin, guilt and retribution. His later writings also reflect his negative view of the Transcendentalism movement.

Hawthorne was predominantly a short story writer in his early career. Upon publishing Twice-Told Tales, however, he noted, "I do not think much of them," and he expected little response from the public. His four major romances were written between 1850 and 1860: The Scarlet Letter (1850), The House of the Seven Gables (1851), The Blithedale Romance (1852) and The Marble Faun (1860). Another novel-length romance, Fanshawe, was published anonymously in 1828. Hawthorne defined a romance as being radically different from a novel by not being concerned with the possible or probable course of ordinary experience. In the preface to The House of the Seven Gables, Hawthorne describes his romance-writing as using "atmospherical medium as to bring out or mellow the lights and deepen and enrich the shadows of the picture". The picture, Daniel Hoffman found, was one of "the primitive energies of fecundity and creation."

Critics have applied feminist perspectives and historicist approaches to Hawthorne's depictions of women. Feminist scholars are interested particularly in Hester Prynne: they recognize that while she herself could not be the "destined prophetess" of the future, the "angel and apostle of the coming revelation" must nevertheless "be a woman." Camille Paglia saw Hester as mystical, "a wandering goddess still bearing the mark of her Asiatic origins ... moving serenely in the magic circle of her sexual nature". Lauren Berlant termed Hester "the citizen as woman [personifying] love as a quality of the body that contains the purest light of nature," her resulting "traitorous political theory" a "Female Symbolic" literalization of futile Puritan metaphors. Historicists view Hester as a protofeminist and avatar of the self-reliance and responsibility that led to women's suffrage and reproductive emancipation. Anthony Splendora found her literary genealogy among other archetypally fallen but redeemed women, both historic and mythic. As examples, he offers Psyche of ancient legend; Heloise of twelfth-century France's tragedy involving world-renowned philosopher Peter Abelard; Anne Hutchinson (America's first heretic, circa 1636), and Hawthorne family friend Margaret Fuller. In Hester's first appearance, Hawthorne likens her, "infant at her bosom", to Mary, Mother of Jesus, "the image of Divine Maternity". In her study of Victorian literature, in which such "galvanic outcasts" as Hester feature prominently, Nina Auerbach went so far as to name Hester's fall and subsequent redemption, "the novel's one unequivocally religious activity". Regarding Hester as a deity figure, Meredith A. Powers found in Hester's characterization "the earliest in American fiction that the archetypal Goddess appears quite graphically," like a Goddess "not the wife of traditional marriage, permanently subject to a male overlord"; Powers noted "her syncretism, her flexibility, her inherent ability to alter and so avoid the defeat of secondary status in a goal-oriented civilization".

Aside from Hester Prynne, the model women of Hawthorne's other novels—from Ellen Langton of Fanshawe to Zenobia and Priscilla of The Blithedale Romance, Hilda and Miriam of The Marble Faun and Phoebe and Hepzibah of The House of the Seven Gables—are more fully realized than his male characters, who merely orbit them. This observation is equally true of his short-stories, in which central females serve as allegorical figures: Rappaccini's beautiful but life-altering, garden-bound, daughter; almost-perfect Georgiana of "The Birthmark"; the sinned-against (abandoned) Ester of "Ethan Brand"; and goodwife Faith Brown, linchpin of Young Goodman Brown's very belief in God. "My Faith is gone!" Brown exclaims in despair upon seeing his wife at the Witches' Sabbath. Perhaps the most sweeping statement of Hawthorne's impetus comes from Mark Van Doren: "Somewhere, if not in the New England of his time, Hawthorne unearthed the image of a goddess supreme in beauty and power."

Hawthorne also wrote nonfiction. In 2008, the Library of America selected Hawthorne's "A show of wax-figures" for inclusion in its two-century retrospective of American True Crime.

234

Criticism

In "Hawthorne and His Mosses", Herman Melville wrote a passionate argument for Hawthorne to be among the burgeoning American literary canon, "He is one of the new, and far better generation of your writers." In this review of Mosses from an Old Manse, Melville describes an affinity for Hawthorne that would only increase: "I feel that this Hawthorne has dropped germinous seeds into my soul. He expands and deepens down, the more I contemplate him; and further, and further, shoots his strong New-England roots into the hot soil of my Southern soul." Edgar Allan Poe wrote important reviews of both Twice-Told Tales and Mosses from an Old Manse. Poe's assessment was partly informed by his contempt of allegory and moral tales, and his chronic accusations of plagiarism, though he admitted,

> The style of Mr. Hawthorne is purity itself. His tone is singularly effective—wild, plaintive, thoughtful, and in full accordance with his themes ... We look upon him as one of the few men of indisputable genius to whom our country has as yet given birth.

Ralph Waldo Emerson wrote, "Nathaniel Hawthorne's reputation as a writer is a very pleasing fact, because his writing is not good for anything, and this is a tribute to the man." Henry James praised Hawthorne, saying, "The fine thing in Hawthorne is that he cared for the deeper psychology, and that, in his way, he tried to become familiar with it." Poet John Greenleaf Whittier wrote that he admired the "weird and subtle beauty" in Hawthorne's tales. Evert Augustus Duyckinck said of Hawthorne, "Of the American writers destined to live, he is the most original, the one least indebted to foreign models or literary precedents of any kind."

Contemporary response to Hawthorne's work praised his sentimentality and moral purity while more modern evaluations focus on the dark psychological complexity. Beginning in the 1950s, critics have focused on symbolism and didacticism.

The critic Harold Bloom opined that only Henry James and William Faulkner challenge Hawthorne's position as the greatest American novelist, although he admitted that he favored James as the greatest American novelist.

Bloom saw Hawthorne's greatest works to be principally The Scarlet Letter, followed by The Marble Faun and certain short stories, including "My Kinsman, Major Molineux", "Young Goodman Brown", "Wakefield", and "Feathertop". (Source: Wikipedia)

NOTABLE WORKS

NOVELS

Fanshawe (published anonymously, 1828)

The Scarlet Letter (1850)

The House of the Seven Gables (1851)

The Blithedale Romance (1852)

The Marble Faun: Or, The Romance of Monte Beni (1860) (as Transformation: Or, The Romance of Monte Beni, UK publication, same year)

The Dolliver Romance (1863) (unfinished)

Septimius Felton; or, the Elixir of Life (unfinished, published in the Atlantic Monthly, 1872)

Doctor Grimshawe's Secret: A Romance (unfinished, with preface and notes by Julian Hawthorne, 1882)

SHORT STORY COLLECTIONS

Twice-Told Tales (1837)

Grandfather's Chair (1840)

Mosses from an Old Manse (1846)

A Wonder-Book for Girls and Boys (1851)

The Snow-Image, and Other Twice-Told Tales (1852)

Tanglewood Tales (1853)

The Dolliver Romance and Other Pieces (1876)

The Great Stone Face and Other Tales of the White Mountains (1889)

SELECTED SHORT STORIES

"The Hollow of the Three Hills" (1830)

"Roger Malvin's Burial" (1832)

"My Kinsman, Major Molineux" (1832)

"The Minister's Black Veil" (1832)

"Young Goodman Brown" (1835)

"The Gray Champion" (1835)

"The White Old Maid" (1835)

"Wakefield" (1835)

"The Ambitious Guest" (1835)

"The Man of Adamant" (1837)

"The May-Pole of Merry Mount" (1837)

"The Great Carbuncle" (1837)

"Dr. Heidegger's Experiment" (1837)

"A Virtuoso's Collection" (May 1842)

"The Birth-Mark" (March 1843)

"The Celestial Railroad" (1843)

"Egotism; or, The Bosom-Serpent" (1843)

"Earth's Holocaust" (1844)

"Rappaccini's Daughter" (1844)

"P.'s Correspondence" (1845)

"The Artist of the Beautiful" (1846)

"Fire Worship" (1846)

"Ethan Brand" (1850)

"The Great Stone Face" (1850)

"Feathertop" (1852)

NONFICTION

Twenty Days with Julian & Little Bunny (written 1851, published 1904)

Our Old Home (1863)

Passages from the French and Italian Notebooks (1871)

CPSIA information can be obtained
at www.ICGtesting.com
Printed in the USA
LVHW030505140720
660560LV00012B/468